A.M. Parrish

The Journey The Malevolent Curse

Published by Amazon KDP
Published in the United States of America
ISBN: 9781549681004
1. Fiction/ Science Fiction
2. Fiction/ Historical Fiction/ Spiritual

For Julianna Marcarelli: A strong and exceptionally creative young lady.

Inspiring Quotes and Bible Verses

"But they that wait upon the Lord shall renew their strength; they shall mount up with wings as eagles; they shall run, and not be weary; and they shall walk, and not faint."
-Isaiah 40:31 KJV

I heard the voice of the Lord, saying, Whom shall I send, and who will go for us? Then said I, Here am I; send me.
-Isaiah 6:8 NIV

"Finally, be strong in the Lord and in his mighty power. Put on the full armor of God, so that you can take your stand against the devil's schemes."
-Ephesians 6:10 NIV

"You fail to recognize that it matters not what someone is born, but what they grow up to be."
-J.K. Rowling

"I used to dream my life would be so different from this hell I'm living."
-Les Miserables

There is nothing either good or bad but thinking makes it so.
-William Shakespeare

Prologue

What is faith? Why do we need faith? Can't God just show himself to us? And if there is such a thing as one God, then why does he make such bad things happen to us? I mean, I know there is only one God and I have faith in him one hundred percent, but I still had so many questions for him—questions that needed answers, or else we would be lost and confused forever.

Who is doing this to us? There must be someone who hates us and wants to get back at us. I mean, God would not make my family and I endure all these things that have happened in the last couple eras. The question was: who would?

And eventually we do find out who it is. And we find out from a person we thought we knew well but realized we didn't know at all. And, of course, it had to be after the tragedy—the tragedy that would change each of our lives drastically, even more so than how the cell phone and the storm did.

Most of the time I wished that it would just end! Too much pain. Too much confusion. Too much suffering. It was not how I preferred to live my teenage years. I'm pretty sure that no one my age has endured as much as I have. Couldn't God make it stop? Couldn't he just wake me up from this nightmare? And what if even worse things happen? Would I be able to take it all? Or would I just crack and decide that this life I am living isn't worth it. . .?

It's just, I thought God never gave someone more than they could handle! I'm pretty sure I couldn't handle all of this and I don't think that it is really worth handling. Did God really believe in me this much? Did he have faith in me the way I had faith in Him?

And then what about all these impossible dreams of traveling through time? I had heard once from a scientist that if you traveled back in time, then a black hole might be created. Is that why we can't get back to the future? Is it because the future is the black hole and God is protecting us from that fatal storm?

I guess time traveling plays with the mind, as well as the heart. How could I fall for Liam so fast, anyway? It's as if time sped up, and I fell in love with him so quickly because of that. I know I love Liam, especially because of everything going on. He is mine, no matter what. I just think it is crazy how fast we fell in love.

If it all was true and these dreams were possible, then wouldn't there be a way to bring back someone from the dead?

Chapter I
The Castle

I slowly stood up and felt dampness on my back, for the grass below me was wet from rain. The sun had just broken through the dense clouds. It must be a little after noon and it was warm, so it felt like summer.

My family was sprawled and scattered on the grass as well and, as they looked around, they stood up one by one. Dad had to help Mom get up because her leg was still bruised and swollen from the dresser that had fallen on her when we crashed on the Titanic. The sun was going down. It felt like we went back in time seeing the sunset again. This time, at least, it wasn't on the Titanic, where it could have been the last time I would see sunlight.

"Where in the world are we?" Bryan asked, once everyone had a chance to stand up and look around.

I had typed the words of our last name in the phone so specifically so that we could go home, but we ended up, once again, in an unknown place. At least I had my whole family with me this time. We could all help each other through it, but first, we had to figure out where we were.

"I lost the phone again," I said, jumping back to the place I had landed, searching the grass, pulling it apart, but with no luck. I felt tears come to my eyes. We were, once again, lost in time without the phone.

"Here we go again," Bryan said, outraged, but I could tell he wasn't mad at me.

I held my hands up, as if in surrender.

"No. We're stuck again," Bryan said, falling into a sitting position.

"Do you think we are back in the future, just in a different place?" Liam inquired. "And if you lost the phone again, that might mean that we are done traveling through different times. But the question remains—where are we?" Liam looked around at the trees. They were large and thick oaks, and I noticed that their roots were long and jutting through the surface of some parts of the grass.

"Good question," Bryan said. "Let's at least try and find where we are. Let's head that way." He pointed to a clearing in the trees where the sun was peeking through.

"I feel like a secondary character in a movie," Dad said. "You guys are like the main characters. You've found the phone every other time, so it seems you know what you're doing. I trust your instincts."

"Mommy," Amy said. "I want to go home." She scurried to Mom's side and hugged her.

"I know sweetie," Mom said. She didn't know what else to say, I could tell, so she just held her close.

We pressed on through the trees without anybody else saying a word. Dad put an arm around Mom's shoulder, supporting her weight as she limped. Amy was on her other side.

I had so many questions for Mom. She probably had just as many for us. We all knew that once we found out where we were, we could all exchange stories.

We walked for what felt like a mile, through roots and trees, every now and then someone tripping over a root, or getting slight cuts having to wedge through close trees, finally coming to a large meadow. We heard voices as we poked our heads into the clearing. Whoever they were, they did not look happy to see us.

"What are you doing?" one man asked. His face had black boils that were pussy and bleeding. A woman and a child were groaning on the ground next to him, and they looked the same as he did, in terrible condition. "Get away. Don't come any closer; it's not safe here. It's not safe anywhere." He wrung his hands in despair.

"I'm sorry, we were just passing through," Dad said. "Do you need help?"

"Just leave," the man said with certain fear in his voice. He pointed in the opposite direction.

We scurried away back the way we came, and went around the meadow, putting as much distance as possible between the frightful man and us before finally coming to a stop in the woods.

"It's not safe anywhere'?" I asked, pondering the man's words. Why wasn't it safe? Why was there so much panic in the man's voice? And why was he covered in a red liquid that was obviously blood? Where were we? And more importantly, when were we?

"I don't think we're back in the future," Dad said, not exactly answering my questions. I knew that was already the case, of course.

"Why do you say that?" Liam asked.

"They didn't have any belongings, their clothes were dated, and did you notice their bodies? They were covered in blood and multiple boils."

"Something isn't right." I shared my thoughts aloud and then pondered what I just saw.

A man covered in blood, panicking and yelling; a woman and a child on the ground a few feet away from where he was, also covered in what looked like blood and boils; the moment of fright in my eyes that I shared with my family. Was there a war going on? Did we just land ourselves on a battlefield? I wanted—no, needed—to find out. We all did.

"Yeah . . ." Bryan said uneasily. Bella held Bryan's arm tightly, pulling him closer.

Liam was walking next to me, but we weren't holding hands or anything. Every now and then, we would meet eyes and then quickly pull away, knowing that our eyes were full of fear. It scared me that Liam was almost as scared as I was. I wondered what was going through his mind right now. I wanted to share the idea that we could be on a battlefield.

Amy and Luke were right behind us, just following like frightened puppies, listening to

11

everything but not talking. I could tell that they felt safer having Mom and Dad both here, but they were definitely sad, knowing that we were not yet home.

The last three times were already hard, seeing them trembling and frightened because none of us knew where we were—hoping that their big siblings could figure everything out. But sometimes we just couldn't. We had simply gotten lucky every time we found the phone.

"Where do you think we are, Ben?" Mom asked, breaking my train of thought again and looking up into Dad's eyes. Dad seemed like he was doing perfectly fine, supporting Mom's weight—not that her weight was much more than one hundred and fifty pounds anyway. Mom was five-foot-eight, slightly taller than me, and carried her weight well.

"After the time of Christ," Dad said. He taught history, so if anybody would know where we were, it would be him.

"How do you know that?" I asked.

"I'm just guessing based on that family's clothing. I do have a hunch about the exact time period and place, but I really hope I'm wrong."

Did he think we were on a battlefield too? "What era are we in?" I asked. I would not let another hunch go by without knowing what that hunch was.

"I want to find out more before I say anything else," Dad said.

That did not sound good. I nodded but felt uneasy as I did.

His eyes darted from one object to the next as he tried to put the pieces of the puzzle together.

Bryan and I looked at each other, trying to figure out what Dad was thinking. Bryan shrugged. It didn't look like he knew any more than I did. I also noticed definite stress in his eyes. That meant he was scared but didn't want to show it.

"I'm getting tired, Daddy," Amy said. "Can't we stop and rest?"

"Let's keep moving until we find the next open place," Dad said. "We'll sleep there and get a fresh start in the morning."

Amy started walking slower.

"Want to get on my back?" Bryan asked. He leaned down, and she climbed on. She rested her head on his shoulder and closed her eyes.

"Luke, do you want a ride?" I asked. He looked even more tired than Amy as he climbed onto my back and rested his head on my shoulder.

We traveled for another hour before we came to an open field. The sun was going down, so we decided to stop for the night. We staked out spots that looked to be comfortable and curled up for the evening.

In less than a minute, we had all fallen asleep.

~ ~ ~

"Kyara?" Liam whispered.

"Mmm?" I opened my eyes.

"Come on."

I really didn't want to go anywhere. Who knows what we might run into? But maybe Liam found something that could help us understand what time we were in. As I stood, I could see the outlines of trees up ahead but not much more. It was a good thing the moon was so bright and full tonight.

Liam put his index finger over his lips. "Shh."

It was impossible to sneak away from the campsite without stepping on twigs and dead leaves, both of which made way more noise than I ever imagined. But no one stirred.

Once we were out of earshot, Liam spoke. "I couldn't sleep, so I went for a walk."

"Did you find anything?"

"No, but I missed you."

He kissed me, and I realized it felt like ages since we last kissed. I had missed the way I felt when we were kissing, and this kiss was finally one where I wasn't worried about dying from the ship sinking. I was on solid ground now, and, though I didn't know exactly where I was, I, at least, felt safe with Liam.

"You're so adorable."

I smiled and looked down at my shoes in embarrassment. His compliments always made me blush because they made me feel so special.

"So, I'm curious—what did you enter into the phone that brought us to this place?"

"Our last name and the word 'home.'"

"And we ended up in a forest. How crazy is that?"

"It makes me wonder . . . if I had entered the word 'forest,' would it have taken us home?"

"You found the phone in the water," Liam said. "Maybe the water damaged it to the point where it won't work properly anymore."

"It was already broken. It took us to Rome when I entered the word 'home' and to the Titanic when I entered '2012.'"

"Hmm."

Apparently, our thoughts on the key to success were wrong. We already found everyone we loved. We had both Mom and Dad back, and Bryan had found his one true love, and I found Liam. What else or who else would it be that needed to be found? Why did we have to go to another time? And especially one where we knew something was wrong but could not figure out what.

But then what if there was something I was missing? My eyes grew wide. What if we were here to find someone close to Liam?

~ ~ ~

We decided to take a look around. Maybe we could find a clue regarding our whereabouts, which we could share with everybody when they woke up. "Should we leave a trail to find our way back?"

"What should we use?" Liam asked.

"Sticks? Rocks?"

"Why not both?"

We gathered an armful of both and headed down our trail. We were faithful to leave the sticks and rocks behind us as we went, stopping every once in a while, to figure out if we should keep going or turn back. After what seemed like several miles, I was ready to give up. "This is pointless, there's nothing but forest here."

"I wouldn't be too sure about that. Look." Liam pointed toward a group of houses off in the distance that could just barely be seen through the trees.

We continued down the trail, drawing closer to the houses that were wooden with steep, thatched roofs. At least we were uphill, above all the houses, making it easier to notice them.

"This is definitely not the future," I said.

"No, it's not." Liam dropped his head. "Those houses are too old."

As we got through more dense trees, I could see a massive stone building with round towers, and I pointed to it and asked, "What is that?"

Liam followed my pointer finger. "Looks like a castle."

And then everything clicked. The man telling us to go away, with all those bloody bumps and boils. The trees. The castle. It looked like the picture of Windsor Castle—which had belonged to Edward III, our ancestor. What if we are in the medieval times of King Edward—that would mean we would be here during the time of the Black Death!

Chapter II
The Plague

The sun started to peek its way through the trees.

"Kyara?" Liam's voice rang in my ears. I hoped that it was a dream.

"I know where we are. We have to go back," I said, and I started walking back through the trees. I didn't want it to be true. Black Death could mean the death of all of us.

I heard Liam's worried voice behind me as we walked but could not understand what he was saying. He stopped talking when he realized I wasn't going to respond, so the rest of the trek was filled with an eerie silence.

Fifteen minutes later we were back at the campsite; Liam and I hadn't spoken a word since we had started walking back, but I knew he was busy picking up and throwing off into the distance each piece of rock and stick we had left, as a trail. I didn't think twice about it though.

Everyone was fast asleep. They looked so peaceful and happy, and I did not want to wake them up for something bad, like this. But I knew it had to be done. It would help us figure out what we could do and how we could get through this time. Together.

"Hey, everyone, it's morning. Wake up! Come on, get up!" I said with as much enthusiasm as I could muster.

Several of them stirred and opened their eyes, looking around, yawning. Some, like Bella and Amy, were still fast asleep. Bryan went over to wake Bella up as Dad went to wake Amy up. Mom was sitting, looking at her bruised leg. It looked much better and not as purple, but I could tell she was still in pain.

"What's going on, Kyara?" Dad asked, after everyone was awake and looking at Liam and me.

"Liam and I . . ." I hesitated. Liam didn't know where we were, so I rephrased my sentence. "I. . . know where we are." I said. I bit my lip and looked from person to person. Many had relieved but frightened looks on their faces.

"You do? Well, where are we?" Dad asked. He was the only one that seemed able to speak. We looked at each other in the eyes and I knew he was thinking the same thing I was. No wonder he didn't want to tell us his hunch last night.

"We found a castle. We think we're in medieval times." I said, not letting them know exactly what was happening yet. Dad nodded and noticed I didn't tell everything. I gave him a look like "not yet", and he understood.

"Really?" Mom asked, but there was a hopeful smile on her face. And then everyone else started to awkwardly smile. Something about the medieval times must make them think that this would be fun, or at least, not as hard as the other times we had visited. They didn't even know the half of it though. Should I let them have their fun and then tell them later, or should I just let them know now and get it over with?

"But it's not what you think—"

"Why don't you two show us the castle?" Dad interrupted me, his eyes stern. He must want to tell everyone later. I didn't know why though, so I figured I would ask him as we walked to where we found the town.

"Yeah, come on, we'll show you." Liam said, sharing an eager and uncertain look with me. I felt bad not telling Liam where we were, on our way back to camp, a few minutes ago, but I didn't want him to know anything because I was too frightened to even say what was happening. I think Liam understood; or, at least, I hoped he did.

"Alright, let's go then," Dad said, helping Mom to her feet. Everyone else stood up, walked towards us, and stopped as Liam and I looked at each other, nodded, and then walked through the trees from which we had just entered from.

I had absolutely no idea how we had gotten back so fast this morning. Had we really walked that fast? I knew I was just following the trail, but we had been walking for at least an hour last night—or had it only felt like an hour? —and had gotten back to the family in fifteen minutes this morning.

I asked Liam if he had known the way back to the castle as we started walking, with my family following closely behind.

"I think so," he pursed his lips and kept walking forward confidently.

About three minutes in, Dad caught up to us as everyone else followed like the walking dead.

"Do you know where you are going?" Dad asked me with tentative eyes.

"Uh," I stuttered. "He does. I think." I raised my eyebrows at Liam.

"Yes, I believe I do."
"Okay?" Dad said, probably questioning our sanity, and then walked back to mom, who was wobbling a little.

As we walked slowly through the trees, they became less and less familiar. The idea of getting lost became more and more possible.

"Is this the right way?" I asked Liam in a whisper.

"I don't know, Kyara." He said, slightly upset. I had basically just followed the trail back, because my mind was racing through so many different things, and Liam had somehow decided that getting rid of our trail was a good idea. He, on the other hand, should have known the way because he, at least, wasn't dealing with the fact that we were in a deadly time.

"How do you not remember?" I asked him.

"How do *you* not remember? You were with me this morning and probably have a better memory than me. I don't have photographic memory. . ." He trailed off.

"Well, I was slightly zoned out earlier. I was just following the trail, which is now nowhere to be found."

I scrunched my eyebrows together, as he looked at me with slightly angry eyes, and we both stopped walking. Several family members behind me asked why we had stopped, but I didn't answer.

"I *told* you, we needed to get rid of the trail because I assumed that there would be people around and I didn't want them to find or follow us. Did you not hear me?" His voice became slightly louder as he got somewhat angrier with the last sentence.

"I was too scared," I started walking randomly through the trees as Liam followed me with his eyebrows scrunched. I could tell he was calming down, as we walked on because he must have realized how scared I truly was.

"Why are you scared?" He asked after a minute or so.

"Because. . ." I stopped talking as I noticed Dad was coming toward us again.

"So, do you two know where you're going now?" Dad asked, timidly.

"No," I looked down at the ground awaiting an angry retort from my father. Instead, he seemed solemn when he spoke up.

"Then?" I looked up and Dad looked at me as if he thought I was kidding.

"We actually have no idea where we are going, sir. We had made a trail this morning, but I got rid of it on our way back because I knew there may be people around and I didn't want them to follow us. So, we're

21

just walking in that general area, hoping we'll find the castle." Liam said and scrunched his nose.

Dad opened his mouth to speak, and then closed it. He must think we were crazy, but he shrugged, shared one more apprehensive look with us, and then walked back to Mom.

"I think your Dad is losing respect for me. . ." Liam frowned.

"No, I think he just hopes that we know what we're doing. And he also knows exactly where we are, so—"

"Then, where are we?!" It seemed like he had just hit his boiling point. "You walk back this morning in silence. All you say after we see the castle is, 'I know where we are; we have to go back,' and then you just walk off, and I. . . I follow you like a puppy." He paused and regained his composure. "You're not making any sense. It's like this time has taken the Kyara I knew, and I don't know where she is or what's happened to her. I want the Kyara I know so well, back. Is she still in there?"

I half smiled but then let it fall into a frown. "I don't know," was all I could say.

Liam searched my eyes for some sort of answer.

"You are acting worse than when we were on the Titanic. Could this possibly be worse than the Titanic?"

I nodded carefully.

"Kyara, please tell me where we are. Maybe I can help."

I shook my head. "No one can help." I said and then heard those painful words the man had said the previous day, "It's not safe anywhere."

I looked back down at the rooted ground, as we walked on, because I could not bear to look at Liam's face. I felt anger radiating from his body through each breath, and I felt like I was about to cry.

"Fine. Do you really want to know?" I asked.

"Of course."

"Even if it means we can all die?"

"Well, we could have all died on the Titanic."

"But this is worse."

"How is it worse?!"

"Shhhh! Don't tell anyone, okay. They can't know now, not yet."

"Fine. Just tell me already then."

"I think we're during the time of Black Death." I gasped, but Liam just nodded.

"Yeah . . . That makes sense." He shared an understanding look with me.

"You knew?" I asked.

"Well I figured it was something like that. Black Death. The Hundred Years War or another war or invasion . . . Any of those would make sense. And what makes you guess that it is Black Death?"

"The people we've seen and the big boils on their bodies. Also, the castle we saw is my ancestor's castle: King Edward's Windsor Castle."

"You are related to a king? How do you know for sure that he is your ancestor?"

"Stories. Ones that were passed down to us."

And I told him of the diary that had been passed down

through the ages from King Edward's son that no one knew about. For the king had had an affair with a woman and had a child with her. This had not been recorded in any history book, but it was in the diary of Edmund, the king's son.

"How do you know the diary is true, then?" Liam interrupted.

"We have tons of evidence. The diary was translated by my third great grandfather into proper English. We have the real one, written in the French they spoke at court back in this time, and then the readable one. Also, because my Dad is a history teacher, he had traced our ancestry all the way back until about this time."

"Oh wow, okay. So, you think that because of the diary and because your ancestry begins here, King Edward is a very great grandfather to you all."

"Well, yeah. And also because of our last name."

"But then how would that work. A male in every generation, back until Edmund?" He asked, a little confused.

"Yes, and because Edmund did not have a last name when he married, he took the name of his father, which was Edward. On Ellis Island, when Edmund's descendants came to America in the early 1890s, the people at the registry added an "s" by accident to Edward, which is why our last name is Edwards," I explained.

"And, did King Edward know about his son?"

I smiled because now I could tell the full story. It was such an amazing story full of love, surprises, and conquering hard times in one's life. So, I started the tale as we walked, recalling Edmund's words in his diary. "He was fifteen when he wrote his very first journal entry, and that was the day that changed his life forever.

"Edmund learned from his mother that he was the son of King Edward on the morning of his fifteenth birthday. She said how she was a servant and maid of the grounds of the castle, and how King Edward thought she was the most beautiful woman in the world. One day, Edward had left his sleeping room and went to see Marguerite, Edmund's mother, and they talked and had wine and then slept together. Edward had told Marguerite never to tell anyone of their affair; however, he told Marguerite that he loved her dearly and wished that she could become his wife.

"The next day Marguerite despised herself because she was a Christian and had just had an affair with the king. In the Ten Commandments, one of the commandments requires the people of God not to commit adultery. She felt unclean for this reason and decided to run away that night. She successfully left the castle and ran to Winchester where she found out that she was pregnant, and Edmund was born nine months later. That was all Edmund knew of his mother's life, and all that Marguerite would tell him. Edmund then made it his mission to one day meet his father.

"His second journal entry was pretty depressing because he was angry at his mother for not letting him go to Windsor to meet his father. He knew that his mother was trying to protect him, but Edmund called his mother a coward for leaving, and there was a huge dispute between him and Marguerite. His last line of the journal entry said, 'I am a man now and I will not let my mother stop me from going to see my father. He needs to know that I exist.'

"The third, fourth, and fifth entries were about his journey: how he was almost kidnapped, how he also almost got sick from the great plague which had been spreading through the country, and also how he had finally reached Windsor. He saw many sad and lost people throughout the kingdom.

"Then, he tells of the incredible story of going up to the castle and meeting his father. 'I saw the two towers and in between them was the entrance to my father's home. My hands were trembling. What would I say to the guards at the foot of the entrance? What would I say to my father when I saw him? I am now looking up at the marvelous castle, the castle in which I could have grown up in. I was scared to meet my father, but, at the same time I was excited. And what if the guards wouldn't let me see him? What would I do then? Well I came all this way! I must try!' That was the end of the sixth journal entry.

"The next entry tells of how he had finally summed up the courage to go to the guard at the castle entrance, and how he pleaded to enter. The old guard realized that Edmund looked exactly as Edward did when he was a boy and had actually helped Marguerite escape the night she found out that she was pregnant. So, the guard had led Edmund into the castle to meet his father. And that was all that was stated in the journal entry, until Edmund sat down with the king.

"It is found out in the next entry that the King was deeply distressed when he learned that Marguerite had run away. He was happy to learn that he had another son, and begged Edmund to live with him, for he had another son named Edmund, who was only two years younger than him. Then the King told Edmund that his seven-year-old daughter was named after his mother because he deeply loved Marguerite and wanted to see her once again. Edward would gladly support her and keep her at court as his courtesan. This greatly pleased Edmund because he thought his mother would be well taken care of by Edward. He said that he would surely go back to Winchester and bring his mother back to Edward.

"Then, of course, the sad story begins. When Edmund goes back to Winchester he found out that his mother had died from the plague. Now Edmund was alone and did not know what to do. He did not want to go back to the castle and bring bad news to the king when he was in the middle of so much else with the Black Plague and the wars and problems with the French.

"So, he never went back and stopped writing in his diary until about six years later," I said to Liam, whose mouth was wide open. I realized then that we had been walking for a long time and still had gotten nowhere.

"Keep going," Liam pleaded as Dad walked up to us and asked how much farther we would have to go.

"I'm telling Liam the story of Edmund." I smiled, and Dad exchanged a smile and then asked again where we were. I could tell he knew what was going on and that he knew the castle we had seen was our ancestor's.

"We haven't exactly been paying attention, and we believe that we are once again, lost." I shrugged. Dad rolled his eyes.

"Well, people are getting hungry." He said as my stomach growled.

"How are we going to eat? There's no food around."

"Which is why we needed to find the castle so that we could get to the town and get food!" He wasn't angry, yet he was annoyed.

"Oh." My head dropped. "But what about money? How are we going to get food?"

"We'll figure it out. There must be someone who will help us," Dad said.

"There are probably not many people around, though. With the Black Death and all. We're hopeless," I said.

Before I could go on about our hopelessness, the sound of a loud scream followed by heavy weeping came from ahead. The three of us ran up to where the terrible sound was coming from, and everyone else closely following behind. We saw a woman, holding a baby in her arms, crying.

"Are you alright?" Dad asked the woman. I looked closer at her and the baby and saw boils on the baby's arms and face. The woman looked up, and I saw that her face was oozing with blood.

"My baby has died," she said, "and I'm sure that I'll die soon too. The curse has swept across my whole family and has killed us all! You must get away from me before you catch the plague as well! Go! Now!"

Dad nodded and bellowed to everyone to back away from her. We all listened and ran for a few minutes until we were well away from the woman.

If the plague was spreading so rapidly through the woods, and we had already seen several people with the plague in less than a day, would that mean that we would get it too?

Chapter III
Hope

There were no people in sight, and I heard the sound of water flowing somewhere near us, making me realize how thirsty I was.

However, the realization of what we were facing made me forget my own discomfort for the moment, as Dad, Liam, and I shared frightened looks.

"Ben?" Mom hobbled up to us. She noticed our looks of fright and nodded. "I'll get everyone else." I looked back on Bryan, Bella and the kids, who were a little farther behind us.

"Hey, give me a second, guys." Bryan said, looking up, and then heading towards us. "Is it what I think it is?"

"Yes." I nodded as Bryan stood next to me, his eyes reflecting mine.

"What are we going to do then?" He asked as Bella, Amy, and Luke ran up to us asking what was going on.

"We have to tell them. They need to know." I whispered to my parents. I hated seeing my younger siblings hurt, knowing that they shouldn't understand everything they did by this age. But they did need to know what was going on, in order to keep them safe and close to us.

And so, Dad began telling the story behind Black Death. "In the thirteenth century, a deadly plague came across Europe, parts of Asia, and parts of Africa, killing nearly 20 million people," he explained. "And we are in that dreadful time. This plague sweeps across the different countries like wildfire, killing everyone in its path."

"Ben . . ." Mom scolded Dad with the look saying that they are just kids and they shouldn't know this much.

"They need to know, Maggie. As painful as it may be to hear, they have to know so that we can keep them safe," Dad explained with a poignant frown.

"How long did it last?" Bella spoke up.

"Eight years, I think," Bryan said.

Dad nodded. "But, it is assumed that we are in England right now, considering what Kyara has explained to me." Then he whispered low enough for only me to hear, "What part are you at in the story?"

Believing that he was talking of Edmund's story, I whispered back, "Just about to get to the part when he meets Genevieve."

Dad nodded, understanding.

"Some people believed that the plague was a punishment from God because of their sin and worldliness, assuming it would end the world. It nearly did—almost one-third of Europe's population died," Bryan said, bringing Dad and me back to the previous conversation.

"That must have been really terrible," Bella said, miserably.

Amy had tears in her eyes, but I could see Luke trying not to cry. He had the tough face on, like the one he sometimes had after he gets really hurt and tries his hardest to be a man and not cry.

Amy; however, always shared her feelings, but this time she said nothing, and wiped her tears away as I looked at her. Then I noticed that she and Luke were holding hands, clenched together. I felt chills roll up my arms and down my spine. This meant that they were both more petrified than they ever have been.

Their sweet faces, once full of childhood innocence and joy, had been replaced by something so terrible that I couldn't bear to look away. They were frightened, terrified, in utter horror that they and their family could actually die.

"We really need to find that cell phone before things get worse and one of us ends up with the plague," I said, wretchedly.

Bryan was the first to nod, and then everyone else nodded as well.

"So, are we almost at the castle?" Mom asked.

"No. . . um, we got lost. . . Sorry." I shuffled my feet a bit.

And then it was completely silent. All that was heard was the sound of stomachs grumbling.

"Hey, do you hear that?" Bryan asked, breaking the silence. *Well yes, obviously we are all hungry. No need to rub it in, Bryan.*

But then I noticed what I had heard about ten minutes prior. The sound of water. If there was water that meant our thirst would be quenched, and that could also mean that there could be fish, meaning food!

"Water!" I said as I ran towards the sound, everyone following close behind me.

Finally, the ground started to feel damper, there was promising moss sprouting on the trees, and then our prayers were answered, and we spotted the flowing stream. I ran so fast I could feel myself becoming thirstier every second because of the exercise. I hadn't realized how dry my mouth was until now, until that beautiful stream flowed in front of me, glistening in my eyes. Once I reached it, I fell straight into it and gulped up the clear water. I didn't care that I was wet. I didn't care if the water didn't taste like it was purified, all I cared about was that wonderful taste; that chilly and moist touch; and that fresh smell of what I had been waiting for.

"Kyara, don't drink the water. It's not purified. You'll get sick," Dad said, and I looked up wiping my mouth.

"Oh," I said. "I'm thirsty though."

"We all are. But we don't want to get sick. I'm sure the town is close, so we should head down the stream to the river, which I'm sure is also close."

I nodded.

Liam jumped in after Dad finished his last sentence and covered himself in cold water. Then Bryan waded in, and Luke followed shortly thereafter. The others walked around the water.

I followed, still in the water pushing Liam down as I got up, trying to act funny.

"Hey!" I heard from behind me as I splashed on towards Bryan. The sound of more splashing was coming from behind me but was getting louder and louder and I knew he was getting closer to me.

Then I felt those familiar arms around me, and the next thing I knew, I was face down in the water, Liam on top of me. I rolled over, pushing Liam off and started laughing so hard I could barely breathe. Liam managed to get up and then helped me up as I sputtered with laughter.

"Hey. Don't you dare think that I won't get you back after you do something to me." He winked, and I hugged him.

"PDA!" Bryan yelled.

"Kyara," I heard Dad say sternly, but with a hint of teasing in his voice.

I let go of the hug, smiled at Liam, and then started splashing again toward Bryan, who had kept walking and hadn't stopped. The sound of water falling was beginning and I assumed we were getting closer to the river. I looked at Liam, it seemed like he was thinking what I was.

The stream started to widen out, turning into more of a river. Trees started to get thinner as they backed away from the edge of the water, until there were barely any to be seen. There was a small waterfall, falling into a quite large river. Then, as I neared closer to the river, I saw it. Up ahead was the castle. It was a side view of the castle, and I realized that we were on the complete opposite side of it than we were last night. I laughed at the thought, and then yelled for everyone else to come look. Liam had been gazing at it, smiling with me, but Bryan had completely missed it, because he had jumped into the river, which looked to be quite deep.

"And there it is!" Dad said when he was next to me. "Kyara and Liam weren't both dreaming the same dream! And this means that this is the Thames River!"

I rolled my eyes. Dad knew so much about geography and history it was crazy. My mind couldn't even begin to remember all the facts he does.

Liam's arm was around mine. "You want to join Bryan?" He raised his eyebrows.

"Let's go!" I said taking Liam's hand and jumping with him into the cold but refreshing river.

I couldn't even feel the bottom as I made my way to the surface, and when I did, I shook my head, spraying water from my hair all over Liam. He returned the favor and then dunked me under the water. I gulped for air because I was half laughing under the water. Then, when Liam let me go and I could get fresh air, I dunked him and then swam away towards the shore.

"Join us!" I roared to my family. Luke didn't take a second to retort, as he ran straight into the water. He was a great swimmer, so I didn't think twice about going to help him.

Amy and Mom sat down together. Dad looked at Mom, who gave him a "go for it" look and he jumped over my head. Bella; however, stood there, at a loss for what to do.

"Come on Bella!" Bryan bellowed at her.

"I don't really want to." She said looking at the water, uncertain.

"It's fun! It's not that cold." I said, smiling up at her and I swam back to Liam. "It's actually quite refreshing!"

"I think I'll just hang with Amy and your mother." She complained about the depth of the water, the strong current and the freezing temperature, making more excuses on why she shouldn't come in. While she was complaining; however, Bryan snuck up out of the water and silently walked over to where Bella was, who had not noticed a single thing because she was looking upstream. We were all staring at him, and I was slightly laughing. Hearing my giggling, she stared at me and looked around at the water. She seemed confused because we were all looking behind her. She turned around quickly, but it was too late. Bryan scooped her up in his arms and raced into the water.

"Bryan, n—" She screamed, but the water stopped her from finishing her exclamation.

Bryan slowly came up, still holding Bella.

"Oh, my goodness, this water is so cold. Bryan, I hate you!" Bella screamed, laughing slightly and spraying water at him.

"Oh, don't be chicken." Bryan smiled, letting Bella swim on her own.

"You'll get used to the cold soon enough," I said to Bella.

"Hey kids! Are there any fish in there? Because we need to eat somehow," Mom hollered at us.

"Yes!" Dad said, and I looked at him uncertainly. "I've felt a few swim by me."

"I haven't felt any." I raised an eyebrow. "And how are we supposed to catch them? Aren't they really fast?"

"I have." Bryan said, paying no attention to the second part of my statement. He dove under.

Liam swam a little upstream and dove under as well.

Both didn't come out for an unreasonable amount of time, and I was about to go under and try to find one of them, when Bryan finally broke the surface. "Kyara's right. They are impossible to catch."

Liam then popped his head up and said, "I almost got one, but ran out of breath before I could catch it." He tried again, going back under.

Dad went under as well, and I looked at Bryan, pursing my lips.

"They won't be able to catch one. Plus, how are we supposed to make a fire? We have no matches or anything," he said.

I nodded. "We need to get into town."

Luke swam toward Bryan and me and asked if he could try and catch fish. Both Bryan and I were quick to say "no."

Then Liam came up and started coughing. I swam over to him. "You okay?" I asked, after he finished coughing.

"Yeah, but they are literally impossible to catch," Liam said, referring to the fish.

Dad projected through the surface, then, and shook his head, sadly. "We need to get into town. There might be several deserted homes because of the plague. We have to try and make a living there. It's impossible to get fish and we need shelter, especially because it may take some time to find the phone." He said, matter-of-factly.

I nodded and looked around as everyone else did the same.

"Yeah, I'm super hungry," I said, and everyone agreed.

I started swimming toward the bank and pulled myself up out of the water. Everyone followed my lead.

I already felt myself drying off. The heat was radiating through my clothes and heating my body as well, and I didn't feel cold at all. It must be summertime here.

"In order to get to the town, we are going to have to swim across the river," Dad began. "There probably isn't a bridge anywhere close by."

I groaned. I didn't want to get back in the water, but I was hungry, and I'd do anything to get food, so I jumped back in the river, and followed Dad in pursuit of the other side.

"I don't want to go in! It'll be cold," Amy whined.

"I'll swim with you." Mom said. "We'll dry off pretty quickly. It's warm out."

Amy sighed and then started toward the water. Mom followed, limping slightly. Her bruise was becoming less definite, but I knew it would take a few more days until she could walk completely normal.

Liam caught up to me and started doing the butterfly stroke, quite well, I thought to myself.

"Is there anything you can't do?" I asked, laughing slightly.

"What do you mean?"

"You can do the butterfly, play almost any sport. . ." I trailed off, wondering what else he could do.

"So? I'm good at sports. Not much else," he raised his eyebrows at me.

We had reached the other side of the river and when we got out I whispered in his ear, "You're good at loving me."

He blushed, and then gave me a quick kiss on the cheek.

Dad had already started through the trees, as Bryan came out of the water next, closely followed by Luke and Bella. Mom and Amy were the last to join us.

"We should probably catch up to him, so that he doesn't get lost," Mom said and started after Dad, with Amy next to her for support. Then everyone else started following.

Liam took my hand as we neared the trees. I clutched it tightly and smiled at him, slightly. I was happy, yes, but I was also a little nervous and scared. We were in a difficult time—maybe the most difficult one yet, but I did have Liam with me. And I would not let him go.

We caught up to Dad and the rest of the group and started toward the town that was now able to be seen through the trees. The first thing I saw through the completely opened, metal gate was the cathedral—it was the most beautiful thing in area and in the center of the town. Beyond were several homes—ones Liam and I had seen about five hours ago—made of pure wood, two to three stories in height, but not many townspeople were around. There were a few stragglers here and there, but not many. Most must be in their homes—which was strange, considering it was midday—or they had mostly cleared out.

We tiptoed through the gate, as if the town was haunted, and still hardly anyone was in sight.

"I have a bad feeling about this," Mom said, her eyes glazed over with fear.

"We need food and water; our only hope is to go into town," Dad said.

Mom's eyes darted to Dad's and she returned to her normal, hopeful expression. "You're right. I'm probably imagining things."

And so, we carefully made our way through the town.

"Where is everyone?" Bryan said, and I could hear him gulping down fear.

I nodded and followed Dad, who was in the front of our pack. I felt like I was in a pack of wolves, and Dad was our alpha. We went through an alley between two houses and found a well. A woman walked up to the well and didn't even look at us, though we were quite visible and a large group. She fetched her water, and then went back to where she came from—to the left of us and into a house that was made of perfect white washed wood.

"That was weird," Bryan stated. Most everyone in the group seemed frozen. What was going on? Why was everyone acting so strange?

"Come on," I said and started toward the well. I was thirsty and pure water seemed like it would be satisfying. I sure hoped I wouldn't get sick from the stream water.

Liam, still holding my hand, walked with me, and Bryan followed, with Bella still holding tightly to his hand. I didn't know who else had followed, because I didn't look back, but I assumed most had. Liam helped me pull the bucket out of the well and I scooped some water into my mouth with my hands.

Everyone took handfuls of water and then Dad lowered the bucket back into the abyss after all our thirsts were quenched.

"We should stay on the outer side of town," Dad said. "Maybe at an abandoned farm somewhere because we don't want too many people asking questions about us."

I nodded, and he led us to the right, out past some houses.

Right before a hill, I saw a bridge off to our right, and I laughed slightly at how we had gone through the water for no reason. But how would we know that a bridge was there?

A few others noticed the bridge too.

"That's just our luck," Bryan said, and we all laughed feebly.

Then we started up a hill and I finally noticed a few buildings cluttered on a field. I saw a barn and some more fields beyond and knew right away that Dad had let us up to a farm.

"Did you know about this place already?" I asked, confused on how he knew a farm would be over here.

"No, I was hoping there would be based on my historical knowledge of the medieval era. Farms are always placed outside the city."

I shrugged and smiled slightly, but as we neared closer to the farmland, I noticed some type of animal in the distance, and my smile turned into a frown. I knew when a horse was sick—we had a few growing up, and Mom was a vet—and this horse seemed very sick, meaning that the people who used to be here, must have left a while ago. The horse was thin and out of shape, and it was tied up by a few long ropes, to the fence. I could see its eyes were fading, trying to stay open. When it saw me, it tried to swing its tail, but it couldn't do it without neighing heavily.

He didn't budge when I put my hand on him and started pulling off his ropes.

"He needs food and a vet. Mom, can you save him?" I asked.

Mom came up behind me and told me to go get water in the well that I had not seen until now. It stood right next to the house and I ran up to it as Mom started feeling around the horse's body. As I reached the well, Liam, helped me yank the bucket out of the water.

Then I asked him, "Can you go into the house and find something to put the water in?"

"Yeah," he said and hurried inside.

Bryan, Amy, Luke, and Bella walked past me into the barn, and I could hear Bryan's heavy groan of dismay.

"There's two cows in here, Mom," he yelled out to her. "They don't look too good either."

Mom scrunched her eyebrows and muttered something to herself and then whispered what seemed like instructions to Dad.

Liam then came out of the house, carrying a large wooden bowl and put it on the ground next to me. I filled it up, and then put the bucket back in the well and walked with Liam, with the bowl in our hands, back to Mom who was leaving the horse and heading toward Bryan.

"Where are you going?" I asked.

"Cows are more important right now. The horse will be fine if you give him food and water. He just hasn't eaten in a few days," she said. I looked around for piles of hay or patches of grass but noticed only dirt. All the hay and grass had been eaten or torn from the soil. The cows must have gotten to it all. But the poor horse had probably not eaten in days.

Liam and I reached the horse and helped it drink. He drank the whole bowl. Then Bryan and Bella came with a big pile of hay. They dropped it next to the horse and he started munching right on it. He neighed happily as he ate.

"We should go help my mom," I said to Liam. He nodded, and we went to the barn where the cows were.

Mom had started milking one of the cows. They looked much more fed than the horse. There was still a lot of grass and hay in the barn and there was still some water in the trough. Good thing, too. Cows would be a good source for us.

Amy and Luke were shoveling cow poop and running outside with it. Amy almost ran into me as she ran past me and I yelled at her to be more careful.

"You need any help, Mom?" I asked after Amy apologized and continued on outside.

"Why don't you go and see if there's any food in the house. Be careful on what you find; make sure it's not old and moldy. Your father is in there trying to find a clue on where the family, who lived here, is."

I nodded, and Liam and I exited the barn.

Bryan and Bella were still with the horse, but Dad was not in sight.

Bryan looked up and said, "He went inside—"

"I know. Mom told me. Thanks," I said loud enough for Bryan to hear me and went to the house to find Dad.

It was quite beautiful. The door was some type of dark wood, but as we entered, the door creaked, and I noticed that the house smelled like rotting animals.

The first room was the kitchen with all sorts of cupboards and counters. There were pots, pans, and skillets scattered on the counters and there was a fireplace with a kettle, spits, and a pot hook. There were two doors on the far-left end of the kitchen, but I didn't have time to look in them. I assumed they were pantries, though.

A long hallway led through the center of the kitchen with a ladder at the end of it, and as I looked down it, I got a large knot in my stomach.

"Dad?" I yelled out, slightly fearful.

"Kyara, do not come down here. Is anyone with you?"

"I'm here, Mr. Edwards," Liam said.

"Everything okay?"

"Not particularly. Liam, come here. Kyara, stay in the kitchen and look for food, okay?"

Liam's frightened eyes met mine and then started down the hallway. I stayed put, not only because I was told to, but also because I felt like my shoes were glued to the floor and my body was frozen.

I saw Liam turn into the far-left room and then heard a deep intake of breath. I couldn't take it anymore. I couldn't stay here; I had to see what was going on, so I slowly picked my left foot up, placed it down several inches in front of the right foot, and then the right foot moved in the same fashion. Walking seemed harder than normal, but I was able to make it to the room Liam had just disappeared into.

Once I saw it, I felt my face turn pale, and the knot in my stomach become a boulder, but I kept the bile down.

A man, about the same age as my father, was laying on a bed; his eyes were wide open, but he was not moving. I had never seen a sight like it before. I knew he was dead, but something about the way his

45

body was covered in blood and boils made horror films seem like nothing.

Tears formed quickly around my eyes and I turned away, running back to the kitchen. My breaths became seemingly irrelevant, and I doubled over, but nothing came up. I heaved, but still nothing. I hadn't eaten a meal in several hours, not since the Titanic, and even though I had been starving a few minutes prior, hunger would now be hard to rekindle.

I heard Liam's hurried footsteps, and then felt his arms wrap around me and pull me close. For some strange reason, the tears would not escape my eyes. They just stayed, surrounding my eyes, unable to let go. It was as if the trapped tears were depicting my life, and this, I thought, would be the worst I would ever see. Little did I know how wrong I was.

Chapter IV
Mad World

Dad and Liam wrapped the body up in bed sheets, and, as I looked through the cupboards to see if there was any possible food, trying to ignore what they were doing, they carried it through the kitchen and outside. I stood motionless when I heard the voices of Bryan and Bella ask them what was going on.

I did not want to hear the answer, for I wanted to get the idea of how mad this world was out of my mind, so I skidded to the wide-open door and slammed it shut. I had finished looking through all the cupboards, with all the contents on the kitchen table, so I walked toward the pieces of bread, oats, and the variety of vegetables and gazed down at them. I wasn't hungry, but I wanted to eat the food I had found. And the only reason I could think of as to why, had to do with the fact that I didn't want anyone to get sick or poisoned. I'd rather it be me.

Bryan then came in through the door and stared at me, his mouth gaping open. Bella ran in past

Bryan and stopped in front of me, looking down at the food.

"Can we eat it?" She asked.

"I wouldn't trust it," Bryan found his voice and walked up to us. "We should probably get some more water from the well and wash the vegetables." He picked up the bread and smelled it, breaking it in half.

"Kyara," Bella took a bowl from the counter behind me and headed back toward the door. "Do you want to help me get some water?"

I nodded and followed her outside to the well. Liam and Dad were nowhere in sight, but somehow, I knew they were somewhere burying the body of the man.

"You okay?" Bella asked me as she and I started to pull the bucket up. For some reason, it seemed heavier this time, and I could only guess that it was because I felt weak. The bucket was filled with as much water as there was last time.

I shrugged to her question as she poured the water into the bowl. She looked up at me with questioning eyes. She probably didn't notice me shrug, so I said "yeah" softly, knowing it was a lie.

Bella pursed her lips and placed the bucket back on the pulley, letting it fall slowly back into the void.

We walked back to the house silently, all the while, Bella held the bowl. She was strong, that was for sure, but I was slightly confused on how she was muscular. She hadn't shown much physical strength before, or maybe I just hadn't noticed it.

Entering the house again was something I did not want to do, but this was our new home now, so I knew I would have to get used to it.

Bryan wasn't in the kitchen. Bella called out for him, and I could hear him from upstairs saying, "There's enough beds in here for all of us."

I cleared my throat, wanting to say something about the bed that had held the man a few moments prior, but the words would not escape my mouth. Instead I stared at Bella, my mouth slightly ajar, in hope that she would say something. It wasn't until Bryan came down the ladder that she did.

"How many beds?"

"Seven. Not counting the one in the far-left room. I'm not sure any of us will want to sleep in there," Bryan said awkwardly.

"How are eight of us supposed to fit in seven beds?" I had finally found my voice.

"Two of them are double sized. So, one of us will be sleeping like royalty," Bryan smiled as if he had just said something funny. It may have been funny in different circumstances, but surely not now.

"We probably need to clean the sheets, though," I said.

"When Liam and Dad get back, we will."

"What about soap?" Bella asked.

The door opened, and Mom, Amy, and Luke entered.

"Oh my gosh!" Luke said. "It smells worse in here than it did in the barn."

Amy plugged her nose, "And we were cleaning up poop in the barn."

"Where is Liam?" Mom asked me, placing a bucket of milk on the side of the kitchen's door, taking no notice of the kids' complaining. "And your father?"

"They had to, uh," I stopped, unsure what to say. Amy and Luke could not know the truth.

"They went to look in the field for crops," Bryan said, "Which you should go help Kyara with."

I squinted my eyes at Bryan.

"You said," Bryan began, looking only at me, "that when Mom came in, you would bring her to go help Dad and Liam."

I knew for a fact that I had never said that, so I wondered why Bryan would say that. Then I realized that he either wanted me to tell Mom what Liam and Dad were really doing, or he didn't want to have to explain it himself, possibly because he didn't know what had really happened. So, it could actually be both.

I nodded, "Yeah, I did say that. Let's go, Mom." I took her hand and pulled her outside.

Amy and Luke asked to come with, but Bryan was quick to give them a reason not to go. "I need your help." But the help he needed, I was unsure of, for the door closed behind me before I heard Bryan finish.

Mom and I headed toward the fields, and it was silent for a few seconds until Mom spoke.

"So where are they, really?"

"There, uh, was a dead man in one of the rooms," I said, quicker than I thought I had ever spoken in my entire life. But Mom seemed to understand.

"So, they're burying him?" She asked.

"I'm not sure," I said, and then my question was answered when I heard Liam call my name.

I looked up from the ground that I had been staring at while speaking to Mom, turned around, and saw Liam running toward us from where the town was; Dad was following a few steps behind Liam.

I stopped in my tracks and waited for him to reach me. Mom kept walking but stopped suddenly when she realized what I had a few seconds prior, that both Liam and Dad had panicked looks on their faces.

I wanted to ask what they had seen, but words failed me, once again.

Once they reached us, Dad breathing more heavily than Liam, explained what happened.

"We took the man to the church, for we knew we should bury him on holy ground—that's what they do in this time."

"And there was a priest at the church," Dad continued, "who told us about the man's family."

"All five of his children and his wife had passed away in the past few months, and the priest had said he was waiting to find the father of the farm dead," Liam went on.

"The priest had said that he had come to talk with the man, or farmer, a few days ago, and that he had just started to get the plague. The priest prayed with him and they parted ways. The priest knew that the farmer had very little time left, and that he was worried for the farm."

"When the priest found out that we would start to take care of the farm, he thanked us and said that he'd take the body to bury him with the help of his two nephews."

"So, you left the body with the priest?" Mom asked. "And they will bury him with his family?"

"Yes," Liam said.

"You didn't touch the body, did you?" Mom asked, nervously.

"No," Dad began. "Of course not. But the priest did say that he had seen in the town, that some people may not catch the plague, and that some may be immune to it."

Mom and I nodded.

"Do you think we could be immune?" I asked.

"I'm hoping so," Dad said.

Liam smiled slightly at me and said, "We should probably wash our hands, though."

I nodded, and Liam and Dad started toward the well. Mom said she would start to look through the fields to find crops. I stayed put until Mom told me to come help her.

As we neared fields I noticed that all the crops stood up tall, looking as though they were waiting to be picked.

Liam and Dad came back a few minutes later to help. Barley and wheat were the main crops we found as we searched through the fields. We stuck together as we ranged across the area. Liam taught me what the good stuff was, and what not to pick. I filled as much barley and wheat into the skirt of my dress as I could. Liam had taken his shirt off and tied the two ends of the shirt sleeves into a knot making a sort of bag. Then we went back to the house.

Bella, Amy, and Luke had taken off all of the sheets from the beds and placed them in a pile next to the door. Bryan had started to boil some water in the fireplace by the kitchen. As we placed the wheat and barley on the counter, Dad came in with Mom emptying their bundles, and he said he could take over Bryan's job. Bryan never had been a great cook, so I was glad Dad had taken up the responsibility.

Bryan had also placed three baskets out for us to use, and then we all, except Dad, went out to the fields to retrieve more of the crops. Liam and I stuck together, as we split into three groups to range across the fields, one bucket for each group.

Liam and I were silent for the first few minutes, as we picked at the bean stocks. Then finally he asked the inevitable—which I knew I'd have to answer sooner or later.

"Are you okay?"

It took a few seconds for me to look at him, away from the basket I had just placed another bean sprout in.

"Not really," I said, and then everything that had been on my mind spilled out in an informal fashion. "We're in a terrible place, where I'm certain at least one of us will get the plague. And if not the plague, then we'll die from something else probably! Why can't we just get home? Why do we keep having to live like this? I'd rather be in school, learning about stuff I know for a fact I won't need to know. No one prepared us for this. No one could have prepared us for this.

"We're stuck, not just in this time, but I'm sure there'll be other times too. We've already gone through three different eras and I just don't think I can take it anymore. Yeah, sure I met you, but if we're meant to be, why couldn't I have met you in real life? Rather than in this some sort of fairytale—or more like a nightmare—"

"You think that my love for you isn't real?" He interrupted, dropping the basket full of bean sprouts. "You think that this isn't real life?" He wasn't mad—I knew that for sure—but he was disappointed.

Tears formed my eyes. I didn't know what to say. It had just slipped from my mouth, and I didn't mean for it to. It was just so difficult, living like this. I wished that it was all a dream, and that I had met Liam some other way.

"Because it's not," he said and took my hand. "It is real. And do you want to know why it is real?" He paused, but not long enough for me to retort. "Because, number one, I haven't met you before. And dreams only show people who we have met in our life. It's impossible for us to create a person in a dream, especially someone so miraculous."

I opened my mouth to speak, but he kept going, a little louder this time as he clenched my hand tighter.

"Number two. Dreams don't last this long, and they certainly can't be as crazy as this. Yes, dreams usually are crazy, but they don't ever stay in chronological order for such a long period of time. And number three," he took a deep breath. "It is impossible to feel so many emotions at once in a dream. And it is impossible for me to fall so in love with someone in a dream. You may wish that this were all a dream. But I don't. It all happened for a reason, and that reason, we may not know for sure, but I have to hope it has something to do with you and me."

I wanted to smile, but for some reason I couldn't lift my lips up into the right position. Instead, I let the tear in my right eye fall. I had read once that if a tear from the right eye fell first, it meant the person was happy. Liam had obviously known that fact, too, for he smiled.

I dropped the last few bean pods into the basket, which I then pulled into my arms.

"We should take this back to my dad. It's almost full," I said.

Liam nodded, took the basket from me, and together we walked back to the house. Mom, Amy, and Luke had just dropped off some vegetables, and were about to go back out for more, when we came in.

"That's enough beans for an army!" Luke said to Liam.

I smiled down at him and ruffled his hair. As he pushed my hand away and walked outside, I noticed something I hadn't noticed for a while. He was smiling—a true smile. He was actually happy, and I couldn't help but think that that happiness may soon fade. I didn't want it to. I mean, the whole family was together, and it seemed like things were going well. And for a six-year-old, I could tell how oblivious he was. He didn't know about the man who had died. He didn't understand about this era as well as we all did. And he certainly didn't understand that one of us

could possibly die, at any given moment. I surely
hoped, however, that he would stay happy, and that he
would never have to see or deal with the pain as
heavily as I was dealing with it.

Liam had dumped the beans on the counter,
and as he walked up to me, he took my hand and said,
"Time to find oats."

We walked outside, and I asked Liam, "Isn't
that what Bryan and Bella are picking?"

"No," he said. "They're picking more wheat and
barley."

I nodded as we walked back to the fields.
Bryan and Bella exited as we entered, and I noticed
that their basket was filled to the top.

"I wonder if this getting picked will be all for
nothing, or if someone knows how to make bread?"
Bryan said as he walked past us.

I laughed awkwardly, "Isn't it easy, though?
You just grind the wheat and water into a dough and
then cook it, right?"

"But we don't have a bread oven. We have a
fireplace. Plus, we need yeast. I wonder . . ." Bryan
trailed off.

"What?" I said, waiting for Bryan to continue.

"There has to be a bakery somewhere. And I'm
sure the baker gets his ingredients from us, or the
farmer, that is. . ."

"The town is dead, Bryan. We're going to have
to make do with what we have." I said.

He shrugged and then walked off with Bella
toward the house.

~ ~ ~

"So, Mom. When are you going to tell us how you ended up on the Titanic?" I asked her, smiling.

All the girls were working on making the barn a good place to sleep, while the boys were cleaning the bedding outside. Pottage had been eaten and we were all happy and full.

It was dark out, but the moon was bright enough to where the boys could see what they were doing. There were only two lanterns, and the boys insisted we had both of them, making me very thankful. It also didn't smell too bad, thanks to Amy and Luke for clearing out the cow poop.

"I don't think your father will like the story very much." She scrunched her eyebrows as she carried another stack of hay to the far side of the barn. I followed her. Bella and Amy were helping make the hay beds as Mom and I distributed the hay across the barn.

"I wouldn't say that. Nothing can beat what Dad did! Remember, we found him in the Roman times." And with that I told Dad's story briefly, all the while distributing hay to Bella and Amy, who listened attentively.

When I had finished telling the story, there were enough hay beds for the eight of us and they all looked fairly comfortable.

Mom finally looked at me, for she had barely gazed up at me while I told the story, and I noticed a tear glinting in her left eye, but she said nothing. Was she upset with Dad? But he didn't know what he was

57

doing. Now I wanted to know what mom had done, to make Dad not like it.

"Tell me this." She finally said. "Is murder or having an affair worse?"

Chapter V
Marriage and Divorce

"You had an affair!" I said, astounded.

Amy looked slightly confused. I don't think she knew exactly what an affair was. Bella; however, was shocked, but I knew I was even more shocked.

"You said it yourself: Adults lose their memory when they go back in time. Kids only remember what happened and where they were the night of the storm." Mom tried to explain. And I understood. She didn't know she was married.

"But what about the ring? Wasn't it on your finger the night of the storm?" I asked, confused.

"I had taken it off while Daddy and I were at dinner because I was eating something messy. So, when I ended up in England, I had no ring on my finger, I didn't know where I was or who I was, and this nice man came up to me, noticing that something was wrong. And we had dinner. . ." Mom trailed off and tears were in her eyes.

I felt tears fall out of my eyes as well. We all sat down on a bed of hay as Mom told her story.

"He found out I didn't have a place to stay because I had forgotten everything. He tried to help me remember my past, but I couldn't. So, after dinner, he said I could stay with him at his manor. His parents had recently passed away and left their land to their oldest son, Richard, the man who I had dinner with. So, we went back to his manor and I stayed in my own room.

"I did not know about predators or rapists because I had forgotten every bad thing—I had not a care in the world. I was vulnerable. Thankfully, however, Richard was a very nice man, and he had recently had a dream about meeting a woman who he would have to help and care for. He had been married, up until a year before I got there, to a woman who had gotten a very rare disease and died. They had not had children, for she could not bear children. They thought briefly about adopting, but never got to it. Richard's wife had been diagnosed with the disease two years before she had died. And he and his wife, Abigail, were only forty and got married at thirty-four. . ."

At least he wasn't that much younger than Mom. Mom was a little over forty.

"Sorry, I'm rambling so much. Not all of this is relevant, but I do need to tell you how I got on the Titanic, I'm sure you are wondering about that . . ."

We all nodded, slowly but surely.

"Well I had stayed with him, for two weeks, and we got to know each other really well, before. . .

before," Mom took a deep breath and a single tear fell down her face.

I could only guess what happened. . . But what she said was not what I had expected.

"He asked me to marry him. I said yes, but something in my mind made me feel like I should've said no. Something didn't seem right." She took another deep breath and began again. "A week passed and as we made plans for the wedding, I kept feeling that there was something missing. But I couldn't quite understand what it was. Then I had a dream about giving birth to Luke, and that was when I realized, not just that I had a family, but that my family was in America. So, one night, when Richard was working late—he was a lawyer—I took the tickets for the Titanic—the ones that he had bought for our honeymoon—and ran away. It was the night before the Titanic departed and, because I took his ticket, he wasn't able to get on the Titanic to follow me. I had successfully escaped."

"So, if it was the day before the Titanic took off, and the Titanic was where your honeymoon was supposed to take place, did that mean. . ." I gulped back tears, "that you had married Richard?"

Tears began to stream down her face. "Yes. We had gotten married the day before he had his court case, and two days before the Titanic was supposed to depart."

"So. . ." I had to ask the inevitable. "The night you got married, you guys . . ." I couldn't bring myself to say it. But by Mom's reaction of more tears

61

streaming down her face, I knew the answer. Mom had had a true affair.

All was silent for a few minutes.

"The day before you found me, on the Titanic," Mom began again, composing herself, "the truth began to come back to me and I realized where I was. I found the phone in the dresser in my room, the night before the Titanic sunk. But what it said in the messages, you probably won't believe me."

"Why do you say that?" I asked.

"It's a riddle, but it helped me figure out who I was and what happened the past few days. I memorized it, as well."

"What did it say?"

"It said this:

'I am a moment in time
You will become love's first grime
When you find out your offense
Everything will make sense.

The one you think is candid
Is one that has been handed
To your kindred's oldest lad
His first lover will be sad

I am your competitor
But not your first predator
Some have hated you I'm sure
Before me; I am your cure.'"

"What does that even mean?" I asked. I played it over in my head a few times, but it was too confusing to help me get anywhere.

I finally took my eyes off Mom and made eye contact with Bella, who looked quite distressed and gave me a half-smile. I then looked at Amy who had tear streaks on her face.

"What's going on?" My heart jumped, and I looked up. The boys had just entered the barn looking tired and wet.

I met Mom's eyes, which began to water again. She must not want Dad to know about what happened with her.

"Maggie?" Dad came over to us and knelt down beside her, starting to rub her back. "Does she know my story?" He looked over at me.

I nodded my head.

"Is that why she is sad? Is she angry with me?"

"No. She thinks her story is worse. And I can't tell which one is actually worse." I looked up at Dad.

"Maggie? What happened?" Dad asked, delicately, still rubbing her back.

"Dad. Come here." I stood up. I did not want to watch Mom tell the story again. And anyway, I don't think she would be able to.

I gave Liam a look of, "I'll tell you later," right before I walked outside with Dad and Bryan. We walked toward the house, where no one could hear us.

Bryan and Dad looked at me, worriedly.

I opened my mouth to speak, but realized my mouth was dry.

"It's okay, Kyara. You can tell me. I don't think it can be worse than murder. And anyway, just like me, she didn't know what she was doing." Dad was trying to utter a smile.

"Well you both broke one of the Ten Commandments. The two worst ones in my opinion." I hiccupped.

"Adultery." Bryan said, and his eyes were wide.

Dad looked me straight in the eyes asking if that was it. I nodded.

Dad took a deep breath and walked away from me and started pacing.

Bryan and I looked at each other, his mouth was open, and he was surely shocked.

Dad's eyes closed, and he kept pacing, saying words under his breath that I could not quite hear perfectly, but figured it was something like "murder" and "affair".

"Should we let him be alone to think?" Bryan asked me, his face all puckered up into a frown. I was biting my lip so hard that I actually tasted blood. Something about the pinecone under my feet seemed very interesting. I would not look up. Tears were still in my eyes, but I did not let them fall down my face. I had to be strong—for Mom.

"Kyara?" He lifted up my chin to see my face. My face must not have looked very pretty because Bryan's frown turned into a tremor. But all the same, he wiped the tears away from my eyes. "Come on. We need to give Dad a little time alone." He pulled me back towards the barn.

"Wait," I said, halting mid-step.

"What?" Bryan said and stopped as well.

"When Mom found the phone, there was something in the messages. Mom has it memorized, and what I remember wasn't good. Something about the one we think is telling the truth is a liar, and, like, the person who wrote the message is our cure . . ." I paused. "I don't know. Mom will have to say it again."

Bryan didn't say anything, but he looked like he was thinking hard.

"Let's have Mom repeat it," Bryan said. "Come on."

We walked through the barn doors and saw that no one had moved, except for Amy who was now in Mom's lap and Luke who had moved over to a hay bed.

Liam walked over and gave me a hug. Bryan went to sit down next to Bella. Mom didn't dare look up, even when Amy moved and said "hi" to me.

"Where's Daddy?" Luke managed to ask, looking up at me.

"He needs a little time." Bryan said to him and I gave him a look of thanks.

"Why?" Luke said.

"We'll tell you later, okay buddy?" I said.

Liam led me toward the other side of the barn and asked me what had happened. I explained Mom's story in short and Liam didn't interject until the very end when I had told him about the poem.

"We should ask your Mom to repeat it so that we can try and figure it out," Liam said.

"Yes, Bryan and I think so too, but she seems so down, I don't know if this is good time to make her repeat it."

Liam shrugged. "Up to you. We should go back over there, though."

I nodded, and we walked back toward the others. Bryan met my eyes and cocked his head toward Mom and mouthed the word "poem".
I nodded. Might as well ask her.

"Mom?" I said, and Mom looked up at me, her eyes red and blotchy.

"Yes dear?" She wiped away a tear.

I sat down on a hay bed and Liam sat next to me. "Could you say the message again? I want to try to figure out what it means. . ."

She sniffed and then repeated the poem.

"'I am a moment in time
You will become love's first grime
When you find out your offense
Everything will make sense.

The one you think is candid
Is one that has been handed
To your kindred's oldest lad
His first lover will be sad

I am your competitor
But not your first predator
Some have hated you I'm sure
Before me; I am your cure.'

"I don't know what it means though. I feel like maybe it wasn't meant for me. . ." She sniffled.

I pursed my lips and thought about the message. I played it over and over again in my head and figured out little of it by the time Dad re-entered the barn.

"Maggie, dear. Can we talk?" He smiled at Mom. He seemed okay, and the smile was real, but as Mom stood up and went over to him, I could tell she was nervous.

They exited the barn and disappeared toward the house. I wanted to know what they were saying, but I knew I should give them space. Spying on Bryan and Bella was different than spying on Mom and Dad.

Bryan and I looked at each other, tentatively, and then I turned my head to look up at Liam.

"I wonder what time it is." Liam said.

I shrugged. "It's been dark for more than an hour, but I'm pretty tired, so it's got to be at least eight o'clock."

I looked away from Liam and noticed Bella and Bryan were whispering—well it was mostly Bryan doing the whispering, and Bella was listening. She looked like she was about to cry, and she looked away every now and then.

I scrunched my eyebrows and craned my neck trying to listen to them, but I couldn't quite catch what he was saying. If there were ever a champion whisperer, Bryan would be it. He was the best at whispering.

Liam nudged me, and I looked at him. He smiled and then kissed my lips, muttering, "I love you."

I said those same, meaningful words back to him, smiling.

I lay back on the bed and Liam lay down next to me.

"Are you scared?" He asked, turning his head toward me. I turned my head and our noses were only inches from each other.

"A little. . . yeah. I just can't bear to think if one of us got the plague."

"Oh. I meant about your parents. . ." He trailed off and I could tell he felt uncomfortable.

"Oh." And I shared that same feeling. "I think they will work it out. I mean they both didn't know what they were doing. All adults *must* have lost their memories when they traveled through time."

"Must be. But what about that woman who told Mr. Murdoch that the Titanic wasn't safe?" Liam asked me.

"I don't know."

"I was thinking, it could have been your mom, but now that we know her story, it wouldn't make any sense."

"Yeah. . ." I trailed off not knowing what to say next.

"What do you think the message on the phone means?" He asked.

"Honestly, I have no idea." I began. I had some ideas on what it meant, but they didn't make sense. I was always good at interpreting riddles and poems, especially anything having to do with Shakespeare, and I thought I might have an idea on this one. But I couldn't make sense of it . . .

"Your eyes say something different." He knew me too well. I couldn't keep anything a secret from him.

"Well, I may have an idea or two. . . Some of it I was able to interpret, but I could be completely wrong."

"Tell me." He rested his head on his bent arm, as he turned towards me more.

I closed my eyes. "I'd have to hear it again or see it written down to make sure, but I think, 'I am a moment in time,' means that the writer is the one who made the time machine. 'You will become love's first grime' may have something to do with mom cheating? 'When you find out your offense. Everything will make sense.' My mom must have an enemy—like someone who is trying to get back at her. That's the gist of the first stanza. The second one makes sense to the point where someone we think is telling the truth is actually not, 'The one you think is candid.' And I think it's Bella. But I don't know what she could be lying about."

"How did you even understand the second stanza? I had no idea what it meant." Liam scrunched his eyebrows.

"Kindred means family, and lad means, in this sense, boy, so I think "kindred's oldest lad" means Bryan. And then the line before that is 'the one that has been handed'—"

"How do you even memorize this?" Liam's mouth was wide open.

"I have a good memory. . . Anyway. The one who has been handed to Bryan is Bella. So, it has to be Bella that has a secret. I want to ask her, but I don't know exactly how to. You know?"

69

"Ok," Liam said, seeming more confused than ever. "What's the last stanza mean?"

"'I am your competitor. But not your first predator. Some have hated you I'm sure.' This means that the person who wrote this message hates us, or we hate them, for some reason I don't know. And then, 'I am your cure,' means that the person who wrote the message will be our savior, basically. That he, or she, has the power to take us home," I said.

Liam raised an eyebrow. "You really think that?"

"Yes."

"Then why hasn't he, or she, taken us home yet?" Liam asked.

"Well, I don't think they can or want to," I said.

"What do you mean by 'want to'?"

"We are their competitor, it said. The writer hates us, but I don't know what it has to do with anything. I'm trying to figure it out. Just give me some time to process it."

Liam nodded and pursed his lips. It was then silent for a few minutes.

"So? How do you think your parents' talk will go?" He said, changing the subject again back to our previous one.

"I think they will forgive each other. I mean both made a huge mistake." I shrugged.

"Yeah I know. But do you think one will think the other is worse? Do you think one is worse than the other?" Liam asked.

"No. In God's sight we are all sinners. But I don't know what he is going to do about this one because neither of them knew what they were doing." I sighed.

"I hope they work it out."

"Me too." I nodded and then it was silent. I noticed that everyone else had lain down as well. I then proceeded to look back up at the ceiling.

They had to work it out. If they didn't then that could only create more problems, and we had way enough problems to figure out already. Both Mom and Dad crossed a line and committed a sin they thought they would never commit. And both of them didn't mean to. They didn't know what they were doing. Satan was trying to break up their marriage right now and I couldn't let him. And so, I prayed, *Lord, be with my parents through this hard time and don't let Satan break them apart! Jesus, help us! Please! We need you.*

I could feel the break down coming. Just as it did on the Titanic and Liam had to bring me to my bed and let me sleep it off. But would I be able to sleep it off this time? Especially with the possibility of all of us dying? That was a possibility on the Titanic as well, but we had four days to figure everything out, and we knew the exact time and day that we had to find the phone by or have an escape plan. This time; however, we had no escape plan because there was nowhere to escape to. The Black Plague could hit us at any moment, without us even knowing it. We didn't have a time of possible death now. This time was different than all of the others.

Water came to my eyes. What was going to happen to us? I felt sick. Not only because of the pain I was going through, but, I actually felt like I was going

71

to vomit. I sat up quickly and the next thing I knew, I was puking up everything in my stomach.

Chapter VI
The Red Sunrise

"Kyara!" Liam said, or at least, I think it was Liam. I could barely hear over my vomiting. He held my hair back. There was a huge puddle of bile beneath me, mostly consisting of the dinner we had and what looked like a yellow liquid. The smell was terrible.

Bryan ran over to us.

"Get your parents!" I heard Liam tell Bryan.

I could barely keep my head up as Bryan ran outside the barn to find our parents. The vomiting stopped, giving me enough time to catch my breath, but then I started to vomit again.

I felt lightheaded. More lightheaded than I ever had before, and it seemed like I was going to faint. But I had to stay wake. I could not pass out. Mom and Dad would be back soon. Stay awake!

~ ~ ~

I slowly came to. My stomach didn't feel as gross and I didn't feel as much nausea. But, I had no sensation in my legs or my arms. Was I paralyzed? Would this be the end? Was the plague already trapping me from life? I felt cold. My heart was pumping fast and I could feel the blood run through my head and chest, and there was a searing pain in my throat on each beat.

Were there already bumps and bruises covering my body? Were my arms and legs numb from what would surely end my life? I tried to open my eyes but couldn't. My mouth was dry, and I needed water. I opened my mouth to ask and that was when several people called my name, "Kyara!" But it seemed as though they were someplace in the distance.

I started coughing, but I had no more substance in my stomach to throw up.

"Can we help you sit up so that you can drink some water?" Liam's voice came from right next to me. I saw the ceiling of the barn, but not the same part I had seen before I started puking. They must have moved me away from the pile of vomit.

There was a hand stroking my hair, which I could guess was also Liam. But it started to feel more feminine after a while and I realized it was Mom.

I now had feeling in my hand, and I could move my fingers, which were held by Liam's smooth, familiar hand.

They helped me into a sitting position, Liam, all the while, held my hand tightly. I knew he loved me a lot because of how much he cared for me, and how much he had been there for me in the past, and I know he will be there for me in the future. Through sickness and in health. No matter what.

I opened up my eyes and drank from a cup. The cold water rushed through my throat into my stomach and I felt better.

"What happened?" I asked.

"You puked because of the water you drank from the stream," Mom began. "You don't have a fever, which is a sign of the plague. So, we think it was just from the water you drank earlier. You don't have the plague, though. Other symptoms would start coming up by now."

I nodded. "How long was I out?"

"About thirty minutes. If you were out longer we would've been a little more worried, but. . ." Dad trailed off.

"And you're not worried now? That I could have the plague!" I said. How were they not worried? I was just puking up my guts. I mean, I felt fine now, but that didn't mean that soon I wouldn't be.

"Kyara, calm down," Mom said, in her soothing tone. "You are going to be fine. As long as you stay with us, you should be okay. You don't have a fever, so I promise you, you don't have the plague."

I pursed my lips and scrunched my eyebrows. I tried to stop my worrying, but I was someone who worried a lot, even if what I was worrying about was unnecessary. So, I tried to think of something else.

I then realized that my dress was off, and I was in my undergarments of the early 20th century. It felt slightly awkward to be in all white and just a light shirt and leggings, but I was still covered.

Then the question I had been dying to know came to my mind and I looked at Mom, and then Dad, and then back at Mom who smiled.

"We are okay. Your dad and I have worked it out and we still are deeply and unconditionally in love. We both made terrible mistakes, but God had already forgiven us, so we forgave each other."

"And neither of us knew what we were doing, and we know that. Divorce has never been an option for us because we are children of God and He thinks marriage should never be broken. When we get back to the future; however, which will hopefully be soon, we are going to renew our vows." Dad smiled, and then hugged and kissed Mom.

Bryan came over to sit next to me and hugged me, smiling. Their marriage was saved. The devil didn't get in this time, nor will he any other time. We must stay true to that.

"All right, I think everyone's getting a little tired. We should probably get some rest," Mom said.

I was getting tired and I could tell others were, as well.

"Mama? Can you sing me a song?" Amy asked and went up to her and nuzzled herself into her lap. Mom had the voice that could call the angels down through the clouds and sing along. Her voice was the most beautiful one I had ever heard in my life, and I knew that when she sang, God was smiling from Heaven above.

"What song shall I sing?" Mom asked Amy, and everyone started dispersing toward the beds of hay, with smiles on their faces.

"How He Loves." Amy spoke up. That was her favorite worship song, as well as mine.

And so, she began. "He is jealous for me. Loves like a hurricane, I am a tree, bending beneath the weight of his wind and mercy. . ."

And the rest of us joined in, one after the other, after the other.

As we sang I thought about all the pain we had endured the past few times and all the hardships we had overcome. When we got to the line, "If grace is an ocean, we're all sinking," I started to cry. God had been so gracious with me. I didn't deserve all that he had done for me. None of us did. But somehow God gave us life when we didn't deserve it. It would hopefully be a long time before I understood why, because hopefully I wouldn't be going to Heaven anytime soon. But who knew what would happen? We were in a time of death—Black Death.

I didn't care if I died here. I was not afraid of death because I knew where I would go. I knew God had everything under control and if I were to die here, I would accept it. But would I accept it if someone else died here? Like a sibling or Liam? Would I fall away from God and curse Him for what He had done? I didn't want to. Not now at least, but would that change, due to certain circumstances? Then I thought of how my family would feel if I died. They would be broken and deeply distressed, Liam most of all because I knew how he would feel. In Heaven, I would look down on them and feel bad for them. I would not want them to cry over me because I would be in a happier place.

I would pity them; I would pity the way they cried over me. And then that made me realize, just how several movies, plays, and books had explained death and life. Death was just a part of life. And the living didn't understand it. The dead were almost always happier than the living, and they did not want to come back to life after they had died. Even though life was sometimes a wonderful thing, death was way better if you knew and trusted in Jesus.

So, the question was, if one of us died here would I be able to move on and accept it? Especially if I knew that if I was in their place, I would want them to be happy that I was in a better place? Hopefully I would not have to figure it out, but I did know that it was good to think of this, just in case. And right then, I put everything into God's hands, and I thought, I will accept whatever happens because it is You and only You who has the power over us.

~ ~ ~

I woke up to the sound of the barn door opening. I turned my head and a bright light shined into my eyes. It was surely morning. I didn't know who the source of my waking up was because they had already disappeared outside. But I assumed it was Amy or Luke, for they had left the barn door wide open. I heard groaning near me, so I sat up.

Amy was still on the hay bed next to me, turning her face toward the other side of the barn so she would not have the sun shining on her. It must have been Luke who had left then. Looking around,

Mom and Dad had left their bed, as well as Luke—whose bed was next to theirs. Liam's bed was also deserted. Bryan and Bella were still asleep, however.

I stood up and stretched. I then exited the barn and walked toward the house. The sun was just peeking between the hills in the east and the sunrise was shaded red, almost the color of blood. I wondered why as I walked to the house—it was slightly frightening, but somehow, I thought God was trying to tell me something. I couldn't comprehend what it could be, but it sure was something.

As I entered through the door, Liam was the first to greet me, with a kiss. Mom and Dad came to each give me a hug, then Luke hugged me and gave me a kiss on the cheek.

"How are you feeling, Kyara?" Mom asked.

"Hungry," I said, and everyone chuckled.

"Well, we are making porridge," Dad said. "It won't be as good as the homemade oatmeal that Mom makes because we have no cinnamon or brown sugar, but I'm sure it'll still be filling."

"Yes, it will surely be filling, just not tasty," Mom laughed.

I could smell something cooking, and saw that Dad was cooking the porridge in the pot above the fire.

"Are the sheets dry yet?" I asked, referring to the bed sheets.

"No, but they should be dry by the time the sun goes down. We'll place the sheets on right when they are completely dry."

79

"Ok, I feel a little sore from sleeping on hay last night," I twisted my back so that it would crack. Liam started to rub my shoulders for me.

"So, Liam," Mom looked at Liam, smiling, "It has been so busy the past few days I haven't been able to ask. How did you come to find us? I assume you are from the future, right?"

"I am from the future, Mrs. Edwards." He stopped massaging me and went to sit on a chair at the table. I followed and sat next to him. "I was transferred back to New York the night that everyone disappeared and found the family that I was with on the Titanic." And he shared the story on how he ended up with us and held my hand the whole time

"So, you are an orphan?" Mom said after he finished, apparently taking note of the saddest part of his story. "Are you in a foster care back in our time, or?"

"No. You see Foster Care is a sad way to go because sometimes it doesn't work out with Foster Parents, and you just move from home to home and it makes it very hard on the kid." Liam hadn't told this story. I had not even thought of Foster Care as he told his story of being an orphan. "So, in 2000, a Catholic Church bought out a business facility and made it into an orphanage. Very few know about the orphanage, but hospitals around the area take kids there if their parents died and CPS brings kids there rather than a Foster Care facility to give kids a more normal life. We also go to a school in the area and have as much as a normal life as an orphan can have. I am very thankful for the care and love they give there. They saved my life." Liam finished.

Mom had tears in her eyes as everyone was listening closely to his story.

"May I ask? When did you become an orphan?" Mom asked, as politely as she could.

"I was nine. We were in a car accident. I shouldn't have survived, but apparently God had something better planned for me." Liam smiled and clenched my hand.

It was silent. A good silence. Everyone was pondering his words. I felt bad that I hadn't heard this story yet. But then I reminded myself that I had only known Liam for six days. I could not understand that. These days had been so long, and it definitely felt like I had known Liam for a lifetime. We had gone through a lot together in the past six days, though. We had fallen in love. We had learned each other's life stories. We knew what each other's weaknesses and strengths were. We probably knew more about each other than some married couples knew about their spouses.

It blew my mind to think of this. Six days with someone and you could know every detail about them. And three days to fall in love. But, then I remembered the first time I saw Liam, on the deck of the Titanic. It's like I fell in love with him before I even knew him. Love at first sight? And then when we ran into each other. I liked him even more then. Something I had never felt for any other guy.

The door opened, and Bryan and Bella entered.

"What did we just walk in on?" Bryan asked.

I looked around and noticed Mom had tears streaming down her face, and she held Dad's hand. Luke had a frown covering the lower part of his face, and I could tell he was trying not to cry. He smiled up at Bryan.

"We are getting ready to eat," Mom said and turned around toward the pot above the fire, shaking her head and wiping her face with her hands, probably clearing the sad look off her face and the tears out of her eyes.

Bryan looked at me with a look as if to say, "what's going on."

"Liam was just sharing his story."

Bryan nodded. "Where's Amy?"

"She's still in the barn." I said, wondering why Bryan asked that.

Bryan shook his head. "I didn't see her—thought she was in here with you."

My face scrunched up.

"Yeah we thought she had come inside." Bella said. "The door of the barn opened and closed, to wake me up, and looking around, I noticed Bryan and I were the only ones in the barn, so I woke Bryan up—"

She was rambling, and I didn't care what else she had to say, so I cut her off. "Amy isn't in here."

"Then, where is she?" Mom asked and started toward the door.

"She couldn't have gone far," Dad said, and followed Mom outside.

I sat frozen in place, holding Liam's hand tighter than ever. Something didn't seem right. He stood up and pulled me toward the door—I resisted at first then joined him outside.

"The horse isn't on the property," Mom said.

Bryan, Bella, and Luke came out as well.

"She wouldn't have just taken the horse, without asking us. Something is obviously wrong," I said.

Mom started yelling out Amy's name. Soon we were all yelling out her name. After about five minutes of searching the entire property for any sign of Amy, or the horse, Dad said he would check out through the woods beyond the farm. Bryan said he would go toward town, and Liam said he'd search over toward the woods we had come from yesterday. They were off in a matter of seconds.

My heart would not stop racing. I *could not* just stand here and wait for the boys to come back. I had to help. I wanted to run after Liam. I was a good runner, and I had gotten more in shape with all the walking we had done the past several days, and the running on the Titanic, so I decided, about a minute after the boys had disappeared, I would go after Liam.

Several members of my family yelled my name to stop, but I would not.

As I reached town, about to turn left toward the forest, Bryan screamed my name. I stopped for a second and waited for Bryan to catch up to me.

"I'm going after Liam," I said, wondering why Bryan had stopped me if he did not have Amy.

"You can't, it's not safe," he said.

Of course, it's not safe. There is an outbreak of the plague. Bryan realized what I was thinking and said, "You must come back with me to the farm. I'll explain it to everyone."

I hesitated and looked toward the bridge that went over the river into the forest. Bryan took my arm as if knowing what I might do.

"Okay." And we started running back to the farm.

As we reached the gates to the property, I noticed Dad had returned, as well with no sign of Amy.

"Why did you come back without her?" I asked, disappointed and confused.

"That takes us toward the castle, and there's no sign of hoof-prints anywhere."

"Dad," Bryan began, breathing heavily. I knew it wasn't from the running. He was in shape. Something was obviously wrong. "There're kidnappers!"

Chapter VII
Gone

I bit my lip. Kidnappers? During the time of Black
Death? Why? That didn't make sense. Especially if the
kidnappers had Black Death as well. Were they
possibly apart of the king's army? But then why would
he want young girls? I didn't remember hearing that
our ancestor was a molester, nor did I hear that there
were kidnappers during the plague. Nothing made
sense.

"Kidnappers?" Dad asked, aghast. "Do you
mean highwaymen?"

"Yes. I was running around town screaming
Amy's name when someone came up to me and said
that she was probably abducted by the highwaymen."

"No. There was never any historical evidence of
children being abducted during this time."

"Well Dad, there is now." Bryan said, slightly
agitated.

"Okay." Dad nodded. "Go after Liam. I'll stay
here. You're faster and stronger."

Bryan started running back towards town, but Dad stopped him. "Wait!"

"What?" Bryan was getting steadily angrier.

"You may need protection." Dad ran inside and came back out a few seconds later with a knife. "It's dull, but you can probably do something with it."

Bryan nodded, took the knife and was off.

Tears started streaming out of my eyes, and I knew why.

Amy being gone was one thing; highwaymen was a whole other story.

I began to pace. Mom and Dad started talking, but I didn't have the patience to hear what they were saying. Bella and Luke came towards me. I stopped pacing and looked into Bella's eyes. Though mine were hazy from the tears, I could see Bella was crying harder.

Luke had the strong, tough face on, but I could see how hard it was for him not to let the tears flow. I knelt down to Luke's level and hugged him tight. I was glad he had not been taken, but was fearful, still, about Amy.

"Kyara," Bella said. I looked up.

"Yeah?" I said with slight venom in my mouth. For some reason, I was mad at her. I couldn't say why, but I was.

"I feel like this is my fault," she said, sincere.

"Why would you say that?"

"Well. . . Bryan and I didn't exactly leave to come to you when Amy had left the barn. I thought she would be fine, but she's, of course, not." She paused.

"I don't understand. . ."

"We waited in the barn for a while, enjoying our time alone."

I put my hand up to stop her. "It's fine," I was slightly shocked that Bella wanted to tell me that. And I didn't want to hear what they had done, so I kept talking. "Liam and I would have done the same."

"Oh," she said and looked down at the ground. "Well, there's something else, too."

"Kyara," Dad said, and I looked up to see him walking toward us, with an axe in his hand. "I need you to go after them as well."

"What?" I was slightly shocked that he had an axe.

He handed the axe to me. It was quite heavy, but I managed to hold it steady.

"You're fast. Faster than Bryan, and I have a feeling they will need more help. I need to stay here to protect the rest of us. So, you're my number one option."

I did want to go, but at the same time I didn't. I was fearful and quite surprised Dad thought I'd be okay out there. I did have protection, but I was still confused.

"Okay." I said and started jogging toward the bridge.

It was hard to run fast, because I was carrying a heavy axe, but I went as fast as I could manage. After crossing the bridge, I ran straight, hoping to hear a sound that would not normally be heard in the trees. Then I reached an open area that I had not seen before. Grass hills and bushes filled the space. I could see trees beyond the hills, but it was probably 200 yards away.

I was at a loss on what to do. Where would Liam or Bryan have gone? And then my question was answered from far beyond, when I saw Bryan walking up a hill, holding Liam under his arm. Liam was limping, and I thought I saw blood.

"Bryan!" I yelled and started running towards them.

"Kyara!" Liam and Bryan both said simultaneously.

I dropped the axe and ran as fast as I could to the two of them. As I reached them, I noticed that Liam's entire leg was bleeding, staining the ground that he walked on. Bryan had wrapped his shirt around Liam's leg.

"What happ—"

"I saw her." Liam interrupted and began talking very quickly. "She had been taken by men who had the plague. They said they took her so that she could serve them. They needed a healthy girl to help them because they were so sick. I tried to fight them off, but I couldn't. They had swords. There was no sign of the horse, but Kyara—" I could only barely understand him.

"Slow down, slow down! You saw Amy? Was she okay?" My heart was beating so fast, I felt like I was about to throw up.

"Yes, she was okay, when I saw her at least. She had cried out for me and I saw her with three other men. One of which was carrying her. She was trying to get away when she saw me. I ran up to the men and started fighting them, and I almost got her, but then one of them hit me in the leg with the sword. I had hurt them pretty bad, though, because they were limping as they ran away from me. Amy was crying. It was so hard watching her go. I was in too much pain to go after her. And then I heard someone coming through the trees and I called out for help. It was Bryan. We would have gone after her together, but I'm losing too much blood. I'm so sorry, Kyara." Liam was breathing very deeply, and his eyes were watering.

"It's okay. You tried. Thank you."

"Kyara, we need to get him back before he loses too much blood. Mom will know what to do. I already wrapped my shirt around the wound. It's really deep. Can you help me get him back to the farm?"

I nodded, and Bryan and I lifted him into our arms. So much blood was pouring onto my arms as we ran, but my stomach was strong, and this was Liam. I loved him, and I didn't care how much blood was covering me. All I cared about was getting him back to the farm and getting Mom to stop the bleeding, or he would not last.

But Liam had been brave. He tried to get my sister back, and almost died trying. I couldn't imagine how scared Amy would have looked as the men took her away from Liam. Tears were pouring down my face and I didn't have the hands to wipe them away, so I let them fall. When Bryan and I got back we would tell them what happened, and Dad and Bryan would probably go after her as Mom and I tried to stop the bleeding.

Liam was staring into my eyes and he tried to open his mouth to talk a few times, but nothing came out. Every few minutes I would say, "Don't waste your breath," and, "You will be okay."

Going over the bridge and through part of town would be a slight problem. It was a good thing it was usually barren, but I was still worried someone would see us and start freaking out. Thankfully, though, we made it through town unseen.

When we finally reached the farm, Liam had passed out.

Dad and Mom saw us first, and both their mouths were dropped. Bella and Luke weren't in sight. Dad rushed over and took Liam from my arms. They went inside, and I followed with Mom on my tail. Bella and Luke were sitting inside at the dining table when we entered.

"Oh, my goodness," Bella said.

"Is he okay?" Luke asked.

I didn't dare take my eyes off Liam as Bryan and Dad took him into the first bedroom. They placed him on the bed, and I rushed over to him and held his hand. Mom rushed over and started to listen to his heart.

"Dad. We need to go back. Liam saw Amy with the kidnappers, and he tried to fight them off to get Amy, but they sliced him in the leg. I found him a few minutes after, and then Kyara saw us coming over a hill and helped me carry him back. But Dad, he saw Amy! She could still be alive! We have to go! Now!" Bryan was stumbling over his words as Dad nodded.

"You get Liam well. We will be back with Amy soon! We promise!" Dad said to Mom and me, and then he and Bryan swept back outside and started after Amy.

I prayed hard for both of them, hoping everything would be okay.

Bella and Luke came in after Dad and Bryan left.

"Luke, honey, give me your shirt," Mom said and then she turned to Bella. "Bella get water and leftover porridge please. He's going to need sustenance."

They obeyed, and I asked Mom what we were going to do and if he would be okay.

Mom took Luke's shirt and went down to his leg, without answering me. She was in life saving mode. She was a vet, and a damn good one, so I knew Liam was in good hands.

Mom began undoing Bryan's shirt and took it off Liam's leg. Blood gushed over the bed.

"Was that supposed to happen?!" I asked, but knew Mom was smart enough to help him, so I shut up and just held Liam's hand tight.

Mom tied Luke's shirt hard around Liam's leg and placed Bryan's shirt on the ground. The bleeding slowed down very slightly.

"He'll need stitches, but we don't have those tools!" Mom said.

"Wouldn't they have thread and needles somewhere? Don't they make their own clothes in this time?" I asked, unsure how I had thought of something like this.

Mom met my eyes and then ran out of the room to find what I assumed was a needle and thread. She came back in, not twenty second later, with a needle and thick thread in her hands.

I wanted to ask where she had found it all but realized again that there was no time for questions.

Bella came in and placed the water and porridge on the table by the bed.

"Thank you, Bella," Mom said and began to feel for Liam's pulse.

Luke and Bella stood in the door frame watching.

"Kyara," Mom said. "I need you to feel for Liam's pulse as I stitch him up, okay?"

I did as she said, placing two fingers at Liam's throat as Mom began to stitch up Liam. The bleeding slowly began to stop as she stitched up my lover's leg, all the while, his pulse stayed consistent.

After she finished stitching Liam, she picked up the water and started pouring it on the stitches, cleaning the blood away. I watched fervently and hoped to God that he would wake up.

After a few seconds of sheer anxiety, Liam took a deep breath and opened his eyes. Mom helped him sit up and gave him the water to drink, which he gulped down, while I held his hand tight.

He smiled at me and slowly clenched my hand. A single tear escaped my eyes.

"Don't," Liam began after Mom put the water down and picked up the porridge, "don't cry." He coughed. I sniffled.

"All right, Liam. Time to eat. You're going to need your strength," Mom said.

Liam nodded, and Mom began to feed him.

"I love you so much," I said and kissed his hand. As Liam ate, I explained what happened while he was passed out. He thanked my mom and told her that he would be careful not to break the stitching.

"You will be on bed rest, for a few days, for sure, if not more. You will not be walking on that. We will try to find or make wooden crutches for you, but for now, you're on bed rest," Mom said, cautioning.

Liam nodded, understanding.

"Where did you find the thread and needle?" I asked Mom.

"In the pantry. I had noticed it this morning, but didn't think anything of it until now," she said and then told me she'd give us a little time alone to talk. I thanked her as she left.

"I'll be in the kitchen. Let me know if you need me," she said and disappeared out of the room. Luke and Bella followed.

"Thank you, my love. I could never ask for a stronger and more caring girlfriend. You mean everything to me." He smiled up at me. I smiled brightly back at him.

"Well, I don't want to lose you. I love you more than you could understand."

"Oh, I do understand," Liam said. He was talking slowly, trying to regain his strength.

Another tear fell from my eyes and I nuzzled my head into his chest. I heard his heartbeat and was so happy it was still beating. I could not bear to lose him.

After I counted ten heartbeats, for they were slow heartbeats, I heard the door open from the kitchen to the outside. Hoping it was Amy and Bryan and Dad, I ran out to the kitchen, after telling Liam I loved him, and I'd be right back.

It was Bryan and Dad, but Amy was not with them. I then noticed that both their shirts were off and that a body was wrapped up in Dad's arms.

Chapter VIII
Sacred Words

I shook my head and tears began to stream down my face.

"No!" I said. Several others shouted Amy's name, as if shouting it would bring her back to life. She was wrapped up in their shirts and no part of her body was showing. Dad and Bryan must not want anyone to see her, other than themselves. The sight must have been terrible.

I felt as if my heart was out of my body and it was on the ground screaming for someone to pick it up. My heart wanted to keep beating, but it couldn't. Just like how Amy's heart had stopped, mine had too. I fell to my knees and hit the floor so hard with my fists. I could now only hear hard breathing, weeping, and my deafening cries.

Amy was gone. How could this happen? Why did this happen? Why did God do this to us? And she hadn't died from Black Death either! How did she die? But as I thought that, I wasn't sure if I would want to know. It would only make the reality more. . . real. This had to be a dream. I must have passed out from all of Liam's blood.

As the tears fell, I felt pain. Was that pain real though? Pain is just in the mind. If it was a dream, I needed to wake up, now. Dad and Bryan had to be on their way back with a happy and laughing Amy.

A laughing Amy. . . I would never hear her laugh again. Her perfect and beautiful laugh. She would never grow up. She would never be my age and go through things I went through. She would never have a boyfriend. She would never marry. She was gone. Gone from this earth and never to come back. Life was no longer an option for her.

Pain. Brokenness. Heart-wrenching sorrow. An ache that would never be healed. Damage that could never be fixed. My heart was broken, and it would never be fully mended. A piece of my heart was missing. And it was a piece that Amy and I had shared. She was my little sister and mini-me. She was a part of me that would never come back. A part of me that was now. . . dead.

Why? I may have thought last night that I would accept anything God threw at me. That I would accept it if someone in my family died. But I didn't think I could live out that promise, now. Not when a part of me was missing. I thought that losing Liam would be worse. And I had a taste of what it would feel like without Liam. But this was worse. I had known Amy her entire life. I was there when she first became part of this world. I was there when she took her first breath of life. I was there when she first rolled over, and when she first crawled, when she said her first word, and when she tried to say my name, but it came out as "Kikar". Then her first steps, and her first time on a bike; I was there for all of it. Then when Luke was three and Amy was four we took a professional photo. One with just the four kids, which hung in our living room. And then one with the whole family, which hung in the hallway at the front door.

It would never be the same. We were the four Edwards' kids. Some called us the double twin Edwards' because Luke and Amy were only eleven months apart. Luke had lost his twin. Bryan and I had lost our little sister. I would never have a sister again. I should have had two sisters, but now I had none. Was I some sort of curse?

What was going to happen now? My family's arms were wrapped around each other. Mom's hand was on my shoulder. Bryan's arm was wrapped around my back, his sobs becoming more prominent every few breaths. He had been there. He had seen her body, motionless, without breath. I could not even imagine what it could have been like.

Dad hadn't let Amy go from his arms. He was holding her so close that if someone tried to pull her away, they would have to pry her away from Dad's strong clutch. Though one of Mom's hands was on my shoulder, her other one was on Dad's hands.

I slowly looked up to where Liam's room was. I wanted to go in there and tell him what had happened, but I figured he already knew, from our sobs. He was probably almost as distraught as we were because he knew the feeling.

I now knew what Liam had felt about Rosie's death. And I also felt the guilt, not as major as his would have been, but I did feel it. If I had stayed with Amy this morning and not gone into the house, or if I had woken her up and asked her to come into the house with me, she would still be here. Liam's leg would not be stitched up, and he would not have had a near death experience today. We would probably all be laughing, singing worship songs again, and eating our second meal of the day. However, we had not eaten at all, and we all felt the complete opposite of happy.

I felt as if all the joy had drained out of my body, just like how all the blood had drained out of Liam, and how all the life had now drained out of Amy. What would happen now? Would we bury her? Would we have a funeral and tell of all the "happy" memories of my perfect little sister? It would be hard to talk of her. I couldn't understand how people were able to do that at funerals or memorials.

She may be in a better place, but that didn't mean that we all were. I could just imagine her beautiful face looking down on all of us now, holding the hand of Jesus. It would be an absolutely perfect sight. I wish I could see into what she was thinking right now and whether she understood why we were all crying. She would probably want us to be happy. I knew Amy well enough to know her thoughts, most of the time.

And then the picture of me holding Amy in my arms on the bed on the Titanic, swarmed through my mind. We were both crying and in pain because we did not know if we would make it through the crash. I had felt every breath she took and every tear she shed. With that thought, I became self-conscious of my own breaths. As my chest moved up and down, up and down, all I could think of was Amy and how she would no longer have that. But I knew she wouldn't want me to be thinking like this. She would want me to be happy that she was with Jesus.

Those thoughts of her face next to the face of Jesus kept on popping up every time I would think of something sad. Was that her telling me to be strong?

I tried to open my mouth to speak, but I just couldn't. *Amy, give me the strength. The strength to tell our family what you are telling me. I love you, Amy, and you will be in my heart forever.*

I didn't know what had come over me. I was as depressed as I had ever been, until that moment. Until I felt Amy's presence over me. I had almost heard her voice telling me to be strong. I knew Jesus had His arms around me. Both Him and Amy were radiating their light on me and were telling me to be strong, for my family. Jesus was helping me with what I had promised last night. Accepting anything that would happen. As hard as it may be, I knew I had to do it.

"Um." I managed to say, and only Bryan looked up at me. No one else had heard because of how hard they were sobbing. His eyes met mine, and both were very blurry. Bryan slightly raised an eyebrow as if asking why I had spoken in this silent time.

"Amy would want us to be strong." I whispered, and I could tell he knew what I said because he nodded slightly, but he did not stop his tears from falling.

I could not talk any louder, so I decided to stand up and walk over to Liam's room. Each person looked up in turn and then back down at the ground or at Amy. I walked through the door, and my eyes met Liam's. I sat down next to him on the bed and he said, "I'm. . . so. . . sorry."

I nodded and said, "Now I know what it's like."

His lip twitched downward, and he wiped his eyes with his hand. I lay down next to him and started to cry, harder than I had ever cried before.

~ ~ ~

There was a hole in the ground near the barn and we all had quite a bit of dirt under our fingers. The hole wasn't perfect, but it was large enough to hold her petite little body. The clouds shadowed over Amy as if they were meant to, and her body was right next to the dug-up pit. We all stood around the grave but said nothing.

As we had dug the grave, Dad and Bryan told us of the tragic story on how they had found Amy. Once they had gotten to the place where Bryan had found Liam, they followed a break in the trees, which had been recently walked on. They had walked about a hundred yards before they saw it. The men that Liam had fought off, all had arrows in their chests or backs, as well had many boils and bruises on their bodies. They had had the Black Plague. Amy had an arrow in her stomach but had no sign of the plague. She was still breathing when Dad and Bryan reached her.

When Amy saw them, she cried out for them, happy that they had come for her. Bryan and Dad told her not to speak because she was losing too much blood and would soon run out of breath. Knowing that if they took the arrow out, she would only lose more blood and it would surely kill her, they left it in and just stayed by her side. They had watched as Amy breathed her last breaths and prayed over her, telling her that she would soon be with Jesus.

Amy had been smiling as they said all the fun things she could do in Heaven. Bryan had told her that she could play soccer and dance all she wanted—her two favorite things to do. Dad had told her that she could fly—something that she had always wanted to do. Also, they told her that she could be with Jesus every single day and have the most fun she would ever have. Then the time came when Amy's breaths came to be less and less regular.

Bryan and Dad told Amy they loved her so much and then the last words Amy said, after "I love you" were "I'll miss you." And then she was gone. Bryan and Dad took out the arrow and just sat there for a while, staring at the motionless Amy. Knowing that everyone was waiting for them to come back, they wrapped her up because they didn't want anyone to see the terrible sight that they had and started to walk back. They had not spoken a single word on their way back.

"I love you, Amy." Bryan broke the silence. "And I was happy to spend the last few minutes you had with you. I know you are in a better place. I know you want us to be happy for you. We know that you are looking over us right now and that you are dancing with Jesus. I'll miss you, too and you will forever be in my heart. I love you."

A few seconds of silence, and all of us pondered Bryan's perfect words. I couldn't have said any of that better than how he did. They were words that meant more than anything I had heard before. Even if they were few words, they were very meaningful.

Then Dad decided to start talking. "Amy, you'll be in our hearts forever and will never leave us. You were a wonderful girl who always knew when to say no, and yes. You never looked back and always moved forward with your life. You were a wonderful Christian child who told her friends that Jesus was real and died on the cross to save our sins. You changed people's lives in your seven years of life. When you were born," tears started falling down his face, "you looked into my eyes and I saw that they were mine. With your mama's face and my eyes, you were so beautiful.

"At ten months old, you said your first word, 'Dada'. Then you started walking a few months later. You were such a wonderful girl as you grew up. I was proud to call you my daughter. And now you are dancing with your true Father. He will be happy to have you so soon, even if I don't get to have more years with you. You will be happier in Heaven, and I will be happy to see you on the day of my judgment. I know we all will.

"And though it is hard to watch a child die before their parent, we will soon understand why Jesus decided this. It was hard to watch you go, and right now I don't understand why you had to so soon. I love you, my sweet, sweet girl. Showing your love to all you knew, you'll be in our hearts forever." Dad finished. His touching words were so powerful. They may have been more than Bryan had, but they both had the same meaning.

"Good bye, Amy." Liam said. We had sat him up against the barn so that he could watch as we buried her. I did not think that he would say anything, but I was happy when he did. "It was so wonderful to know you for this week that felt like a lifetime. I know that you and Rosie will be great friends up there. Say hi to her for me and tell her I love her. I love you." He finished.

I could tell that Liam had loved her like she was his sister. I was certain Amy had reminded Liam of Rosie, and I felt bad that Liam had to witness her death. But I knew that Rosie and Amy would be great friends, and that they were probably both looking down on us now, holding hands with Jesus.

"Thank you for telling me to stay strong." I began and smiled, tears of joy falling down my face. "You were the best sister I could ever ask for and you were an exact replica of me when I was your age. I know you will have the happiest time ever in Heaven. Tell Kaylee I love her, and I wish that we could have grown up together. Wish you didn't have to meet her so soon, and before I did, but I know you are happier up there. You be good, and I'll see you in my dreams. I love you so much." I took a deep breath and let a small smile stretch on my face.

Mom opened her mouth to speak, but nothing came out. A mom losing their child is probably one of the worst things in the world. Hopefully I would never have to go through that. Losing my little sister was bad enough.

"The moment. . ." Mom took a deep breath. "The moment I laid eyes on you. . ." She stopped again, and I could see that she could barely say another word. Dad put his arms around her and hugged her tightly. It was good their marriage was saved, but I knew that if they hadn't made up, they would have by know. Something about losing their daughter would bring husband and wife together. At least that's what made sense in my mind.

It was silent until Luke opened his mouth and said, "I'll miss you, sis. I love you." He said through strangled breaths. I could tell that he wanted to say more, but for some reason he didn't open his mouth again.

"I'm so sorry this had to happen, Amy. I feel just terrible about it. It was great knowing you." Bella said, and I could see in her eyes that something, besides this, was troubling her. And she was the only one that said "sorry". Why? Was that how it was in the Roman times?

And then, after a few more minutes of silence, Bryan and Dad picked Amy up and set her in her grave. Everyone else started throwing the dirt over her and I went out walking through the trees to pick some flowers. After picking a few pink and yellow flowers, I went back to Amy's grave, which was now completely covered, and made a bouquet with the flowers. Bryan had gone off as well, and when he came back, he had two sticks and a few pieces of grass, and a long flexible branch.

I understood when he put one stick perpendicular to another and used the grass and branch to tie them together, that he was making a cross. He then stuck it in the ground, above the flowers that I had set down. We all smiled gratefully at him, and after each of us went to kiss the ground in which Amy was now below, we went back inside, barely anyone speaking a word.

We had brought Liam's bed out to the kitchen so that he could spend time with us. He was now lying there with his head propped up against a pillow, and every now and then we would meet each other's eyes, and then turn away, knowing that if we looked much longer, we would start to cry again. My stomach started to grumble, and I knew I was hungry, but we probably wouldn't eat until later tonight. I don't think any of us had the energy to make a meal.

Several minutes, maybe even hours, passed— the concept of time having lost meaning—and no one said a single thing. We didn't know what to do next. I could barely think anymore. All my tears had been shed, and my eyes were the driest they had ever been. I wondered what Heaven was like, and right now I really wanted to be there. Not because I wanted to die, but because I had so many questions for Jesus and because I wanted to see Amy.

For the next few days, we probably wouldn't do much, meaning that it would take longer to find the phone. Then, if we did find the phone, would we just be sent to a completely different time? Would we ever get home? But now home would be entirely different. There would be no Amy. But there would be Liam and Bella. Life would change, and it would be almost like we were restarting life. Everything had changed, but both for better and for worse. The question was: Did the better outweigh the worse or vice versa?

I had found Liam; the one I would be with for the rest of my life. But my sister that I had known my entire life, and loved since the day she was conceived, was gone. Bryan found the girl he would be with for the rest of his life. But Mom and Dad both made two of the worst possible sins. Even though they had made up, their sins would haunt them forever.

I've traveled through time, which I thought to be impossible. But in each time, there was always something bad that happened, other than when we found Jesus. Jesus. . . And that made me remember the day we saw him as a baby, and he touched our foreheads, and blessed us. That had been the best thing I had ever felt in my entire life. Would I rather have Amy back, or have the wisdom and strength I had received when Jesus blessed me?

I looked up toward Liam, again. He looked at me and smiled warily. Bryan had his head on the table. Luke's head was on one of Bryan's outstretched arms, his face towards me, but eyes closed. Mom and Dad were sitting, holding hands, and had been whispering for the past few minutes. Bella was sitting next to Bryan. She had a strange and troubled look in her eyes, just as she had during the funeral. What was up with her?

Bryan pulled his head off the table and looked around, as if he was thinking hard.

"Bryan?" I said and scrunched my eyebrows. "You okay?"

"Yeah. I just thought of something," he said.

"And what might that be?" Dad said, his voice low and somber.

"I mean, this had slightly crossed my mind before, but we were too focused on Amy for me to say something."

We all waited patiently for him to continue.

"The kidnappers had Black Death. Amy didn't have a single boil or sign of the plague on her and she had been carried by them. How did she not get the plague?" Bryan turned to look at Dad as he spoke, knowing he would have the best answer.

"Well, first off, the plague usually spread and infected its source between two and five days. However, we have been around the plague for three days now, and none of us have ended up with it. So, either we are really lucky, or, like the priest said, we may be immune to it. But I honestly don't know."

"You think we're immune to it?" Bryan interrupted, his mouth dropped.

"Possibly, but not all of us. Bella, Liam and your mother may not be. But those directly related to me, could almost certainly be."

It was my turn to interrupt. "How are you immune?"

"Because I am related to King Edward, who was also immune. And you three are too," he said pointing to Bryan, Luke, and me.

"King Edward was immune to the plague?" Liam said.

"Yes. Edmund explains that in his journal," Dad said.

"Oh, right." I said and remembered when Edmund had explained that. For when Edmund had gone to see his father, Edward had told Edmund that it was impossible for him to get the plague, and for him not to worry about getting it. Edmund had asked why, and Edward responded with a very conceited answer, saying he was invincible. Which was slightly true, because he never got the plague, but he did die from a stroke at the age of sixty-four.

Dad explained then where it said that we were immune and then went on to say, "but I think Mom and Liam must also be immune because they don't have signs of the plague. And Liam fought the men off with his bare hands, so I'm sure we'll find out soon for sure. I'm sure Bella is possibly immune to it, but you," he turned to Bella, "were from an older time so it's hard to tell. We must be careful. And in two days, if there is no sign of you three getting the plague, then we are very lucky."

We all nodded. Bella had a worried, as well as a troubled, look on her face.

Liam sighed when we met eyes. I walked over to him and asked him how he was feeling, taking his hand.

He shrugged. "Could be worse."

I nodded and felt the tears come to my eyes again. Liam reached my face with his hand and wiped my tears away.

I smiled slightly.

It was silent for the next few minutes.

Everyone was pondering like I was, I'm sure, about our next few days. If we really were immune, or if it all was a hoax. And if we were, but Liam, Mom, and Bella got the plague, what could we do? I knew Liam would not be strong enough to fight it off. Mom and Bella may be able to if we found the phone in time, but what was "in time"? We really needed to find that phone and get back to our time.

I looked up, and around at everyone.

"Uh." I cleared my throat. Mom and Dad turned their heads towards me, and Bryan moved his eyes slightly.

"Kyara?" Dad caught my eyes and I stared at him for a few seconds, then at Mom.

"I was just . . . I think . . . We shouldn't just mope here forever . . . That's not what Amy would want." As I said it, I felt as if someone else was saying the words through me. Amy . . . She'd want us to find that phone and get back home, but I knew none of us would have the ability or energy to go look for the phone right now, so I kept that part to myself.

"I agree." Dad nodded, and Bryan pulled his arm out from under Luke and placed his head slowly down on the table. Luke didn't budge, and I knew he was sound asleep. I was glad he had fallen asleep; he needed to rest. It's not healthy for a six-year-old boy to have to go through all this.

Bryan opened his mouth to say something, but nothing came out. After a few more attempts at speaking, something finally came out of his mouth.

"Why not talk about the good times with Amy—maybe some funny times?"

I bit my lip and nodded. "That's a good idea." Bryan nodded back at me and pulled Luke onto his lap who still did not wake up.

"Sure, why not." Dad said but said nothing else.

"Well, I remember something that would probably cheer everyone up." Bryan said, smiling slightly. And I had an idea of what he was thinking. We had done several things with the kids that Mom and Dad had never found out about. But they couldn't get mad at us now. And that made me think of Costco. Riding on the shopping carts and almost hurting ourselves, but that was what we always did. We did stupid things, got hurt, and then tried it again. That was the thing. We had no fear because of how much we did.

"Go for it, then." Dad said, a little uneasily though.

I looked at Bryan and he took a deep breath, summoned up a smile, and began to talk.

"You and Mom were out on a date while Kyara and I were babysitting Luke and Amy two years ago. We were all eating dinner and when Kyara and I had finished, our plates as clean as could be, we started spinning them on our fingers like a basketball."

"You did what!" Dad asked shocked, and it looked like all the sorrow drained from his eyes and filled up with surprise. Bryan and I had done so many things that Mom and Dad had never found out about, and Bryan had picked a good one to tell.

"Amy said that she wanted to do that too, but we took her glass plate away from her and gave her a plastic plate from the cupboard. She looked at it for quite a while, put it on one finger, but it fell off, so she put it on two fingers and began to spin it, carefully and slowly. Then, as she kind of got the hang of it, she started spinning it faster and faster until! It flew across the room and hit the wall, almost taking my head off. Thankfully I had ducked just in time, or else I would have had a huge bump on my forehead, or worse, a broken nose." Bryan laughed slightly, and I laughed with him. I didn't realize how hard it was to laugh. . .

"Was that what the dent in the wall was?" Mom asked, raising an eyebrow, somewhat smiling.

"Maybe," Bryan made a puppy-dog-face. "It was one of the cutest things ever. Her mouth had dropped open and her face was so apologetic. It was so adorable." Bryan finished, taking a deep breath.

I remembered it like it was yesterday. That face was so clear in my mind and so pure, I almost began to cry again. I stared at Luke, who had woken up, and he was laughing, acting as if it was the funniest thing in the world. It was good he was able to laugh, and because his happiness was so vibrant, it permeated the air, and everyone felt that happiness we had all been dreading. Joy had finally filled everyone's face again.

Then it was completely silent. One by one the smiles faded from our faces. No one could find the right words to say. I looked into my water cup and thought deeply. And I wished that I were water. There was nothing you had to worry about. All of life was an adventure. You would be in a new place every day, surrounded by new things. Each day would bring new experiences, especially if you fell down a waterfall, or collided with a river, or swam with the currents. Your life would never end, even if you were swept onto the ground. For you would evaporate, live in the clouds, and then fall when it was your time to fall. You would never feel pain or suffering. Everything would be perfect.

Human life, however, was different. Though there may be adventures, there would also be suffering. Life would end. But you would be in Heaven afterwards, if you believed. Either way you would have eternal life, but the question was: How much pain and suffering will you have to endure?

Then I heard footsteps, and I glanced toward the sound. Bryan and Bella had gotten up. They were moving toward the door.

"What are you doing?" I asked; my voice was quiet and unsteady. Everyone else was now looking at them with confused eyes.

"We are just going to take a walk. I. . . I need to talk with Bryan." Bella told us.

I looked at Bryan. He managed to shrug his shoulders, showing me that he didn't know what she wanted to talk about. Mom and Dad were too distraught to care what Bryan and Bella were going to do.

Bryan and Bella started out the door. I stood up and went over to Liam, and whispered in his ear, "I'm going to go follow them. There's nothing else to do and I want to see what Bella wanted to tell Bryan. Is that okay?"

"Sure, if that's what you would like to do. I'm stuck here anyway. Don't want to take away your fun." Liam whispered, slightly agitated.

"You know you could have just said, 'I'd rather you stay here and keep me company' rather than 'go have fun without me.' Gosh." I lifted my hands up like I was surrendering.

"No. I didn't mean it like that." He whispered in an apologetic tone. "I wasn't angry at you. I was angry at myself. I could have saved her. Just like I could have saved Rosie." His teeth were clenched, and the apologetic tone was drowned out by fury. I felt tears come to my eyes, but I would not let them fall. Liam had closed his eyes and taken his hand away from mine. I bit my lip and then started toward the door. It would not be good for me to be around Liam whilst he was angry.

Mom and Dad barely noticed as I went through the door and outside.

I looked around and noticed the sun was starting to go down. The day was almost over. I started walking toward the fields where I heard talking. I found them near some crops, staring at one another. Bella seemed very uneasy and Bryan looked confused. I hid behind a few denser crops, so that I could see what was happening, but they would have to look hard to see me.

"Bryan, it's. . . it's gone too far. I. . . I think it's time for you to know." Bella started after a few more prolonged minutes, stuttering on her words.

"Time for me to know what?" Bryan asked. His voice was uneven, and it sounded depressed.

113

"Everything." Bella said.

"I'm afraid I don't know what you mean." Bryan said, still very confused.

"What I am going to tell you is going to be very, very hard for you to believe and take in, but it's time for you to know because it's gone . . . it's gone way too far . . . Before I go any further, though, I need you to know one thing," She took a deep breath, "I am completely in love with you and I will never lie about that. I hope that after you hear this, you will still love me. But I can understand if you don't."

Bryan opened his mouth, as if he was about to speak, but closed it quickly, unsure of what to say. I was positive I was just as confused as Bryan. What would Bella have done to make Bryan possibly not love her?

"Bryan, I'm . . ." she took a deep breath. "I'm from the future, too."

Chapter IX
Stages of Grief

"What?" I screamed and came out from behind my hiding place. Bryan looked over in my direction, but then back at Bella with his mouth wide open. It seemed as if he didn't care that I had followed them. My mouth was wide open, too. How could this be?!

"You can't be serious. You would have told us earlier." Bryan said after a few seconds of utter disbelief in both mine and Bryan's eyes.

"I am serious. I am from the future. I was just, not supposed to tell you guys." Bella said.

"Not supposed to?" I asked, and my voice sounded angrier than I meant it to be.

"No. . ." Bella took a few deep breaths while rubbing her forehead with her hand. "Bryan and Kyara, has your dad ever talked about Blake Munccello?" She asked, hesitantly.

That name did seem familiar. I remembered Dad talking to Bryan and me about him. It had been a few years ago, but the story was fresh in my mind because of how angry Dad was with him, and how much Dad wanted to try and teach us a lesson about high school.

Blake had been Dad's best friend from high school. They had met freshman year and became great friends because both of them were on the football team and were pretty much the most popular kids in school. And it seemed as if nothing could destroy their friendship, until this. In their junior year, Blake had a girlfriend that he had been with since the end of their sophomore year. He and his girlfriend got into a disagreement, and they didn't talk to each other for a few days. Dad, Blake, and Mia, Blake's girlfriend, were all great friends, especially in junior year. When Blake and Mia broke up, Dad had been there for Mia, but just as a friend. Blake thought differently when he heard a rumor.

The rumor went around school that Dad and Mia were going out. When Blake found out, he and Dad had a huge fight. To make it worse, the fight was in front of the entire school. Teachers stopped the brawl and they were taken to the principal's office. Blake had cussed a few times in front of the principal, and the principal suspended him for four days with a warning. Because of the suspension, Blake missed several exams that were important to his grade, and he was not able to make them up. His grades dropped immensely, and he was kicked off the football team.

Everything was becoming a slippery slope of bad choices for Blake, and when he got back to school he got in another fight with both Dad and Mia. Dad and Mia were so physically hurt by Blake that they were sent to the hospital, and Mia had a knife wound. Blake had meant to stab Dad, but Mia had gotten in the way and saved him. Blake was expelled and sent to a juvenile hall for a year and then to jail for three years when he came of age. Dad took a few days to recover from the fight. Mia had been hurt so badly that she had forgotten who she was and had become so crazy and mentally confused that she was put into a mental hospital. That was the last time Dad had ever heard from Blake and Mia.

But why was this story pertinent to Bella?

"Bryan, Kyara?" Bella asked, looking at us waiting for us to answer. Bryan must have been thinking about Dad's story as well.

"Yeah." I shook my head, coming back to my senses. "Dad told us about him. Why?"

"Well, he's. . . my father. I'm Isabelle Sofia Munccello." Bella said. My eyes grew wide. I had not even thought about that. Her father?

Her father was the one who caused my dad to miss the biggest football game in his high school career. Her father caused my dad's best friend to turn insane. Her father was the only thing my dad was afraid of. But how did that make any sense? Was her father getting my dad back? Is he making this happen to us? Is this really all just a set of a play! Is Amy still alive and that was just a scene!

"Wait! Then why are we here! We can get out! Amy's still alive!" I could barely think straight. This was great! I started toward the house.

"No! Kyara!" Bella's voice cracked. And I turned around, confused. "It's true. . . Amy is dead." She held her breath.

"No, she's not! This is fake! We are on the set of a show! Get us off it! I want to see Amy!" I didn't understand why Bella couldn't just take us home. Tears were streaming down her face now. Her sobs were so distant because I was so angry at her. She let us believe that Amy was dead. What the hell?

Bryan was looking from me, to Bella, unsure of what to do.

"Is it true Bella? Are we on the set of a show? Is Amy alive?" Bryan asked slowly, but with slight anger in his voice. If Amy wasn't dead and this was all a show, then we would both never want to see Bella again. She had hurt us way too much.

Bella's entire body was shaking, and with a hard shake of her head, Bryan and I stared at each other.

"Then what the hell is going on?" I was screaming. I had been so sure that Amy could possibly still be alive. But then this didn't make sense! Were we really travelling through time? Did that mean Bella's father made the time machine? Dad had said that Blake was really smart and that he would have gone to Princeton if it weren't for him being kicked out of high school and put in jail.

"Tell us, Bella. Stop crying and tell us why our sister is dead!" Bryan was now as angry as I was.

"Bryan! Please! Remember what I told you before I said I was from the future?" She wasn't crying as much now. She was now mad. But why should she be? "I LOVE YOU!"

"That's bull shit!" Bryan was pacing, cracking his knuckles, and looking at Bella and me and then back at the ground.

"You killed our sister!"

"Will you please just let me explain!" She was screaming now, breathing hard and unsteadily. Explain? Explain what? Explain how she put us through hell? Explain how she lied to my brother for so long? Explain how she is hurting both of us now? She didn't have a chance! If Amy really was dead and we really were in a different time, and Bella's father was putting us through this, then wouldn't she be able to take us back to the future? None of this made any sense! I thought I had figured it out! I thought Liam and I had. But now everything seemed incomplete.

Bryan still paced. I still searched through my thoughts. Bella tried to speak but knew if she did that we would both quickly shut her up.

"If you want to explain," Bryan began, still with clenched fists, pacing back and forth. "You will explain to my entire family!" And he walked towards me. I nodded, and we started walking back to the house.

Bella didn't follow us right away. I could feel Bryan's anger exuding from his body and from each breath. Then Bryan suddenly stopped, right before we were about to enter the house. His arm stopped me, so I turned and looked at him perplexed.

"Wait. Do you think this is a good idea? Making Mom and Dad listen to her story? Do you think it will be hard for them to hear? Especially when they

119

know that Blake is her father. . ." He trailed off, with a very indecisive look.

I bit my lip and took a deep breath. "Well they need to find out one way or another. And if you and I just hear her story, then we will have to hear it again or say it with Mom and Dad there."

"That's true." Bryan took a deep breath. "Okay, let me go make sure Bella is coming."

Liam was the first to look up when I entered the house. He must have noticed my eyes were red and I had been crying because he asked, "Kyara are you okay? What's going on?"

"Uh. We have to wait. . ." I couldn't go on, so I asked Liam how his leg was.

"It's okay. Throbbing, but there's nothing I can really do. There're no pain killers around." He shrugged.

I nodded but said nothing.

"So, what's going on?" He began rubbing my back, looking at me sympathetically.

I decided that he at least needed to know that she was from the future, so I told him. Then Bryan and Bella came through the door. Right as they entered, Luke opened his eyes and sat up. He had been sleeping in Mom's lap, until now.

Bella's entire body was still shaking, but she wasn't crying. She folded and unfolded her hands over and over again as we all stared at her. Dad, taking his gaze off her, looked at Bryan and then to me asking what was going on.

"Bella's from the future, Dad." Bryan spit out, anger flooding his words.

Dad's eyes widened and then he bit his lip, acting as if he already knew.

"I knew you looked familiar. I couldn't figure out how, but now I know. You're Blake's daughter." Dad gazed at her, and Bryan and I stared at Dad. How could he know? Was it another one of those hunches? Uh, I hated when people had hunches and they didn't tell me. It made me feel so pissed off!

Bella nodded slightly, and Bryan spat, "How did you know?"

"She has her father's nose and eyes. . . and smile. . ." Dad trailed off and then looked quickly back at Bella. "Where is he? Is he here?" Dad stood up.

Bella traced backwards, putting her hands up in surrender. "I don't know. I haven't heard from him in a week."

"He did this to us? And he used you? How revolting." Dad wasn't angry with Bella.

Bella nodded slightly and frowned, her eyebrows scrunched together.

"Why don't we let her tell her story, Ben?" Mom said, putting Luke aside and standing up and taking Dad's arm. Her voice was somber and calming. I always knew Mom to be the one to settle disputes, without getting angry, no matter what the deal was.

"Fine." He pulled his arm away and sat down. All of us, except Liam turned to face Bella, who tottered forward and then sat down on a chair, facing us.

"First, I wanted to, uh, know what exactly happened between you and my father." Bella asked Dad.

"Your father didn't tell you?" Dad began.

121

"No, he did, but I know what he said was partially to completely a lie. And you should know that I am. . . scared of my dad." She bit her lip again.

"What did he tell you?" Dad raised an eyebrow.

"That it was all your fault that my father got kicked out of high school; lost his girlfriend; that she ended up in a mental hospital; and that he got put into jail."

"Bella, do you understand how crazy that sounds? That I would be at fault for all of those things?" He said calmly.

"My father said that you were always jealous of him and schemed for a way to get back at him," Bella said.

"That's a lie. Dad! Tell her it's a lie and tell her what her father really did." Bryan stood up, towering over all of us. Dad closed his eyes, shaking his head.

Had Dad lied to us? Had Dad really plotted for all of that to happen?

Then Dad stood up as well and began pacing from the door back to us.

"It was my fault Mia got stabbed." He began, rubbing his hands on his thighs.

"What?" Bryan and I shouted simultaneously.

"Well she saved you, so that doesn't mean it's your—"

"No." His voice cracked as he spoke. I had never known Dad to be this upset and sad about something. He had cried just a few minutes ago when Amy had been buried, but he wasn't mad.

"I shouldn't have let Mia and I grow close together after she and Blake broke up. I knew Mia

122

liked me, even when she and Blake were dating, and, it wasn't just a rumor. We did go out, but secretly. On our dates, she would always talk of how I was always there for her and that I was her angel that had saved her. I shouldn't have let it happen. She had fallen so in love with me. . ." He stopped, and I could see a shining tear falling down his cheek.

"But how does that make it your fault?" Bryan asked, but before he could say more, Dad started yelling.

"If I hadn't let us grow close or go out. If I had just pushed her away and gotten her angry at me. If I hadn't fallen in love with her!" Bryan's and my mouth dropped. "She wouldn't be dead."

"I thought you said—"

"She was in there for three years until she killed herself. She may have been insane, but she was smart. I had gone in to see her every few months. And every time I did, she acted completely normal around me. She thought we were still going out, and that we were still in high school. She had acted as if we were on a date every time I saw her, and I had pretended we were. But then I met your mom at the end of sophomore year of college at a party. . ." He was speaking to Bryan and me now. He took a deep breath.

"We got together, and I had to tell Mia. Your mother didn't even know about it, and I wish I had told her when I had asked her out. I knew it wasn't cheating, though. . . But I realized that if I told Mia, her heart would be broken, and she would turn even crazier; but if I didn't tell her, then I would feel like I was cheating on your mom."

Dad looked at Mom and she nodded, closing her eyes.

"So, I decided to tell Mia. And that was the biggest mistake I ever made. I should have talked to you first." He said to Mom. "Because, if I had, everything would have been okay. At least, I think it would have. . ." He trailed off again, staring at the door now.

I wanted to know what happened next, but I did not want to make Dad talk more. I figured I knew what happened, though. But how did Dad tell Mia? Did he say that he couldn't see her anymore? Did he say they actually weren't going out and that it's really been three years since the incident? Did he say he found someone else? Someone better? Someone who was not insane? There were several things he could have said.

"So, I went to see her, and she was as happy as ever. Her face was the brightest it ever was. I couldn't bring myself to do it. But I had to. I had to make the choice between her and Maggie." Dad wasn't looking at anyone. Rather, he was staring at the door, his back turned away from us.

Bryan and I exchanged several looks. Had he even told Mom this story? I looked at Mom to see if she seemed confused or if she was right on track with Dad. But she looked solemn, and there was no telling whether she knew or not.

"I had known Mia for years. She had given up her life for me; I loved her. But I knew that we wouldn't be able to be together because she was only normal when she was with me, which made barely any sense. I wanted to be there for her and when I saw her that day, I said I always would be.

"I thought that I would never find a girl that was right for me. But I did. And because of that, I lost a friend; but gained a wonderful woman and four beautiful kids," his voice broke and I knew he couldn't bring himself to say that now it was only three kids. I felt tears fall down my face.

If Dad had decided to be with Mia, he probably would have never had kids, meaning I wouldn't be here. If he had chosen Mia, he wouldn't have had to lose a daughter. Because he married Mom, he lost a friend that he loved, that he said he would always be there for. But none of this was his fault. He was blaming himself for things he had no control over!

Blake was the one who hurt and ultimately killed Mia. Mia wouldn't have killed herself if she wasn't crazy. And it was Blake who caused her insanity! Blake caused Dad to go through horrible things, and what's worse? He is doing this to us. He killed Amy! Amy wouldn't have died if this didn't happen! Because of Blake, we are going through the worst type of pain. Not only did Blake take it out on Dad, but he took it out on us. And he took it out on Amy. An innocent child who should not have died. He had better pay for this. I was so angry that if I saw him, he would be dead in a minute!

Then everything hit me. I'm in a different time and I don't know how to get back home. I lost my little sister. Liam almost died, and he is in a lot of pain right now. Bella was all a lie. She lied to me, to my family, and the worst part was she lied to my brother, her "so called" *boyfriend*. She broke Bryan's heart, after his heart had already been broken several times before. And after he lost his little sister. Could my heart or his crack even more? Everything I knew was a lie. Everything that's going on is because one guy—ONE GUY—wanted to get back at my dad for something that wasn't his fault!

I could not imagine what Bryan was going through. At least I had Liam. But how do I know he won't make it through either? What if we all just die here? Except Bella of course! Her father would save her before she got the plague, if she wasn't immune. But why were we here? Why would Blake put his daughter in such a dangerous place? Did he really only care about himself? Was Dad right in saying that Blake used Bella to do this? Was Bella slightly innocent? Now I wanted to know Bella's story, so that everything could be figured out.

But there were a few things in which I was undeniably certain of:

Bella lied to us.

Dad's best friend in high school caused this to happen to us and made a time machine.

I shouldn't have been born.

Chapter X
The Story of a Liar

"When I was four, my mom left us because she thought that my dad was spending too much time on scientific stuff and not enough with his family. She decided not to take me with her, and I still don't know the reason why." Bella began.

We had all calmed down slightly and decided that we wanted to give Bella a chance to explain.

"When I was ten years old, Dad made a cell phone into a phone that would be able to call to any place in the world and needed no service in order to do so. Then that led him to another idea that many people have dreamed of making a reality. A time machine. He loved cell phones, so he decided he would transform one into a time machine.

"Two years ago, he finished making one, and he tested it out, going back to the day I was born. The time machine worked perfectly and then I realized that my Dad did care about me, even if it seemed like he didn't, and he was always working. He came back from

127

the past and started making another based on the ways he made the first. I basically raised myself since I was ten because he never had time for me. But that also meant that I could do whatever I wanted. I had stayed at friends' houses most days, and Dad didn't even notice. . ." She shrugged her shoulders, making it seem like she was used to it. "Last year he finished the second and started working on a third.

"A few days after school ended this year, I was in his office where he was creating the third time machine and picked up the second time machine he had already finished—or so he thought. I dropped it accidentally, but it didn't break. Dad looked at me and told me that he made a protection guard on the phone so that if it were dropped, it wouldn't crack. Also, if it went into the water, it would not break, which gives you the answer on how we got off the Titanic.

"I went down to pick it up, but next thing I knew, I was spinning out of control. I stopped but did not have a clue to where I was. The time machine wasn't in my hands and I was looking around for it, when I felt a vibration in my pocket. I took out the cell phone that Dad transformed into one that would take calls from anywhere around the world. There was a text on the screen asking where I was. I said that I had no idea. He told me to start walking and see where I could be, so I obeyed.

"After a while I saw a village with a large round building in the middle. I took a picture of the scene with my phone and sent it to my dad. He told me I was in Rome and told me that I should go into the Coliseum and see if gladiator fights were going on. If there were, I was about 2,000 years back in time. So, I went into town, and sure enough, there were fights going on. That's when my dad realized that the second time machine had a glitch in it. The glitch, we came to find out, was that once you travel to a different time, the phone disappears and ends up somewhere else in that time. Dad said he would make the third as quickly as he could so that he could come see me."

"He couldn't use the first one he made?" Bryan asked, and I understood that it didn't make sense either.

"He had let one of his "friends" borrow it to go back in time to change something so his life would be better. After that, we never heard from him again. Which was one reason why the second phone had a glitch in it because he didn't have the first, working one to help him fully. So, he began making the third one, telling me to stay calm and that if I somehow find the phone, to not do anything with it because things could only get worse. So, I "stayed calm" and walked around town and realized that I could understand everyone. My dad told me that the time machine makes it possible for the owner of the machine to understand the language of that time, as well as speak the language of that time, without even knowing it."

"Wait!" Bryan interrupted.

"So, we are speaking in a different language right now?" I asked, on the same track as Bryan.

"And you spoke Latin in Rome, but thought you were speaking English." Bella said shrugging and smiling slightly.

"Now it all makes sense!" Bryan said.

Bella nodded her head and started to speak again. "A few days passed, and my dad didn't text me. I started to get worried. Then on the fourth day of being trapped in a world I barely knew about, my dad texted me. He told me that he was sorry he didn't text me earlier, but he was so busy working on the new time machine. I understood. He never really paid attention to me that much at home anyway. . ." she trailed off and looked down at the ground.

"Two weeks later and I still heard nothing. I had made a little camp in the outskirts of Rome and stole food to eat because I didn't have any money." She shrugged again, and everyone nodded in comprehension.

"A little more than four weeks after—"

"Four weeks! Four weeks without any sign of your father?" Dad asked with pity in his tone.

Bella nodded. "I was more scared than I ever had been in my entire life. My phone had died, of course, because my dad's battery pack, that I had luckily had in my pocket, which kept my phone alive for almost three weeks, had died as well. I thought I would have to make a living in the Roman times. I had no clue what would happen, but I was worried about my father and everything." Bella told us.

No one said anything, so she went on. "On the thirty-second day—for I had been counting the days—I was sitting against a tree, contemplating my life. I had texted my father every single day, until my phone died, and I had not heard from him since the fourth day."

I could see the disgust and loathing in Dad's facial expression, as he groaned hard. Bella looked at the ground and blinked a few times before going on.

"Then I saw something, like a random blob in the middle of the trees and stuff coming towards me. It came into view, and I saw it was my dad. I screamed, and ran towards him, hitting almost every part of him, saying things like "why didn't you text me" and "it's been four weeks" and "I thought you abandoned me" cursing at him. But he pushed me to the ground and said that he was working on the time machine so that he could save me and that I was a selfish brat, and that if I didn't listen to him, that he would just leave me here and never come back for me." Bella gulped, and I could see a tear falling down her face. "But the worst part was," wiping away her tears, "he said that he wished my mom had taken me with her twelve years ago. And I did too. I had ever since she left. . ." She trailed off and looked out the window, letting her tears fall.

Nothing happened for several minutes. Then Dad spoke up. "Do you want to take a small break?"

Bella nodded, got up, and walked outside, leaving the door open. Bryan watched her, with a loss of what to do. I knew he was mad at her, but I think he had begun to feel more like how Dad was: Mad at Blake and not at Bella because he used her, abandoned her, and abused her. Finally, Bryan stood up and ran after her.

It was getting hot and I could feel sweat on my forehead. I got up from Liam's bed and went to get some water. After I had gulped quite a bit, I took it to Liam and gave him some.

Liam thanked me, and I laid down next to him. He held me tight as I sobbed, my whole body shaking. As he rubbed my back, he told me he loved me and said that we would figure things out and get home soon. He sounded certain of it, but I didn't. What if Blake was watching us right now? Doing absolutely nothing about our pain? Making a joke out of it and thinking that this was what Dad deserved?

Blake was pure evil. He was the worst father and the worst friend. He took his anger out on innocent people. He was a murderer and he was proud to be one. Blake was the antagonist of my life, and my family's life, and the worst one of all people.

"Why?" I croaked.

"I've been asking myself the same question for almost ten years."

"Hasn't it," I looked up into Liam's eyes, "hasn't it been enough for one day?"

"I know exactly how you feel." He brushed his perfect hand over my cheek, wiping away the tears.

"Yeah," I smiled slightly, taking a deep breath. "I just wish everything could undo itself. I wish none of this had happened. Was there really a reason that it had to be our family that had to be left all alone? I just. . . I don't get it."

"Well, it looks like all your questions are being answered by a person we never thought would answer our questions. I have several questions as well. And I've been through the same things you have."

"No, you haven't." I interrupted, sitting up, but still in Liam's arms. "You don't have parents. You don't have a home. You don't—"

"Kyara," he put his hand over my lips. "I may have been through more, but that doesn't make it any different. We've been through a lot, and I was just saying I know how it feels. . . to. . . to lose a sister."

His eyes were glowing with tears, but I knew he would not let them fall. Liam may be called a "wimp" for crying, and he may be sensitive, but that didn't make him any less strong! He and Bryan were the strongest boys I knew. Liam had gone through quite a lot. Things that I could barely even imagine, and he had made it. He had made it through the worst.

"But we can't control anyone's lives." Liam began again. "If I could have anything to do over again, it would be to have watched Rosie when I was supposed to. If I had, though, I wouldn't know if she'd make it through the car crash. I was lucky to have survived, but I shouldn't have been the one to. I should have died."

"No, you shouldn't—"

"Kyara. Stop." He took a deep breath. "You don't know about one thing. I didn't want to tell you because it would just make it that much worse. . ." Another deep breath. "We were supposed to be in Anaheim for another day, but I was acting disobedient. We hadn't even talked on the way home. We were just silent. I never even had a chance to say sorry." His sorrow turned into anger. "If I had been a good kid. If I had just respected them. They would still be here!" I could feel his heart beating fast; his stomach moving

133

up and down as he took long, deep, tragic breaths. He was biting his lower lip so hard that I thought that I would surely see blood.

"Liam stop." All my tears were away and all I cared about now, was making sure Liam would be safe. I pulled him into a kiss, so that he would stop biting his lip, but he didn't kiss me back. I let go and looked at him, straight in the eyes that were blank and filled with pain. "Stop. Please. Just take a deep breath. Liam, please. You need to stop thinking everything is your fault." And I realized then that he was just like my father.

Mom, Dad, and Luke looked back when they heard my shouting, and noticing that Liam was in pain, swept over to us. They asked no questions, but just put their arms around Liam and we all began to cry.

Mom; however, began to sing "You Never Let Go" reminding us that God is here for us and will never let us go. And though we were walking down that valley of pain and torture and death, God was here, and he would come through and save us. He already has. And Mom made that clear. Mom had gone through quite a bit in her life, but I always knew she never gave up on God. She was the most devoted Christian woman I knew.

But sometimes I *didn't* understand. Why did he let us go through this? Why did Amy die? Why did he let so many innocent people die? Why did Mom lose her father to an overdose when she was only ten years old? Why'd he make bad things happen to people who were devoted to him? Why was he letting me fall away from him and letting me hate him, not showing me that he was here for me and he was going to get us out of this treacherous place?

When Mom ended the song, I began to cry again. I didn't think I could cry anymore, but yet the moisture escaped my red eyes.

So much death. No wonder we were witnessing and hearing all about death here. It's because we were in the time of Black Death. Families separated and lost each other here. All around us there was pain and suffering. But why did we, an innocent family, once a full and tight family, have to find out what it feels like to be broken.

I had nothing to say. Liam was staring at his stitched-up leg.

I knew he must be in pain. But not just physical pain; mental as well. Just the type of pain I was feeling. A type of pain I hadn't felt before, a type of pain I hoped I never had to feel.

~ ~ ~

Bryan stomped into the house, his face red with rage, and his fists clenched. The vibration in every step he took rumbled across the room to the spot where I sat on the bed.

We stared at him as he walked to the table and sat on a chair—his focus completely absent. I felt a chill run down my spine as he took a seat, but not because I was cold. Rather, it was because I understood exactly what Bryan felt. It was that twin connection Bryan and I shared on very rare occasions.

135

This was one of those occasions. I felt not only the pain he felt, but also the anger he had towards Bella. The way she kept the truth from us for so long made me feel, the same as Bryan: betrayed.

It may have been because her father was a jerk and that Bella was scared of him, but that still didn't give her the right to lie to us. Especially to Bryan, the one who loved her so much and thought that his life was complete with her there. But now his heart was broken, all because of what her father did to mine all those years ago.

Then Bella appeared and stopped once she saw us all surrounding Liam. Then she turned and saw Bryan sitting at the table by himself. I was the only one to look up as she began taking more, slow steps toward us.

Why was this happening? That question had been swimming through my mind all day. I glanced out the window and noticed that the sky was a dark shade of orange as the final rays of sun disappeared behind the fields. The worst day of my life was almost over. Or was it? For all I knew, this day could go on for as long as it wanted to. Ever since the time machine came into my life, I realized that anything was possible, and the concept of time meant nothing anymore. So, because of that, the worst day of my life could last forever. But would this day get worse? Could it get worse? The answer was already answered right when I thought it. *Of course*, it could get worse. We were in the time of Black Death. Anything could happen.

Good things could happen, too, a voice in my head said.

In the midst of all this bad? I asked, my heart beating unsteadily.

Trust in me. And I felt a weight lifted off my shoulders.

In just one day, I had heard God's voice more times than some people have heard in a lifetime.

"We are ready to listen if you are ready to talk." Dad said standing up and going back to the table.

Bella folded her hands over and over staring at Bryan. She opened her mouth to speak, but nothing came out. Bryan glared at Bella, without a single trace of sympathy in his eyes.

What had happened when Bryan went after her? He must have made her cry because of how red her eyes were. I could tell now; however, that she would not cry and was fighting off her tears.

I knew how she felt. Well not exactly, but I knew how she felt about Bryan. When Bryan is mad, he is really mad. Just like what had happened in Rome, this was probably somewhere close to the same thing. Rome. . . Amy was still alive. But we had asked Augustus to watch after her and Luke so that we wouldn't be distracted from finding the phone. Now I wish we had never done that, and that we had kept Luke and Amy as close to us as we could have. I would have had more time with Amy in her last days.

But there was nothing I could do about that now. The past was the past, and the present was about Bella. And I knew how she felt after Bryan yells. Bryan could make you feel worthless and could make the pain worse than it already was. It was one of the biggest problems Bryan had, and he needed to learn a way to get over it. He may always apologize after, but that didn't mean it wasn't a bad thing. He needed to learn that anger wouldn't solve anything and that it could only make it worse.

I could tell, in the past few minutes that Bryan had calmed down, slightly, but was still glaring at Bella.

Bella bit her lip, looked outside, and then back at us. "Ok, so my dad tells his story and why he is late and what he has been doing in the past four weeks. It is very long, but you need to know pretty much everything for most of your questions to be answered. But, I will tell you ahead of time that I was forced to do this, and I did not want to hurt you guys in any way possible. My dad, as you know, scares me and if I don't do what he says. . . well let's just say it's not very pretty." She stopped for a second, took a deep breath, and I could tell that she was angry rather than sad. There was no sign of tears in her eyes anymore.

"So, he started saying that he was sorry for not getting back to me for four weeks, but it was because he was working all day and night. He said he had to hire a maid to make food for him and everything. A week and a half before he came to Rome, he told me he was creating a few more things, even an extra time machine—don't ask me why—that he might need to use when he came to where I was.

"The evening before he came to Rome, he said that something that he was making exploded, the storm going on that night had randomly ended, and some radar he made a couple years ago that said the exact number of people in the world, for some strange, creepy reason, only read 5. The names: Blake Munccello, Bryan Edwards, Kyara Edwards, Amy Edwards, and Lucas Edwards. He knew right then and there that these were the names of his longest and worst enemy: Ben. He could barely believe that you four, out of the billions of people in the world, were the four that were somehow left all alone in the world; that was when he knew that that was the perfect time to get back at Ben. I hated the idea when I heard it. You were four innocent kids, but I could never change my dad's mind. . .

"After he screwed tight a few things on the second time machine that he had made and hoped that it would work a little, he ran to the nearest Costco, which was nowhere near where you four were. He told me that he thought awhile on how you would find it, but he didn't care at the moment because he needed to get back to me. So, he ran back to our house and used the third time machine, which worked perfectly, to get to me." She stopped for a few seconds to give herself a break from talking. "Any questions so far?"

"What about the dust storm the next day?" I asked.

"I'll get to that, but you may not believe me on the answer." Bella said.

"Hey, there was a time machine able to be built; no one ever thought that was possible." Liam said, talking for the first time in a while.

"True, but this is. . . this next thing is like magic."

"Let's hear it then." I said.

139

"I'll talk about that in a few minutes when I get to it," Bella took a deep breath and started talking again. "The night he came, he was carrying a ton of stuff, hoping it would be useful for us in Rome. I didn't bother to ask what the stuff was; I just didn't care too much. All the stuff he made was apparently "better" and "cooler" than me."

"Your dad said that?" I asked.

"No, he just acted like it all was." She shrugged, and started again, "The next day, Dad was watching you guys on some computer screen that he must have transformed into a type of device that watched people—"

"He was watching us!" Bryan screamed in anger. Dad's mouth had dropped as well.

"That's what I thought at first, and I asked him about it. He was only able to see you through street cameras." Bella told him.

Several of us nodded, comprehending

"Something else he had brought with him was something he called the WAFE. It controls the four elements—"

"You can't control the elements! Only God can!" I shouted, interrupting.

"Oh, but you can. My dad figured out a way." Bella raised her eyebrows and pursed her lips. I could tell she was angry and also surprised. If Bella didn't understand her father, then probably no one could.

"I remember that." Dad said. After he heard the word "WAFE" he had gasped, and his eyes had widened.

We all stared at Dad.

"He talked about a way to control the elements in sophomore year. I thought he was joking and because of that, we made a joke out of it. We would imagine what we could do if it truly could be made. And together we came up with the name, WAFE— Water. Air. Fire. Earth." His words ceased to continue.

Everyone became silent. We all knew what this meant. Blake could now have all the power in the world. He could kill off anyone. But would he? He could have killed us by putting a fire or a tsunami on us rather than a sand storm. Was he waiting to use worse on our father? He would have had the chance in Rome, though. Why didn't he? Was he not that bad of a person? Or maybe he thought that Dad would ultimately die in a gladiator fight.

Whatever it was, Dad was still alive, and that was what mattered most.

Then, for the first time in several hours, my stomach groaned. I wanted food, but at the same time I didn't. We would have to work for food and I don't think any of us were in the mood to get dinner started. I would just have to wait. Hunger wasn't the first thing on my mind, anyway. There were much more important things going on.

"All right." Dad broke the silence. "Go on with your story."

"But wait." I said just as Bella opened her mouth to speak. "If we had never gone into that Costco, and never found the cell phone, what would have happened? Would we still be there without anyone in the world?" I asked and thought hard about what would have happened. I would have much rather stayed in our time. We would have found food easier and learned to live on our own. Amy would still be alive. And maybe we would have figured out what to do about getting everyone back. . .

"I think my dad would have done something—"

"You think, or you hope?" Bryan asked and stood up. His anger had grown as Bella talked more, and I knew he was just about to burst.

"Bryan, stop." Dad said, leveling with Bryan.

"NO!" He pushed Dad aside and ran toward the door. Before he disappeared; however, he stopped and glowered at Bella. "You never really loved me. You just made it all up. You're on your dad's side! I'm sure your dad put you up to this! Amy would not have died if none of this had happened. If your dad hadn't done all this shit to us!" He was at his boiling point. I had only seen his face this red once before.

"Bryan, you know nothing!" She stood up, too. Dad began to go after Bryan, but Bella shoed him back. "I never wanted to hurt you! I wouldn't even be telling you this if I didn't love you! I have no idea where my dad is right now! I haven't seen him since Rome! I'm very angry with him for everything and I know that you are angry with me for "fake" falling in love with you at first, but now I do love you! That is why I'm telling you everything!" Bella screamed back at him, but tears started falling down her cheeks. She seemed not to care. I was glad that Bella was yelling back at him because that was what always brought him away from anger. I learned that when I just ran away from him and cried, it would make Bryan even angrier.

"I thought you loved me." Bryan said in a calmer voice. "I thought I loved you. But now, I don't even know you." He started towards the door again.

"Bryan!" He stopped. "I do love you! I never meant for this to tear us apart! I'm telling you because I love you! Can you not understand that?" Bella stood in front of him, but still kept her distance.

"No, I can't." Bryan said with pure disgust, and then he disappeared. Bella ran after him.

"No!" Dad and I screamed simultaneously. I got up, told Dad that I could handle this, and ran after my brother and Bella. I had always been better at handling Bryan better than Dad. Dad had never scared Bryan, but somehow, I did. Somehow, I had more force over Bryan than anyone else did.

"None of this even makes sense!" I heard in the distance and ran all the way up to where we had been before. Bryan was pacing again, and Bella stood, watching his every step. When I reached them, I stood next to Bella.

"Bryan, stop it. This isn't going to help anyone," I said.

"You shut up." Bryan pointed at me, stopping his pacing.

"Don't tell me to shut up, Bryan!" I was eye to eye with him now. I wasn't scared of Bryan. This was the only way to get to him, eye to eye, so that he wouldn't lash out. He would never hurt me. At least not physically.

After a few more seconds he backed away and took a deep breath. He then proceeded to look at Bella, and in a calmer tone, talk to her.

"Why are we still not able to find the cell phone? If your dad was all a part of this, wouldn't he be here now?"

"No, he's not. I just told you I haven't seen him since Rome."

"But why did we find the phone with Mom on the Titanic?" I was the one to speak this time.

"I. . . don't. . . know. . ." She said, pronouncing every letter with a hint of irritation.

Was she mad at us or mad at her father?

"So, your dad hasn't contacted you at all in the past six days?" Bryan asked, gentle this time.

"No." Said Bella through gritted teeth.

"Oh? So, you miss him? You wish he was here?" I asked, raising an eyebrow. Anger began to flow through my veins, now.

"Yes, actually. Because then we could get out of here."

"We. Meaning you." I pointed a trembling finger at Bella.

"No. I would talk to him. He's done—"

"Oh? You would talk to him?" Said Bryan, anger rising up once again. This time I didn't think of stopping him. "You're scared of him. You said it yourself. If you asked for us to go home with you, he would probably hit you!"

"No, he wouldn't! You know noth—"

"Just like he wouldn't push you on the ground! Just like he wouldn't abandon you for four weeks in a place far different than your home! Just like," Bella tried to cut in, but Bryan shouted even louder, "He wouldn't kill Amy!"

144

"He did not kill Amy!" Bella was even louder than Bryan, her toes raised, so that she was as tall as him.

"Well not intentionally. Just like what happened with Mia. But it still happened! And it was his fault. It was *all his fault*," said Bryan, stepping away from Bella.

"Bryan don't." I said. I was angry, too, but he had no right to say that. Bella's face turned a dark shade of red, out of fury, and tears fell from her face as fast as pouring rain.

"I'm sure you know where your dad is, but it's all just a con to get back at my father!" Bryan began shouting again. "You're all happy my sister is dead— it's part of the con!" I gasped as he said it. I knew Bryan was wrong, but I felt the same pain Bryan felt at that moment. What if Bella was faking now? It wouldn't be the first time.

"Your dad is a stubborn, sly, devious, and a repulsive coward! And because you are his daughter. Because you didn't tell us this sooner. Because you sided with him on all this, you're a coward too!" Bryan screamed, in the angriest tone I've ever heard him use. But I understood it all. Blake was a coward. And, even though I may have felt sorry for Bella a while back, I didn't anymore. Bella had hurt us far more than anyone could.

Bella looked up, tears streaming down her face. "Well, if that's how you feel, I'm out of here!" She ran away from us, cupping her face, trying to keep more tears from falling.

Bryan and I stared at each other, our breathing heavy—his was heavier—and in sync. I looked away and then fell to the ground. My face fell into my arms and tears began to fall. Bryan hadn't moved a step.

I didn't know what to do anymore. All I wanted to do was die. I wanted Amy back. Everything was going wrong. *Everything.*

I felt Bryan sit down next to me, and I could tell by his uneven breaths, that he was crying as well.

"It sucks, Kyara." He said. And I knew exactly what he meant.

There were so many feelings running through my body, I could barely think straight. Anger. Rage. Fury. Broken-Heartedness. Pity. Hate. Sadness. . . Pain. It was Bella's father's fault for all of this. All of the pain my brothers and sister had gone through, though there was no more pain for Amy anymore. This brought me back to my own pain, my own sorrow, my own. . . hopelessness and depression. Yes, I was depressed. The most depression I've ever felt before. The kind where you didn't know if you wanted to live anymore, not after someone you were so close to, someone you loved deeply, dies. My sister was dead. She would never step foot on this earth again. She was gone forever. I didn't have a sister anymore; it was just my two brothers and me. If, of course, we all survived.

Bella was most of the reason we were even here—why we had to go through all this pain. I would never get back my happiness from when I was back at home, in our time, with my full family. There would always be a hole in my heart, one that would never be mended.

Chapter XI
In the Depths of the Evil Heart

All was silent as we ate our food. The smell of the pottage that I wished was seasoned with spices, had enveloped my senses. This smell—the smell of food—was what had calmed us down. Everyone finally had slight smiles on their faces. Not enough to talk of good times and to try and laugh, but at least they were not frowning.

I looked in the water of my glass and could see in the reflection that my tears were dried, and my cheeks were not red with rage or pink with sorrow anymore. Bella had come back because Dad had run after her and had helped her calm. He felt bad for her for some reason, and I didn't quite understand that. I figured it had to do with him trusting Bella's story because he knew how deceitful and cowardly Blake was.

We had decided unanimously that after dinner, Bella would finish her story without any interruption, and we would try to believe her. Bella had promised to tell the complete truth, not that she had not been before. Bryan hadn't exactly forgiven Bella, but he was giving her another chance to explain.

After each of us had finished our dinner, we sat and waited, giving Bella the signal to start whenever she wanted to. It was about five minutes before Bella began to speak.

"So, we just learned about the WAFE. And as you probably figured out, my father used the earth and air part of the WAFE to cause the sand storm. When you started to get near the Costco where he had put the time machine, he created a tree right where you were driving so that your car would crash. Then, hoping that you were smart enough, which you were, he hoped you would take shelter in a place that would give you food and anything else you would need. The night you got to the store and the following day, he would occasionally go and move the phone to different places hoping you would find it. But all day long you still didn't find it, until you started a movie for . . ." She took a deep breath. We had set up a movie for Amy and Luke to watch. I'm sure she did not want to say "Amy".

Dad must have noticed why Bella didn't go on, for he said, "So they found the phone. . . and then what?"

"Oh." She sent a look of gratitude to Dad. "Yes, and then when you were in Jesus' era, my dad had enough time to figure out how to get you all to Rome."

"Wait." I interrupted Bella from continuing. "Why did Blake let us even go to Jesus' time? He's done all these bad things to us. Why did he let us get blessed by Jesus?"

"He just needed time to figure everything out, I guess? I honestly don't know though." Bella said.

I nodded, but inside I was screaming.

"Wait," Bryan said, cutting off Bella from trying to speak again. "How did we not lose the phone in Jesus' time?"

"Well, my dad has the power to send you wherever he wants. And he actually planned on landing it with a family member in each era you, or we, visit."

"Wait, the phone isn't broken?" Bryan asked.

"Oh, sorry, I didn't quite explain that right. The phone you had in Jesus's time was not broken. Until my dad replaced it with a different one the night you were all asleep in the tent. That one he replaced it with was one he had made so that you could only end up in a time where a family member is," Bella said.

"I'm confused," Bryan and I said.

"The one I had dropped, the day after school this year, was one he had created so that you, the person who used the time machine, could only go to a relative's or ancestor's time. He had created it that way so that the person who uses the time machine would not change history, only something in their life."

We all nodded.

"So, who was your family member in Rome?" I asked.

"What?" Bella said, slightly confused.

"If you used the phone that sent you to a family member, then who did it land with when you dropped it and were sent to Rome?"

150

"Oh, I don't know. . ." she squinted her eyes. "That's odd. I never thought of that. My dad had said he knew where the phone would be in Rome, but I wasn't with him when he retrieved it."

"Ok?" Bryan said, and I knew he felt like I did. Unsure if Bella was actually telling the truth.

"So, we came to Rome because Dad was there. Titanic was because Mom was there," I said.

"And here, England, was because your ancestor, Edward III, is here," Bella said interrupting. "So, Blake knows we are here? He can get us out of this mess," I said.

"Even if he could, he wouldn't want to bring us back home. Right, Bella?" Bryan said with a hint of displeasure in his tone.

Bella nodded. "And, again, I haven't seen him since Rome."

So, everything that Liam and I had talked about that night on the Titanic was a lie and untrue. The phone wasn't broken. Blake was just messing with us, meaning that he was the evilest person on the planet. He did let Amy die. He had had the power to keep Amy alive, but instead he let her die. What kind of person would do that?

Only the evilest person alive.

~ ~ ~

"So, my Dad found a man in Rome that could be my father, so that I could get on the inside. Then, of course, you came to Rome, sat next to Lucious—"

151

"We had a habit of making things easy on your father, didn't we?" Bryan asked, laughing sardonically.

We had all calmed down after finding out that Bella truthfully had no idea where her father was and had no idea how to get us out of this mess. We were lost, and Blake did have all the power to take us home, but there was nothing we could do about it. We needed to figure out Bella's story, so that tomorrow, we could plan what to do, how to find the phone, and how to get out of this.

"Yeah you did. . ." She trailed off, looked out the window, which now reflected the moon's light, and then continued. "So, as I was saying—"

"Wait. How did your dad make Lucious think he was your father?" I asked, interrupting her once again.

"Oh, right. Another one of my father's inventions. . ." She bit her lip.

"Another?" Bryan, Dad, and I said simultaneously.

"Yeah. He made it when I was in Rome for those several weeks I thought I was abandoned." Bella took a deep breath.

"He didn't?" I knew what had to happen. Something that would play with the victim's mind.

"Yes. And he not only used it on Lucious." Bella said, looking at my father.

"He used it on me, too." Dad nodded, understanding. His face was blank, but there was a trace of hate in his eyes. I knew Dad was only thinking about how many people and animals he killed. But that was not the only punishment Blake used against

152

him. Blake was still out there, pulling the strings. And this time he really did abandon his daughter.

"Was I put in that hypnotic state as well?" Mom asked.

"No, I'm sorry, I didn't explain that very well. You see, all the adults lost their minds and all the kids under eighteen remember exactly what happened. Don't ask me how, though. That has something to do with the time machine and its flaws." Bella shrugged.

It was silent once again.

"My dad hypnotized you," she spoke to Dad, "to think that you were a gladiator. That's how you fought so well in the matches and never lost. You see, my dad didn't want to kill you, because he knew that that would be too easy. He wanted to make you live with what you did—"

"So, he killed off Amy instead." My throat croaked at the last two words. I felt like I was going to throw up. I hadn't thought about the previous day much. Having lost my sister, I didn't think that my sickness was as important.

"I don't know if he could have saved her . . ."

"Oh, stop it." Dad was the one to speak. "Your father is *Blake*. He can do whatever the hell he wants. He killed my daughter. And he had the power to stop it from happening." Dad's tone was not loud and thunderous, rather it was calm and still. His anger intensified when he spoke somberly. That was when it was the worst. This anger was the only one I was afraid of.

"I'm not making excuses for him. I'm just saying that he may not have had the power to save her. Those highwaymen are malicious bast—"

"Not as malicious as your father," Dad said, still with his tone calm, but livid.

And with that, Bella began to sob again. "It's not fair." She stood up. "I hate being his daughter." She was screaming now, her eyes gushing with tears. "I wish I wasn't! Trust me. It's absolutely the worst thing in the world."

I couldn't understand. Being abandoned, beaten, and chastised by a father; being left to that man by her mother, and being part of the same blood as a now infamous murderer and devious man. It could be one of the worst things in the world. But was it worse than Liam's life story? Would I rather have parents who hated me and didn't care for me, or parents that were no longer alive?

I thought Bella's story was worse. Liam at least had Christ. Liam still had a person who loved and cared for him, like me. But did Bella have that anymore, now that we knew her story? Would we still love her like we did before any of this happened? Or could this be something no one could forgive her for? Not even Bryan.

~ ~ ~

It took a little while for us to all settle down again, which had kind of been a problem all evening, which wasn't a surprise given all that we've been through today.

The sun had completely disappeared, and candles were lit inside the house, creating enough light for us all to see each other.

"So, what about the guy who trained me?" Dad asked. "Was he put under a trance, too?"

"Yes. He had watched some gladiator fights and picked out the best of the best to train you." Bella said to Dad.

"So, your father hypnotized another guy as well?" I asked. Blake was as cruel as I thought, but also smarter than I could ever imagine—creating all those inventions.

Bella nodded.

"What about Augustus? Or were he, Lydia, and Leia hypnotized, too?"

"Yes, but Augustus is Lucious's son. Lucious's wife probably died giving birth to Augustus, but because I'm his "daughter" he thought his wife died giving birth to me."

Several of us nodded.

"Well, as I'm sure you remember, I had to tell Lucious that you guys were from the future."

"Wait." Bryan interrupted again. Bella looked at him, slightly fearful. "Did your father make you fall in love with me? Was that all a scam?"

Bella nodded slowly. Bryan looked at the ground, his face turning red with rage. "But then I really did fall in love with you! That first kiss. It was real for me! It wasn't fake. I went against my dad because I loved you and I hated my dad for putting me up to this."

"But then why didn't you tell us this before?" I interrupted before it got more awkward.

"Like I said, I was scared."

"Scared? But your Dad abandoned you!"

"Remember that it has only been a week since we were in Rome. . ." Bella said, raising her eyebrows.

My mouth dropped. So much has happened in just a week. Bryan stared into my eyes and I knew he was thinking the exact same thing I was.

I had only known Liam for a week, and it felt like I knew everything about him. We had been through so much together. We had gone through thick and thin and things that several couples don't even witness in a lifetime. Four days on the Titanic and three days here. I couldn't believe that it had been just a week.

"These days have gone on forever!" Bryan whined. But then I thought that that meant I had had more time with Amy. It's been more than a month since the night of the storm. More than a month since my entire life changed. And in this month, everything just kept going downhill. My sister was dead.

"Yeah . . . So, should I go on with the story?" Bella asked, bringing me back to my senses.

"I guess. I mean there's not much left, is there?" I shrugged.

"Well, when Lucious got mad when I told him that you guys were from the future and you were kicked out—"

"Oh yeah!" Bryan interrupted. "What the hell happened there? If we were all part of a "scam", then why did it take so long for you to take us back?" His voice was getting louder and angrier with every word.

"Because I loved you."

"How does that make sense?" I interrupted Bella from speaking and Bryan from trying to.

"Because I didn't want to make you guys come back and put you through more crap."

"So, wait." I interrupted again. "You knew where the phone was the entire time?"

Bella nodded regretfully.

There were a few minutes of silence and then Bella continued her story.

"I was in a fight with my dad for a few days. And even though you did yell at me," she pointed at Bryan, "and for a day I was mad at you, I realized that I had no reason to be angry with you. I was the one who was being deceptive. And because of that—because I loved you, Bryan, I didn't want to make you come back to Lucious's house. That was when my dad, Blake, abandoned me. . ." She took a deep breath.

"But before he did, and before we had the fight that made him leave me," she bit her lip and rubbed her forehead. "I wanted him to stop making me do this. I wanted him not to cause you all so much pain anymore and let you go home. This was all because I loved you, Bryan. But he wouldn't listen to me, so he abandoned me. But then he made Lucious believe that you guys were from the future. So, the day after we got in the fight, I realized that your dad was still fighting gladiators, and he had the shield, with the phone. So just as you," she pointed to me, "came and asked if you could come back to Lucious's house, I was about to tell

157

you guys that you could come back." Bella stopped talking. It was a few minutes before someone spoke up.

"So, you haven't seen your dad? At all? Since your fight?" Mom said. It had been a while since I heard her voice. She must be thinking about quite a bit.

Bella smiled at Mom and said, "nope!" She laughed slightly, acting as if she was used to it and didn't care. I couldn't imagine what it would be like growing up alone. Both Bella and Liam did, one without any parents, and one with parents that didn't care. I didn't know which could be worse. Knowing that your parents were in Heaven and that they were watching over you was something completely different from knowing your parents were on earth, but neither one cared.

"But he sure saw me." Bella breathed deeply.

"Wait. How do you know that if you didn't see him?" I asked, confused. I've had a lot of confusion for one day. Confusion. Pain. Hate. Too much for just one day.

"Well first of all, when you guys came back, Lucious had a completely different heart. He wanted to help Bryan to win the gladiator fight. And I had nothing to do with that. Secondly, my dad said that it's literally impossible to break out of a hypnotic state. But you," she nodded at Dad, "somehow did. And I think my dad may have had something to do with that."

"Ha!" Bryan laughed, but without a single trace of happiness. It was a disgusted laughter. "With all that he's put you through?"

158

"Just wait. That was on purpose. He wanted us to get out of Rome. He wanted me to be away from him. He wanted me to go through what you are all going through. So, he had some men he hypnotized to be Christian Persecutors so that they would come after us and cause us to be sent to the Titanic."

"But then how did I get the phone on the Titanic?" Mom asked and sat up a little straighter.

"Well you know how my dad programmed the phone?" Bella asked.

"Yeah, so that it would take us to a family member in each era we visit."

"Well I assume that he had put that poem in that you read, Mrs. Edwards, while we were on the Titanic, and before you found the phone."

Mom nodded. And Dad asked, "Poem?"

I realized then that Dad must not have heard the poem yet from Mom. So, Mom explained and recited the poem, then.

'I am a moment in time
You will become love's first grime
When you find out your offense
Everything will make sense.

The one you think is candid
Is one that has been handed
To your kindred's oldest lad
His first lover will be sad

I am your competitor
But not your first predator

Some have hated you I'm sure
Before me; I am your cure.'"

When Mom finished, and everyone was caught
up to speed, Bella said to Mom, "You said you didn't
find the phone until the day before the ship crashed,
right?"

"Yes," Mom said.

"So, I'm guessing that the day we all arrived on
the Titanic, the phone had landed with you, but you
didn't find it until a few days later because my dad had
to put the poem in it. He must've placed the phone in
your room the day the ship crashed."

"So, he was on the Titanic at the same time we
were?"

"I assume so." Bella said. I looked around and
noticed we all had perplexed looks on our faces. "This
is all just guessing. I could be wrong."

"But why did he feel the need to put the poem
in?"

"Well I always knew he loved to write poems.
He would read some to me before I fell asleep when I
was younger. But I think the poem was meant for Mr.
Edwards, actually."

"So why did Mom end up with it, then?"

Bella pursed her lips and I could tell she was
also a little puzzled.

"I think that he wanted us to find Mrs.
Edwards, and if Blake had just given the phone to Mr.
Edwards," she looked at Dad, "then we would have left
without your wife."

We all nodded in comprehension. "I guess that makes sense," Bryan said.

Something in my mind seemed off though. I was always good at telling if people were lying, and I had a feeling Bella was keeping something from us.

"Bella, thank you for telling us everything," Dad began. "It must have been hard for you."

Bella nodded. "I was scared that my father would hurt me if I told you earlier or do something worse to you guys. I was trying to protect you. But—"

"Protect us!" I spat. I couldn't take Bella's lies anymore. "Look at what has happened! Look at how far we've come. Look at how near to death each of us have been *and look* at how one of us has already died!" I couldn't control my anger, I couldn't do this anymore. I couldn't stand to be near Bella. There were too many flaws in her story. This was sure to be a part of her plan to help her father.

And I stood up, took a lantern, and ran outside.

~ ~ ~

I was in the barn for about five minutes before Bryan entered.

"It doesn't make sense," he said.

"You're right," I said, my throat was numb yet sore. I barely even had a voice. "Why would Bella be telling us the complete truth right now?"

"So, what are you thinking?"

"That it's all part of their con." I shook my head.

161

"What if it isn't? I mean, who would make up the time machine, the WAFE, and the hypnotizing thing?" He began to play with the hay we sat on, pulling pieces of hay out of the bed.

I didn't know what to say, so I looked at the candlelight and started thinking about everything. This made no sense. I wanted it to, and I wanted Bella to be right and truthful, but it seemed like, because so much of her story didn't add up, and so much of it seemed to be guessed or assumed, that she wasn't telling the full truth.

I saw, out of my peripheral vision that Bryan was now staring at me. I met his eyes and shrugged.

"I don't know what to think anymore, Bryan. I don't know who to trust and the worst part is. . . I don't know if we are going to make it past this time," I said with heavy worry in my tone. I preceded my gaze back at the hay bed I sat on and dug my finger into the hay.

What was going on? Everything and everyone seemed fake. My dad's friend from high school was now making us, my family, go through possibly the worst things imaginable. We were lost and had no idea what to do.

Blake was a murderer and a bastard for doing this to us. And because he placed his daughter in the center of it all, he was not even accepted by Satan; for the depths of Hell would've spat him back out.

Chapter XII
Shattered Faith

"So where do you think your father is now?" I asked
Bella.

Earlier Bryan and I had decided that we
needed to know as much as we could in order to figure
out how to stop Blake from winning the battle of evil
against good.

"He's not going to win, you know," Bryan had
said.

"How do you know?" I had asked while the
tears fell down my face.

"Because we have the most powerful and most
sovereign on our side."

"What do you mean?" I could barely keep the
tears to stop from falling.

"God. He's on our side." Bryan had stood up,
and while I looked up at him, my vision became as
blurry as a blind dog's eyes.

He had outstretched his hand and helped me
up, and then we walked back together to the house.

Bella's voice shocked me out of my reverie, answering my question before I could relive more of mine and Bryan's encounter. "He's probably back in our present time."

"Pulling all the strings, huh?" Liam said, his arm around my back. I was on the bed with him again. He seemed to be doing all right, but every now and again he groaned in pain.

Bella bit her lip. "Look I'm not trying to defend him or anything, but he probably has no idea what's going on here."

"Ha!" I disrupted Bella from continuing. My anger had returned. "I'm sure he has cameras planted in this house! Watching us. Waiting for us to all to die. One by one he'll take us out. Amy was first! Who's next?" I jumped off of Liam's bed and ran to the wall nearest the door. "You see everything don't you, Blake?!" I started to punch it. I just couldn't take it anymore. "And you don't even care." I felt my hands begin to bleed from the splintered wood, but I didn't care.

I didn't care that everyone was watching me. I didn't care about the pain. I didn't care that my life could end at any given moment. I didn't even care that Bryan and Dad had come up behind me and plied my bleeding hands away from the wall and restrained me. And I didn't care that Liam, the love of my life, was watching my outburst. All I cared about was getting back at Blake. And if he ever showed his face, he would be dead in an instant.

~ ~ ~

164

I had had too many outbursts for one day. One day was all it took for my life to change completely.

I didn't want it to be this way. Obviously, I wanted it to get better. I wanted Amy back. I wanted everything to go back to normal. I wished that I was back at home, probably now at school because we've been here for more than a month. Yes, I wished I was at school. I never thought I'd think that.

I mean, what was the point of being here anymore? We were lost and in an unknown place. The situation was hopeless.

I collapsed on Liam's bed and stared at the ceiling. We had put the bed back in the room, and then everyone else, except me, had gone to their bedrooms. Mom said that someone should stay with Liam, and I volunteered. Luke and Bryan were upstairs. Bella in the room next to Liam and me. And my parents were in the room opposite of us.

The worst day of my life was finally coming to an end.

I sat back up and Liam and I met eyes for the first time in a while. After my umpteenth outburst of the day, I was scared to meet his eyes. But I kept them on his because I wanted to show him that I was working through everything. I may be broken, and I may want all of this to end somehow, but I knew I had to stay strong for Liam because he was staying strong for me.

As I stared into Liam's eyes, I noticed that they were glassy and opaque—I couldn't tell what he was thinking or how he felt. He smiled slightly at me. I smiled back, unsure if I should have. I wanted to know what he was thinking. I wanted to be able to have time alone with him. But he couldn't move anywhere. He had been in the same place for hours. His body must be so weak and stiff from sitting in one place for so long and not being able to move.

We had given him two bowls of pottage to eat, while everyone else only got one. But no one seemed to care. I knew I didn't. I wasn't hungry enough and I knew Liam needed to regain his strength and get his blood flowing again.

I looked back at Liam, and his eyes were still on me. I took his hand in mine and told him I loved him and that I was here for him. He smiled but said nothing in response. Was he in too much pain? Both physical and mental? And that was when I realized how pale white his face was.

"Liam. Are you okay?" I asked, squeezing his hand tight. He didn't squeeze back, nor did he say anything or move his eyes.

"Mom! Something's wrong with Liam!" I yelled so that she could hear me and got up from her room. As soon as I got up, his head fell lopsided, and he slid down from the pillows, starting to shake uncontrollably.

~ ~ ~

I had never seen a seizure before in my life. I didn't know how I was supposed to react. Mom rushed into the room as swift as could be. She held Liam down, trying to keep him from shaking. Dad rushed in as well right after Mom had entered.

"Water!" She yelled, and Dad ran back out to the kitchen.

Foam protruded the surface of my lover's mouth. His eyes had turned into the back of his head and blood began to flow from his leg as the stitches came undone. Liam thrashed in pain and utter anguish as Mom and I tried to hold him down. Bryan had come in, then, to help us, trying to hold his bloody leg steady. He had already lost enough blood before this. Why did he have to lose even more?

I couldn't bear to think what would happen if his breathing stopped. For his breaths were unsteady and he would exhale heavily with every thrash but would barely inhale a sliver of air. After a few more painful seconds of Liam thrashing out with throbbing torture, he stopped moving

Several things happened at once. I screamed, "Liam!" Mom began to do chest compressions. Dad came back in with water. Bryan clutched his leg, putting as much pressure as he could on the bloodstained gash.

I opened Liam's mouth and started to breathe as much air into it as he could, holding his nose closed. Every few breaths, I shook his face in my hands, screaming his name. He must breathe again! This could not happen! I could not lose two people I loved so much in one day!

Dad handed Mom the water and she poured it on his face. Nothing happened, so she returned to pumping his chest again.

Just when we thought all was lost, Liam shot up to a sitting position, his eyes opened as wide as they could be. His chest was moving in and out faster than I had ever seen anyone's chest move before. One moment it was completely stopped, and the next it was moving faster than a speeding bullet.

"I saw him." He began speaking very fast. "I saw it! I saw—"

"Liam!" I screamed.

"Stop!" Mom screeched.

"Save your breath." Bryan shrieked.

"Saw what?" I asked, my voice shaking. "Saw who?"

Liam's face was replaced by dark red, and his eyes were watery. I had never seen him so anxious before.

Nothing seemed to be going right. Liam had almost died twice today. My little sister was gone. Everything we had thought to be true about Bella was a lie. Would this ever end? Would even more happen? I thought I had lost Liam just a moment ago, and I could not bear to think what I would do if I lost two of the people I loved most in one day. I would want to die. This time not because I would want to see the ones I loved, but because I would not want to go on with this painful and heart-breaking life anymore. I would lose the will to live.

What was it about losing everything I needed? We had been through four different eras because the phone had disappeared. And our reasoning behind it was completely off. Someone's using us and pulling the strings like we were little puppets.

I was getting sick of it all. Sick of all this hardship and all this death. Sick of crisis after crisis! Sick of traveling through times! Sick of losing everything! Sick of life. I did not want to go on if this was how I would live. We were in a time worse than the Titanic. On the Titanic, there was only a set number of places we could look. And though we only had four days to find the phone, we had a chance at survival. Here; however, we could all die off, one by one by one, if we didn't find that phone soon.

My heart was beating so fast I could barely remember what it felt like to breathe normally. What did he mean he saw it? And saw him? So many things were going through my head right now, I couldn't think straight. Liam was going crazy and I was too!

"Him. It. The. . . the. . ." Liam said, falling backwards. Mom caught him right before he slammed into the bed's headboard. The what? He was still shaking, but not because of the seizure—because of fear. Why was he scared?

In the past few minutes I had not moved an inch. I felt as still as a statue. I thought that I would stay like this forever. Moving seemed impossible. My eyes stared straight into Liam's, immobile. He stared back at me for a second and then looked from person to person with heavy breathing and ongoing trembling.

"Liam. Calm down. Your heart rate is going to cause you a stroke." Mom said, stroking his head with her hand and dripping water slowly into his mouth and on his forehead.

Liam's eyes moved swiftly each breath he took.

169

"He must be at least 160 per minute," Dad said, as he came back with more water, and kneeled down next to Mom.

I didn't know what to do. I felt lost and confused and broken. So much had happened today, I could barely believe it. All this in one day! It seemed impossible, but yet indescribable and dreadful. No. It was more than dreadful. It was deadly and something more. . . that words could not explain. Things happened today that no one could ever take back. The past was the past and it could not be undone. The phone was useless because it was always lost, like how I felt now.

There was that broken piece in my heart that could never be mended. A piece that was lost forever. Just like how all my happiness was. With everything that happened today, happiness seemed impossible. And it would be worse if. . . if Liam. . . I couldn't bring myself to think of it.

Everything happened so fast I didn't even have time to rest! This time was by far the worst time I had ever been to. This place was by far the worst place I would ever have to live through! This day is by far the worst day of my life.

"Liam! Don't speak!" Mom stopped Liam from beginning again, covering his mouth. "You need to calm down. You need to breathe. Breathe." Mom mimicked breathing slowly as she took big deep breaths. "Deep breaths. Liam. Come on."

I could tell that Liam was trying to slow down his breathing, but I knew his heart rate could not slow down. I had had an anxiety attack only once before. It was a day that before this day, I would have named the worst day ever. It was a few months ago, and the day Trevor and I broke up, as well as the day I got my math final back with a 33% on it. Also, that day I had had a dream the night before about the person who I hadn't dreamed about for several years, which was Uncle Scott. That dream had weighed on me throughout the day, which actually, on some crazy note, caused Trevor and me to have the fight. But those four things were not even close to what I heard that night. That night I heard that one of my best friend's grandmothers had died.

When I was alone in my room, just before I went to sleep, I listened to my playlist with depressing songs on it. The one that I heard, that was still completely clear in my head, even if I had not listened to any music in more than a month, was "Fix You" by Coldplay. This song began the breakdown. This song began an anxiety attack that would last no less than thirty minutes.

I thought that my life would surely end there. Something about the heart beating at least double the amount it was supposed to caused me to believe that my life could not go on. I thought that that night was the most pain I had ever felt. I was wrong. This night— this day—was the worst day of my life.

As Liam began to breathe at a better pace, Mom spoke again. "Ok. Tell us what happened. What did you see?"

Liam's eyes began watering and his breathing became slower and slower. What was happening? His breathing hadn't stayed normal all day! What did he see? I could tell that he was trying to speak, but for some reason, nothing came out.

"Liam?" Mom asked, still stroking his hair, giving the cup back to Dad to get more water.

He opened his mouth once more and a small groan came out, his eyes completely stationary on the ceiling above him. Tears would fall from his eyes, gripping onto the pillow below him, making a darker stain than was normal for the sheet.

I still had not moved an inch, nor did I want to. I did not cry, though I was sad, because there were no more tears to shed.

My faith was failing me. I did not want Jesus in my life anymore because of how much pain he has put me through. God lied to me. He lied to us all. Once my favorite verse, Jeremiah 29:11, was all a lie. He said his plans were not to harm us and they were plans to give us hope and a future, but the future seemed devoid. It seemed hopeless and without purpose. Impossible and irredeemable and only filled with pain. Amy no longer had a future. Liam may no longer have a future. And because of that, I could no longer have a future.

Wouldn't Blake want to make a resurrection tool? I would think that he would want to bring Mia back to life if he loved her so much. But then that meant part of this reasoning for us being in this horrible time led back to Mia's death. I wonder if Blake had ever visited Mia at the mental hospital? Did Dad know? I wanted to ask him, but there were other problems going on right now.

Liam neared death every second and none of us had any way to help him. There were no hospitals, no modern doctors, no one around. Black Death wasn't just a disease; it was a curse. A curse that spread across the world, killing everyone in its path. But it had not swept over us. Why? Amy had died from an arrow, rather than a disease. Liam fought death now because of a battle, which caused a sword to rip up his leg, spilling out most his blood.

Dad came back with more water and Liam gulped it up. At least he still had energy to drink and swallow. As his anxiety faded away more and more, and his breathing and heartbeats were more regular, Mom helped Liam sit back up, propping him against the pillows once again.

"I. . . I think I know. . ." Liam breathed heavily as the blood rushed back into his face. "I know where the phone is."

Chapter XIII
Possibilities

"What?" It was the first time I had spoken in several minutes. The words sounded foreign to me and as I moved my head, I got a little dizzy and almost fell over.

Bella and Luke stood at the threshold. I had not noticed them before now.

Everyone else pulled their heads in closer, waiting for Liam to continue. Each face had a different expression. Dad's held surprise, as his eyes grew wide, and lips narrowed. Mom's mouth dropped, and her eyebrows rose in anticipation. Bryan exchanged looks of hope and expectation with me. Luke came in closer out of excitement and I knew that, as a knowing smile filled his face, he was desperate to get out of here. I understood his feelings completely. Bella; however, was the only one who didn't smile. She stayed at the door, out of the way.

The look of bewilderment in her eyes was replaced with fear. Did she not want us to find the phone? Was there more that she was not telling us?

174

Had she not told the complete truth and lied about not seeing her father since Rome? But I could not complete my thoughts in time because Bryan spoke.

"Look. We can understand it is hard to talk, but please. Just name the place you saw it," Bryan said. His face became redder with passion, and the words tumbled from his mouth. He was barely able to contain himself.

"Where?" Luke said, and his legs shook with excitement.

"Hey. Let him regain his breath," said Mom with a slightly stern tone of voice.

"No. It's okay," said Liam, taking another deep breath. "I can't name the place." Another deep breath, "it was in someone's hand. A young person, probably about our age. He was typing in something on the phone."

How could Liam have seen the phone, anyways? If his heart had stopped and he was basically dead, then did that mean he witnessed one of those "Heaven is for real" or "soul outside the body" thing? But all those stories about people in a coma and seeing what happens around them were not what Liam witnessed. He had seen someone with the phone. Who? Why wouldn't he have seen Blake with it?

"Maybe someone found it?" Bryan said.

"What was he typing in?" I asked.

"I can't remember. It's blurry," Liam said.

"Do you remember anything else? What about the background? Where was he? Do you know?" I continued.

175

Dad stood up to get more water, jogging out to the kitchen. I could tell that he did not want to miss anything.

When Dad came back, and Liam gulped up some more water, he began speaking again.

"Oh, now that's coming back. Yeah," Liam began. "It looked like hospital beds were behind him. But not now-a-days hospital beds. Like almost from the early twentieth century."

"What? Is it in a different time then? Is the phone even here?"

"Yes, it is," Liam said, and his eyes shot wide.

"How do you know?" I was eager to hear what he had to say next.

"Because he was typing in 'Black Death'."

~ ~ ~

"You remembered what he typed?" I asked.

"I do now," Liam said.

It was silent for a second as we all thought.

"I think our best hope is going into town," said Liam.

"One of us could go into town tomorrow," said Mom.

"It's too dangerous." Dad said, looking straight into Mom's eyes.

"Yeah. You need at least two people together at all times. Especially with everything going on right now," Bryan said, biting his lip.

"He's right," I said.

176

"So, what is the plan?" Bella asked, speaking up for the first time in a while.

It was completely silent for a few minutes as everyone thought. I wondered what time it could be. The day seemed like it did not want to end. Like it wanted to cause as many crises as it could possibly cause in a twenty-four-hour period. At least now it acted as if it wanted to come to an end. We now had more of an idea on where the phone was, meaning we were closer to getting home. A good thing happened from a bad thing. Thankfully Liam had survived, though he may have been dead for half a minute.

But the problem remained. We could not all travel together. At least not for a few weeks. Liam was stuck where he was for several days. I had no idea how long it would be before Liam could walk again, if he even ever could. I wanted to ask Mom what she thought, but there were more important matters to discuss right now.

"I say we sleep on it. I can tell we are all very tired and I think Liam definitely needs his sleep," Dad said, and everyone nodded.

Everyone, except me and Mom, got up and went back to their rooms. Bella, however, was the last to leave the room. I couldn't imagine how she felt and how ostracized she may think she must feel. I didn't know what to think of her yet, but by the morning, I would decide whether I thought she had been telling the complete truth or not. I needed to sleep on it first.

"I need to re-stitch Liam. I'm quite surprised he's not bleeding right now."

I nodded and then rested my head on Liam's chest as Mom stitched Liam up. His arm wrapped around me and within seconds after that, I drifted into a dream.

~ ~ ~

As the consciousness crept back into my system the next morning, I opened my eyes and noticed I still had my head buried in Liam's chest, and his arm still tight around me. The sun peeked its way through the window and rays of sunlight fell onto my lover and me.

The bandage on Liam's leg was stained with small spots of blood, but that was a great sign that he had not bled through during the night. Mom had done the second stitching well, then. And as the thin and pale right leg was compared to the left, it didn't look as bad as it did yesterday.

No one else seemed to have woken up yet. I assumed that because I heard no one stirring in the kitchen, so I closed my eyes once again, but did not fall asleep. Instead I thought. Thought about everything. About the phone. About this malevolent time. About what would happen if we kept ending up in a time different than our own. About. . . Amy.

I mean, what would the point be of finding the phone and just ending up in more terrible times? Might as well just give up on trying to find the phone and just make a living in this time, until we all die off. I was never one to give up, but this was one of those times that I needed to decide what was and wasn't worth it.

I didn't even think life was worth it anymore. For any of us; especially in this time. It didn't matter if we had a lead on where the phone was. Liam could have been dreaming and it all could just be a hoax. It may bring us into a trap: one worse than we were in now. The thoughts of what is the point took over my mind and kept repeating itself.

Did I even want to do this anymore? I asked myself.

No, said a voice in my head.

Liam's already dead, said another voice.

Don't risk it, said the first voice.

And with that, I was once again pulled through the mist into slumber.

~ ~ ~

"Do you hear that, my love?" Liam said. I knew straight away it was a dream because we were both standing, facing each other, surrounded by trees, with the Thames River on my left. We were back where my family and I were a few days ago. Liam's leg was as perfect as it was on the Titanic, and his cheeks were, once again, the rosy color.

"Hear what?" I asked. I would hold onto this dream as long as I could. I did not want to wake up.

"Music," Liam said. And then I heard the sound of an orchestra playing one of the most beautiful songs I had ever heard. Liam took my hand in his and put his second around my waist and pulled me close.

We swayed back and forth with the music, and every now and then, he would spin me, or pick me up

179

and twirl me in the air. I could dance with him forever. Our bodies moved to the music as if they were meant to. It took no effort at all, but instead, our dance could have been choreographed and no one would know.

As the music slowed to a stop, two beautiful, white horses, with silver manes, sauntered towards us. Two golden saddles wrapped around their pearly backs, and the one that walked straight up to me had shiny blue eyes that reflected the sky. I noticed that the one that greeted Liam had amber green eyes, which met mine when I stared into them.

As swift as a rabbit hopping into its burrow, I jumped onto the saddle, feeling an overwhelming warmth of love from the stallion below. Once Liam had leapt on his, the two charged through the trees, leaving all my cares behind. I felt the cool wind blow my hair back and chills of happiness run down my spine. At exactly the same pace, the stallions quickly strolled upstream. Liam and I met eyes every few moments and our smiles would meet each other across the breeze, dancing together as serenely as Liam and I had moments before.

My heart thumped hard in my chest, but not out of pain, more out of joy. This was the happiest moment I had witnessed since Bryan survived the fight and we found Dad. It did not matter that this was a dream and it did not matter if the hope was only for a little while and until I woke up, but I had it. When we had found Dad, and then Mom, I had had hope that we would finally go home. I did not know that we would be tossed into another time, and another, but the hope still lingered.

Living in the moment was the best way to live. All my cares were lost and all I wanted was the feeling of hope, and I would grasp that for as long as I could. It had been a long time since I had this good of a dream. And I was happy to name this one of those perfect dreams.

Or so I thought.

Chapter XIV
Filling Unfulfilled Promises

"I love you!" Liam said when we met eyes again. I stared into his eyes and let the stunning stallion lead the way. But something else caught Liam's attention. And when he looked away he shrieked, "Stop!"

I followed Liam's gaze and turned my eyes to the front of my horse. Amy had just run out from behind a tree ahead of us. Neither stallion could stop quickly enough! And!

"Kyara." Liam's voice sounded beneath me. I had been shaken awake from the terror in my dream. I couldn't believe it. The dream was so perfect. Why did it have to end. . . end with such grief and horror?

My heart beat fast and my breathing could not sustain itself. I sat up.

"Another bad dream, Kyara?" Liam said, and I turned toward him as he twisted his lip upward to show sympathy.

I nodded.

"The same one as. . ." Liam couldn't finish his sentence. I nodded again and stared at Liam.

"Amy," I whispered, and as I did I felt a great stab in my chest.

Liam groaned in pain and his eyes seemed to be watering slightly.

"You okay?" I asked.

"I mean, I guess. Just hurting," he said. I knew he was trying to suck it up, but that made me feel like somehow, he was lying to me.

I heard rustling in the kitchen, so I stood up, took Liam's cup which was empty and went out to find who was awake.

Mom, Dad, and Luke were in the kitchen. I went to the bucket on the table and scooped up some water as we exchanged our "good mornings".

"How's Liam?" Luke asked.

I smiled. Luke was always so caring and such a sweetheart. It seemed normal that he would ask how my boyfriend was.

"He's doing okay, buddy. Thanks for asking." I brushed his hair back with my right hand, the cup in my left. "I'll be right back," I said and went to bring Liam the water.

"Thanks, love," Liam said when I handed him the water. I lifted his head up and helped him drink.

"No problem," I paused. "You okay?"

"Don't worry about me," he said.

"But I have to. You aren't doing well," I said, sad that he thought that he didn't deserve to be worried about.

"I'm hungry," he said, obviously taking no attention to what I had just said.

"I'll go see if Mom started making the porridge," I said and went back out to the kitchen.

The fire was steaming, and I could smell the scent of oats cooking.

"Is there enough for Liam to have two servings?" I asked.

"Yes, of course. He needs his strength. But we only have enough food for lunch and dinner, then we'll be out." Mom said.

"Good thing we're going into town today. We need to find that person who has the phone," I said.

"We need to get every detail of the boy Liam saw," Dad said.

Mom and I nodded.

"Bella?" I heard Bryan ask from down the hallway. The door to her room creaked open, from Bryan's push, and he called out Bella's name again.

I went down the hallway and saw Bryan standing at the threshold staring down at the floor. His face was pale white, and his eyes were wide with fear.

The words, "You'll be better off without me" were perfectly etched into the dust on the floor.

"That's not true!" Bryan shouted, and Mom rushed to our side. Dad and Luke joined us, as we all stared at the dust on the floor.

"'You'll be better off without me'?" Dad asked, repeating what it said.

"What's going on?" Liam said, and I went to his room. My eyes were wet with tears and my face was glowing with rage as I entered the room. "Kyara?"

184

I had absolutely no strength to say anything. I couldn't. I did not know how I felt or what was going on. I wanted to get inside Bryan's mind to know what he was thinking. The three of them passed my room and Mom and Dad were holding Bryan in between their arms.

She had planned it. That's for sure. But why? Especially after Amy's death? Why would she make the burden bigger on all of us? We had enough to worry about already. Now we had to worry about another life. But what if she was with her dad? Then I had absolutely no pity for her. But I didn't know where she was or whom she was with, so I couldn't judge her just yet.

Something in my stomach turned over and I felt like I was about to puke. And then I heard a voice resounding through my head as if someone was screaming it at me.

Lies! Lies! Lies! It repeated with a slither on the "s". I knew right away that the devil's voice said it. The words were too deplorable and repulsive to be God's.

I let the words repeat over and over again. The anger at God swelled up in me.

You promised! I cried out in my head. *You promised everything would be okay!* And I felt tears roll down my face. I ran outside the room. Liam screamed out for me to stop, but I did not. I needed to be alone, so I ran straight for the door. Mom yelled out my name, but I heard Dad shush her, telling her I'd be all right and to let me go for a bit.

As I ran outside, I shivered—it was a cold morning. I ran into the barn and shut the door behind me and sat on a hay bed.

Nothing's okay! You lied to me! I felt as if the moment Jesus touched me and I witnessed a miracle was fake and worthless. The sacrifice and promise I knew shattered to nothingness. Everything seemed lost—no everything was lost.

Yes! Yes! Yes! The voice resounded once again, and the "s" slithered to a conclusion.

I wanted to die. I wanted to curse the name of the Lord. I wanted to shout out and tell Him that He lied to me and broke His promise, but something held me back. My voice ceased to work, and all sound disappeared. I became mute.

Stop it! This time it was a different voice, and not the voice of the devil. Something invisible pushed me to the ground of the barn and my eyes rolled into the back of my head. And I saw it. An angel.

I sat up and noticed how bright the angel was.

"Do not be afraid!" He said.

My mouth was dry, and I could not speak back, but I could not be unafraid. I was fearful for my life.

The angel glowed bright hovering above me, and my eyes were blinded as four pearly wings with golden streaks outshone everything else around me. After a few seconds, the angel's wings came down and I could see what the angel wore. He had a breastplate of steel that covered his entire upper body. His entire face, except for his oceanic blue eyes, was protected by a shiny copper helmet. Around his waist, the silver belt held his flaming sword. And in his right hand he held a golden shield with a blood red cross, outlined with bronze, carved in the center.

"I have come on orders from the Mighty King Jesus to tell you of His promises that you must not forget," he began.

My mouth stayed wide open, but my voice remained mute—not that I could say anything anyway.

"'Finally, be strong in the Lord and in his mighty power. Put on the full armor of God, so that you can take your stand against the devil's schemes.'" Chills rolled through my body as he continued. "'For our struggle is not against flesh and blood, but against the rulers, against the authorities, against the powers of this dark world and against the spiritual forces of evil in the heavenly realms.'" I did not fulfill this part, for I just fell into the struggle with the devil.

"'Therefore, put on the full armor of God, so that when the day of evil comes, you may be able to stand your ground, and after you have done everything, to stand.'" He let me think for a moment of what he said.

I am about to receive the Armor of God. The *real* Armor of God. *I will have no competition against me, for I will stand firm!* Tears filled my eyes, but tears of joy and hope, not of sadness and grief.

"'Stand firm then, with the belt of truth buckled around your waist,'" he unbuckled his silver belt, but held his flaming sword in his right hand. The Angel helped me to my feet and he buckled it around my waist. The burden of Bella's lies lifted up from my shoulders and I forgave her.

"And with the breastplate of righteousness in place," he untied his breastplate and tied it around me. The burden of lost hope lifted from my shoulders, and pure hope ran through my veins and stuck close to my heart.

"'And with your feet fitted with the readiness that comes from the gospel of peace,'" he said and unhooked his auburn sandals from his feet and took my shoes off. A basket of water appeared, and a golden chair stood behind me. I sat as the angel requested and he bathed my feet in the Holy Water, and then put the sandals on. The burden of anger against Blake lifted from my shoulders, and I forgave him.

"'In addition to all this, take up the shield of faith, with which you can extinguish all the flaming arrows of the evil one.'" He placed it up against my torso, and whence it seemed big on the angel, it now fitted me perfectly. And the burden of emotional, physical, and spiritual pain and loss lifted from my shoulders.

"'Then, take the helmet of salvation,'" he pulled off his copper helmet and fit it onto my head, buckling it tight under my chin. And the burden of Liam's unknown future lifted from my shoulders and I knew that no matter what happened, it was God's plan, for He only could save us.

"And finally! 'The sword of the Spirit, which is the word of God' I present to you." He presented me with the flaming sword, and as I took it, a warm sensation filled my body. And the burden of misery, grief, and sorrow from Amy's death was elevated from my heart. I smiled widely.

"'And pray in the Spirit on all occasions with all kinds of prayers and requests. With this in mind, be alert and always keep on praying for all the Lord's people.'" And with those final words, The Angel vanished as quickly as it appeared.

Chapter XV
Genevieve

"Kyara?" Bryan's voice echoed from a far-off place.

"Kyara?" The far-off place came closer and closer. . .

"Kyara?" I opened my eyes. I had fallen asleep and didn't even know it.

"Bryan," I said, and smiled widely, sitting up. I felt my entire body but found nothing. No breastplate. No sword. No helmet. No shield. No belt. And no sandals, for my feet were bare, but smooth. I stood up.

"What's wrong?" He asked.

"Nothing. Nothing at all." The smile grew wider on my face.

"I came over to check on you—make sure you're okay—but when I found you, you were squirming around on the ground." He bit his lip.

"Oh—"

"Did you have a bad dream?" Bryan asked.

"No. In fact, it was the best dream I have ever had."

Bryan smiled, but I could tell that he was concerned.

"It's a new day, Bryan. We have to use God's armor to shield us from whatever bad comes our way," I said, certainly.

"You are acting. . . Very strangely," was all he could manage.

"It's a new day, Bryan." I jumped a few times, and Bryan's eyes grew wider with concern.

"Kyara?" His voice was trembling.

"Will you wear his armor with me? Will you fight with me?" I asked, staring him straight into his opaque eyes.

He bit his lip and after a few seconds he smiled—this time a smile of hope.

"Sure," he said, taking my hand, leading me toward the door of the barn.

When we returned to the house everyone stared at us. Mom and Dad had brought Liam's bed out into the kitchen again.

I let go of Bryan's hand and ran to Mom and Dad, skipping slightly. I couldn't believe what I had just witnessed.

"Mom, Dad, it's going to be okay." I didn't know what else to say. I wanted to tell them of the angel, but I was frightened that they would think I'm crazy. Was I?

Of course not.

"Kyara?" It was Dad's turn to look concerned. Mom, however, stood up and hugged me.

"I know, sweetheart," she whispered in my ear.

191

I beamed at her. I felt so excited and joyful, I could barely contain myself. I wanted to shout and sing in praise to the Lord.

After Mom let go of the hug, I sprinted to Liam and sat down next to him on the bed.

"Why so happy?" Liam asked.

"I saw an angel." I wanted to tell him everything. I knew he would believe me. A voice in my head was telling me that it was okay to tell him. "He gave me the Armor of God."

Liam sat up straighter and stared me directly in the eyes. "You were given the Armor of God? By an angel? What did the angel look like?" He spoke so fast I had to lean in to hear every word he said.

I remembered his four pearly white wings with golden streaks, his breastplate of steel; his copper helmet and blue eyes; his silver belt around his waist that held the flaming sword; the golden shield with a bronze and crimson outlined cross; and of course, his auburn sandals. I told Liam exactly what I had seen.

Liam's mouth dropped when I finished. "Last night. . ." he took a deep breath, and said, "I had a dream that that angel came to me and read me James 1: 2-4."

My mouth mimicked Liam's. I knew those verses like the back of my hand. The verses tell us how we should have joy for when we face trials. And that when we face those trials, our faith is being tested.

"Consider it pure joy, my brothers and sisters, whenever you face trials of many kinds, because you know that the testing of your faith produces perseverance. Let perseverance finish its work so that

192

you may be mature and complete, not lacking anything." James 1: 2-4.

"So, we both have a dream about an angel who tells us to stay strong and consider it joy whenever we face trials." I said.

"And that we are being tested now." Liam said.

"And if we understand that it is a test and can overcome it, while wearing the armor of God—"

"We will be taken home—the future."

"Bingo." I shrieked in delight. "Our new key to success: Trust in God and he will lead us home."

"What's going on?" Bryan came over to us.

"We figured out how to get home." I was smiling so widely that I could hardly contain myself.

"How?" He sat on the opposite side of Liam's bed.

"Well you know how I had the dream about the Armor of God?" I asked Bryan.

He nodded.

"I had a dream, too," Liam said. "About James 1."

"Oh, the one where it explains that the Lord wants us to consider it joy when we face trials?" There was heavy disdain in Bryan's voice. He didn't seem like he wanted to believe us, nor did he want to listen. His eyes were still filled with yesterday's pain.

"Bryan. . ." I didn't know what else to say. It seemed like just a few minutes ago, he was okay. Had he been faking it?

"He's caused us too much pain, Kyara," Bryan began. "Look outside and you'll see." Bryan stood up to leave.

I looked at the place Bryan was pointing out the window, and I noticed the uneven mound of dirt on the ground and the cross that lay atop the mound. Amy's grave. I held back tears.

Liam rubbed my back. "Hey. Don't let Bryan get in the way of our faith. We know the truth."

"But Bryan needs to understand that we are being tested right now, or else we'll never get home."

"Do you really think that we all need to have the faith that you and I have, so that we can get home?"

"Yes."

"Ok. Then give Bryan time. He will come around. He just needs to think it through logically, or witness something like we did," Liam said.

I rubbed my eyes. "I know. I was just hoping Bryan would see what we saw, now."

"Me too, but remember what happened with Anna? On the Titanic?"

I nodded.

"She had to believe and have faith in the Lord before she was able to see Him. Once she believed . . ." He wiped away my tears and lifted my lips up into a smile with his warm fingers.

I wrapped my hand around his and gave him a quick kiss.

"All right, everyone. Time for breakfast," Mom said.

I got up and sauntered to the table, picked up two bowls, and brought them to Liam. I began to eat out of one bowl, and he ate out of the other.

"I'll get you another serving when you're done with this one," I said.

Liam smiled at me, with his mouth full and I knew he was thanking me with his eyes.

"We need meat." I heard Mom say to Dad. I looked up and noticed the four of them sitting at the table. There were two more chairs, which should have been filled by the two that had left us. One by choice, and one by fate.

"We need to find Bella." Bryan said.

"She's long gone by now," Dad said.

"We don't know that," Mom said.

"I think some of you should go into town. Perhaps there's a butcher shop, so that you can get meat, and then try and find Bella." Liam said.

"Who should go?" I said. "Mom obviously needs to stay back here with you. I'm certainly not leaving you. So, will it be Bryan and Dad who should go into town?"

"I think that sounds like a good idea," Dad said. Bryan nodded.

~ ~ ~

When Bryan and Dad changed into some clothes they had found earlier in a closet in one of the rooms, Mom explained to them before they left what they needed to do.

Liam had told us all exactly what the boy he saw in the vision looked like. With black hair, light skin, and a doctor's coat on, he looked like a doctor at a young age. Then Mom said that as they were trying to find him, they needed to go to each deserted house in the town and get more food if they could. They also needed to try and find Bella, as well as find some type of plant antibiotics for Liam, such as garlic, ginger, onion, or thyme.

After Mom finished, and they said their goodbyes to the four of us, Bryan and Dad were off.

It was silent. Mom and Luke sat at the table, as I lay with Liam.

"So why don't you tell me a story?" Liam said, breaking the silence.

"Do you want me to finish Edmund's story?"

"Oh yeah, I almost forgot about that." Liam sat up a little straighter and looked me straight in the eyes.

"Well, where was I?" I looked toward the ceiling and thought back a couple days. Amy was still alive then. It seemed like a whole new life since yesterday. Everything would change now. Amy was a part of me, and now that part of me was gone.

"Kyara?" Liam said.

"What?" I said.

"I was just saying that you were at the part where there were no entries until six years later."

"Oh, right. Sorry." I shook my head to clear it, and I thought back to the diary. I had photographic memory, so I knew exactly which page the next entry was on. The one with the happy day where he found his bride.

"He became a traveler after he heard the news of his mother's death. He traveled all around the world and on his 2300th day—for he had counted each and

196

every day since he first left on his journey—Edmund was in Southwestern Africa, and there he met his bride. He explained the day perfectly.

"He was about to leave on his boat, which he bought with his mother's secret money, and travel back to Europe. A woman came up to him and asked where he was going, for she had hoped to find someone who would take her to Italy, where her last remaining relative lived, since all her family had perished. Edmund was happy to help, so she boarded the ship and sailed with him to Europe, which would change their lives forever.

"There was a terrible storm, on their fifth day out at sea, and the boat was almost demolished. But somehow Edmund was able to keep the ship afloat, and they made it out of the storm safely. That was when Genevieve, the woman he had brought with him, became infatuated with him. Something about the audacity and hard work Edmund displayed made Genevieve love him. Well, Edmund had saved her life, so that ought to count for something." I shrugged, and Liam stroked my cheek.

"It counts for everything," he said.

I blushed. The way Liam said things made my heart lift and the butterflies in my stomach fly even more. He was so loving and compassionate; sometimes I didn't know how to react. And this was one of those moments.

"I wish you saw what I saw. What I see." Liam said, still stroking my cheeks.

"Well, what do you see?" I said, my voice in a low whisper.

"How you saved my life."

"Liam. . ." I felt a tear in my eye and I quickly wiped it away.

"You did, Kyara. You saved my life—"

"Liam stop—"

"No, you stop," he pulled his hand away from my face and held my hands in his. "If it wasn't for you I would have been in that Titanic crash and could have most likely died." I tried to stop him, but he squeezed my hands and hushed me. "If it wasn't for you I'd be in an emotional wreck and wouldn't want to live. But you showed me what love is. That's why I'm alive, Kyara. It's because you loved me when I thought no one could."

Tears were streaming down my face now. I could never leave him. He and I were destined to be together forever. He loved me, and I loved him. And this love was unconditional.

"I was lost, and you found me." He was starting to get a little cheesy, but I had to admit—it was cute. "I was alone, and you showed me that I had someone there for me. You never gave up on me. You've been there for me through my pain in the past day. You've stayed strong. For me." Now his eyes became slightly watery, but I knew he was trying to be strong.

I hated seeing him like this. He was such an emotional boy, and I appreciated that about him. It made him vulnerable at times, but it also made him strong. He was an orphan—completely alone in this world, and I was one of the only people who loved him. I could not even imagine being alone, with no family. I guess I had just always taken for granted the fact that I had a family. I never really paid attention to those who didn't. And that made me sick inside.

"Won't you say something?" Liam said, raising his eyebrows and clenching my hands in his.

"I. . . I don't know what to say." I said, and his eyes broke my gaze as he looked over to Mom and Luke. I had barely even noticed Mom since I had started the story. There was too much to think about.

"I love you." I finally managed to say as I wiped more tears away, Liam's hands still in mine.

He returned his gaze on me and beamed. "I love you, too. No matter—"

"No matter what," I finished. It was our saying. No matter what happened we would always love each other and be there for each other. That's what unconditional love was.

Liam smiled, a warm and welcoming smile as he squeezed my hand again. *I love it when he does that.*

"So, shall we continue on with the story?" Liam said.

"Oh, yes, of course. Well we didn't hear from Edmund for five days after the storm, because he had thought he lost his diary in the storm. Thankfully, though, he did not, and he was able to tell us exactly what happened in the previous days. Edmund knew Genevieve had fallen for him, but Edmund hadn't quite fallen for her yet. He tells of her beauty and her caring ways, but he was scared to fall in love. He was afraid that if he fell in love, that she would leave him.

"He thought it was brainless, but that was who he was. It happened with his mother, so he thought it

199

could happen to anyone, especially him. But as the days went on, he started to fall for her little by little. One time, he tells of a beautiful day, with the sun shining, and the water perfectly still, but the wind going in the direction where he barely needed to steer the boat. They had had a picnic on that day, and Genevieve had told her life story. She was born in Italy, with a rich and wealthy family of nine children. She was the seventh and her family was any normal family until the plague hit. One by one, the children died, and by the time Genevieve was fourteen, only her mother and two older brothers were alive. The four of them took a ship to Africa, thinking that the plague had not hit Africa. But on the boat, her mother and one of her brothers died. Her seventeen-year-old brother and she were the only ones who made it to Africa, and once they stepped foot on African land, her brother dropped dead from a stroke, not even from the plague.

"Genevieve was told straight away that she must go back to Italy, for the African authorities were frightened that she had brought the plague with her. But Genevieve did not go back; she ran away from the authorities and made it to Southwestern Africa where the plague had ceased to exist. So, once she made it to Southwestern Africa, a generous family took her in and for seven years, lived in peace. The plague had finally died down and on her twenty-second birthday, she received word that her mother's sister was still alive in Italy. And that was how she met Edmund."

Liam clapped. "How do you remember this so well? There's so much, it's hard to believe how much you can remember."

"I've read his diary a million times and my parents used to read the story to us when we were younger. Though there is a lot of death, there is also a lot about love and fulfilling your dreams and moving on. It's really a powerful story." I smiled.

Liam returned one and then said, "So how did they finally fall in love?"

"Well on that beautiful day, after Genevieve finished her story, Edmund kissed her and took her to his quarters, and they made love to one another." I laughed. I knew I would have to get to the awkward part eventually.

"Oh," was all Liam said.

I laughed again and thought about how deep the diary went into his love life. It got very awkward at certain times, for he would explain the "making love" part. My parents had never read those parts to Bryan and me, but I had read it on my own one time. I decided it best not to tell Liam that. So, I moved on to the part where they finally arrived in Italy.

"Once they arrived in Italy, Edmund went with Genny to find her aunt. After looking everywhere, even at her house, they did not find her. They were told by the new house owners of her old house that her aunt had died and left the house for the people who now lived there. Genny was devastated, but Edmund quickly told her that she would live with him—for they were in love. They traveled all the way back to Northern England, where Edmund wanted to spend his later years. Once they got there, they married and had two wonderful children. The end." I said and smiled again. I had done well.

Liam clapped again and then winced as he grasped at his leg. The stitching had opened, slightly and it began to bleed again—no not bleed, gush blood.

Chapter XVI
Dead or Alive

"Mom!" I yelled.

Mom got up and ran over to us.

"It hurts," Liam said, cringing and holding his leg tight. Blood gushed over his hands and onto the already blood-stained bed.

I didn't know what to do, but I rubbed Liam's back, saying things like, "It's going to be okay" and "Just breathe."

When Mom reached us, she told Liam to let go of his leg, but he wouldn't. Luke had now come over to join us.

"Luke, I need you to get your shirt and bring it to me," Mom said, taking control.

"Yes, Mama," said Luke and he ran down the hall and up the stairs.

Mom told me to pull Liam's hands back so that she could look at the stitching.

I held Liam's hands in mine as a billion things flashed through my mind. What would have happened if Mom hadn't stayed back with us? Would I be able to stop the bleeding and keep Liam stable? And what if this kept on happening? Would Liam eventually run out of blood and die? I couldn't think of that possibility. There must be a way to get Liam better. Why was the stitching not working?

Tears were streaming down both mine and Liam's faces. Mom, however, seemed quite calm. She was taking this whole ordeal very well. She always had.

I held Liam's hands away from his leg with all my force.

"It hurts!" Liam repeated, louder this time.

Luke came back, and he gave his shirt to Mom. Mom pulled the rest of the shirts off and looked at the wound. It was so bloody that I could barely see where the stitching was.

Where's your armor, Kyara? A voice, which sounded like the Angel's, said to me. I took a deep breath and prayed silently for Liam. Immediately the bleeding stopped. It was a miracle. But I could see in Liam's eyes he was still in excruciating pain.

"Thank God," Mom said as she wiped all the leftover blood away from the wound. A blood clot must have finally formed, and the only one who could have caused that would be God. The wound, however, was still as deep as it was the day before—the longest and worst day of my life.

"Water," Liam said. I ran to the dining table and started pouring water into a cup. As I came back toward him though, he had passed out.

~ ~ ~

204

Mom felt for a pulse. "He's still breathing but only barely. He's lost too much blood." Mom sighed.

"Pour water into his mouth, Kyara," Mom said. "That might wake him up."

I did as Mom asked, and Luke began to cry. Liam didn't do anything.

"Why is everyone dying, Mama?" Luke asked.

"No one else is going to die, sweetheart. Liam is going to be okay," Mom said.

"Mom," I said, my eyes wide and my body shaking from all the anxiety.

Mom felt for a pulse again.

I was completely frozen. This was not happening. Luke came to my side and I held him tight as Mom felt for the pulse and counted in her head. I was shaking so much I could hardly contain myself.

Mom closed her eyes as she listened to his heart.

"Fifty-seven beats per minute," she said, then opened Liam's eyes and stared into them. His eyes were blank and opaque, with no emotion. Mom bit her lip and stared me straight in the eyes. "He's gone into a coma."

"What? How do you know?" I asked, my voice cracked as it shook.

"His eyes are empty, his beats are irregular, and he would have woken up by now." Mom said. "I'm sorry, Kyara. I don't know how long he will be in a coma, but I know he's not just passed out. I'm sorry." She said again.

205

"What are we supposed to do?" I asked. It felt like my heart had fallen out of my chest.

"Stay with him. Check and make sure he has a pulse every minute. It sucks we don't have any machines to count his beats. We're going to have to be careful with him. I sure hope Dad and Bryan find the young man Liam saw. If he has a doctor's coat, then that must mean he is a doctor. But I wouldn't guess that they would have doctors' coats at this time. Maybe he is from the future? But who knows." Mom kept talking, but I couldn't listen.

My heart was being cut up into little pieces and I knew I could not survive if Liam couldn't. What was happening? Two days in a row of unbearable pain. I didn't think I could go on in life if this was what happened every day.

My insides were deteriorating. Liam was dying. Amy had already died. Bella was gone and could be dead for all we knew. What was going on? And why?

Help us. I prayed silently to myself, crying out for God.

~ ~ ~

Two hours, at least, had passed and Liam was still in his coma. I had lain down and put his arms around me, with my head on his chest so that I could hear his heartbeat.

It was still slow, but at least it was pumping. Mom had redone the stitching right after Liam had gone into a coma and this time it looked like it was tight, and a job well done. She explained that the stitching material was not too strong, but with Liam being in a coma and not moving his leg much now, it should stay in place.

Liam's heart picked up the pace a little and I smiled after taking a deep breath. His face was still as pale as it was two hours ago, but at least his heart was pumping blood around his system, as slight as it was.

My eyes were heavy, and I wanted to sleep, but I knew I shouldn't. If Liam woke up, I'd want to be the first to notice.

I missed Liam. I missed the Titanic. Yes, I missed being on the Titanic with Liam. We were so free then. We knew then when we needed to find the phone. Here our days were limited, and our hours were counted. One of us was already dead. There was no telling when the next would be. I couldn't bear to think that Liam could be the next. He couldn't be.

The Titanic seemed like ages ago, yet it was only a few days since we were on it. Now we were stranded in a completely different time with a whole new set of problems. When would this end?

Stay strong. It was Amy's voice. Man, I missed her. But she was always there for me, and she is even more now. Though she was my little sister, she had always been stronger than me. Now I didn't have her strength with me anymore.

I looked to my left and saw Luke on a chair, his head on the table, and eyes closed. He was always so adorable when he slept. He must miss Amy. I could see large circles around his eyes. He must not have slept well last night. I felt for him. I didn't sleep well either. And the image of Amy running out in front of

Liam's horse and mine flashed through my mind. Why did I have to endure such bad dreams? Ever since Liam told his story, I've had a bad dream every night. It's hard to believe that that was only a week ago though. So much has happened this past week.

I sat up and looked at Mom who sat at the table. She smiled at me, sighed, and then stared at the fire place. She must want to be alone. I felt for her, but I did not want to leave Liam's side. I lay back down, my head on his chest and my ear on his heart. I tried to count the beats per minute, but I couldn't do it without a watch. I knew, however, that his heartbeat had quickened a little.

Before I could think anymore, I had passed out.

~ ~ ~

I woke up to Bryan's soft voice of, "We have food. You hungry?"

I wiped my eyes with my fingers, opened them, and sat up. Mom and Dad were looking at a wagon full of food. Luke was nowhere in sight—he had probably gone upstairs to sleep. Bryan stared at me, sympathetically.

"You okay, Sis?" he asked.

I nodded and wiped my eyes again, clearing out the sleep. I hadn't dreamt this time, which was really good, considering how I'd been the past few nights.

"What food did you get?" I asked and stared at the wagon.

Bryan looked over and then back at me with a smile on my face. "We got some fish that was caught in the Thames River by a fisherman. We got some home cooked bread from a sweet lady. And then we got some beans from an abandoned house."

"Did you find the boy? The one with the phone?" I asked, but realized it was stupid to ask. They would have been much more excited if they had found the phone.

"No. The town is dead right now. Quiet. Barren, with barely anyone around. It's like a graveyard," Bryan said as he dropped his head.

I sighed. "Did you meet anyone with the plague?"

He shook his head. "No, they're all cleared out. Either in the woods or dead. The town and the king make sure that if anyone gets the plague, they clear out. Our ancestor doesn't want it to spread more. It's smart, but it's terrible."

"Anything else I should know? Did you get anything to help Liam?"

"Well, the townspeople don't exactly let anyone in their homes, for they're afraid they have Black Death or that they're kidnappers, or both. They know all about the highwaymen in the woods."

"How do they know?" I asked.

"The fisherman who gave us the fish told us that his daughter was taken. He was able to find her before it was too late, and he made the kidnappers speak before he killed them."

"He killed them?" I interrupted Bryan.

209

"I would too. The ones who took Amy. If they weren't already dead when we got there, they sure would be now."

"Bryan."

"Kyara! They steal kids and use them as slaves!" He said. Mom and Dad looked over at us.

"You guys okay?" Dad asked.

"Just telling Kyara what happened while we were away," said Bryan.

I sighed again and felt Liam's chest. He was still breathing, but the beats had become slower and irregular again.

"How's he doing?" Bryan said raising an eyebrow.

"Do you know what happened?"

"Yeah. Mom told me before I came over to wake you. I'm so sorry, Kyara."

"He's gonna make it. He's strong." I said before Bryan could say more.

"He is," Bryan nodded. "He has a strong will to live. And do you know why?"

I shook my head.

"He's holding on for you." Bryan lifted up one side of his lips in a sort of smile. He was trying so hard to be generous and kind to me. But I knew he was only thinking about Bella and how he wished she were still here.

I patted Bryan's back. "Hang in there."

"I am." Bryan swallowed hard.

"Dinner," Mom said.

"Come and get it while it's hot," Dad said.

Bryan and I got up and walked over to Mom. Dad went to get Luke upstairs.

There were five pieces of fish and five, big cut pieces of bread. There were also some cooked beans in a bowl. Dad must have cooked it all while I was asleep. I went back over to sit by Liam after I had taken a piece of bread, beans, and fish. Bryan stayed with Mom, Dad, and Luke, who looked very tired.

"Wish you were here with me." I said aloud and took a bite of the fish. I had never loved meat so much in my entire life. I liked fish, and I loved this fish. It would have been better if it was soaked in vinegar and seasoned with spices, but it was still good. I imagined what it would taste like with spices on it, which ultimately made it a thousand times better.

I then took a bite of the bread and closed my eyes as I chewed it. Bread had never tasted so good either. I felt like I hadn't eaten in days. Or at least, I hadn't eaten anything other than oats and vegetables in days.

I finished my food in silence. Mom, Dad, Bryan, and Luke hadn't talked much either, so I watched as the sun set in peace out the window. There was only one thing I liked about being here. The sunsets and sunrises were absolutely incredible. God knew that those were two of my favorite creations in life, so even though it was hard here, at least he gave me something to smile at—something to be thankful for.

Chapter XVII
Heartache

I sat up quickly. It was just a dream. I told myself. Just a dream.

The sun was beginning to rise through the window and its rays were bright as they captivated my view. I had fallen asleep with my head on Liam's chest last night, in the Liam's room. My parents said it was okay for me to sleep with him again because someone needed to be with him all night and make sure he was okay.

As I lay back down, I wished I hadn't woken up. I was tired. Even though sleep wasn't kind to me last night, I still wanted to get rest. I had had three dreams and all of them were about Amy or Liam's death. It was Satan trying to mess with my head. I wouldn't let him, though. I had the Armor of God on tight.

I guessed it was about six o'clock in the morning. Liam had been out for more than fifteen hours. Tears began to fall; I thought that I had no more tears left. There had been way too much crying over the past two days. This was the second day I would live without Amy. But I had to be strong. She would want me to be.

I listened closely to Liam's heartbeat. Bum-bum. . . bum-bum. . . bum-bum. . . it was slow, but at least it was going. I feared for Liam and how much longer he had. Was Bryan right yesterday in saying that his will to live was strong because of me? If it was true, then that meant I needed to be here for him through everything. We would be together forever, and there was no way around it. He was mine, no matter what.

~ ~ ~

I heard rustling in the kitchen, but I didn't have the energy to open my eyes. Once a huge clanging sound was heard, though, I did.

"Sorry," I heard Dad say.

"We need to be more careful," Mom said.

"It's a good thing it's not made of glass," Dad said, referring to the pot that was used to cook the porridge.

"Why would a pot be made of glass?" Mom said.

"I'm just saying that I'm glad we don't have to clean up a break," Dad said. He wasn't angry but sounded a little overwhelmed.

I tuned out my parents and listened to Liam's heartbeat. It beat the same pace it did earlier; I wished

213

it would beat the right beats per minute, but that would probably mean he would be awake.

I looked at his leg. It hadn't bled through the bandage this time, but that's probably because he was in a coma and wasn't moving his leg much, or at all. Maybe Mom would go out today to try and find herbs for Liam. I wanted to go into town, but I did not want to leave his side. I wouldn't. I was here for him no matter what and I wanted to be here when he woke up.

"Kyara," I heard Bryan say.

I sat up, holding on to Liam's hand and stared at Bryan, who stood at the door of my room.

"How'd you sleep?" He asked.

I shrugged. I didn't want to tell him that I had slept terribly and had bad dreams in the meantime. But he saw right through me.

"I'm sorry," he said.

"How about you, Bryan?" I asked him.

He mimicked my shrug and looked down at the ground. He must have dreamt of Bella.

"It's hard, isn't it?" Bryan said softly.

"Yeah. Being in the dark—not knowing if your loved one is going to be okay. . ."

"She's not my loved one." His voice was harsh and louder this time.

I didn't say anything, and kept my mouth shut.

"Sorry," he said.

"Me too," I said.

"No need to be sorry. It's not your fault."

Something in my gut made me feel like it was, though. We had been mean to her and told her that she and her father were cowards. We had even blamed her for the death of Amy, or at least I had. She may have been some of the reason to her death but certainly not all of it. But what would happen now, without her? Would we be able to move on? Would Bryan be able to move on from his pain? I wanted to know his thoughts about all this. I wanted to know if he still loved her. No. Surely, he didn't. He couldn't. But then again, it's hard to stop loving a person. I knew from experience with Trevor. Did I even still love him? No. I couldn't. I loved Liam and that was that.

But the question still remained: Is it possible that Bryan could still love Bella? I mean, they were meant to be. At least they were before we found out that Bella lied to us all. But was she sincere about it like she said she was? Was she really trying to protect us from her father? Did she leave to protect us? I shook my head. It couldn't be. She had put us through hell. Why would she try and protect us?

"We should get some breakfast."

I nodded. Liam probably would be fine if I went out to the kitchen for a few minutes.

Mom and Dad ceased their conversation when we entered.

"Oh. I didn't know you two were up. How'd you sleep?" Mom asked.

Bryan and I looked at each other with the "she had to ask" look on.

Mom sighed and got up, walking over to Bryan and me.

"It's going to be okay. I promise," she said, pulling us into a hug.

I felt a tear run down my cheek. How'd she know it was going to be okay? She didn't know the future. No one did. Except Bella maybe. I wondered where she was.

I wiped my eyes. "Mom are you going to town today to try and find medicine?" I asked, pulling away from the hug.

"Yes. I plan on doing so. I think I will be taking Bryan, as well."

"You will?" Bryan asked.

"Yeah. I think you and I need to have some time together," said Mom.

Bryan nodded.

Luke then entered the kitchen.

"Hey kiddo," Mom said. "How'd you sleep?"

"Good," he said, but somehow, I knew he was lying. I didn't want to push him to say anything more though.

I looked up at Bryan and then beyond his head, out the window and assumed it to be around nine o'clock, noticing the sun's shadows. I had been getting good at guessing the time with the sun as my watch. It had always fascinated me, even before the disappearances that people could tell time with the sun. I didn't know what the big deal about it was, but somehow, I was amazed.

"All right. The porridge is ready. It's not quite breakfast food, but it has every food group in it," Dad said.

Everyone went to get bowls full of the porridge. I did too, but for some reason, though, I wasn't that hungry. I took it back to Liam's room and ate slowly

216

and without much enthusiasm. I held his right hand in my left hand and ate with my right hand. I felt his pulse in his wrist and did not let go.

Bryan came into the room right as I finished my breakfast.

"Mom and I are about to go into town. Are you going to be okay here alone?"

I nodded.

"We'll just be in the town so if anything happens with Liam, run and get us. Dad is here as well. But Liam should be fine . . ." Bryan trailed off.

I nodded again.

Bryan took my bowl from my hand and kissed my forehead—a nice gesture.

"It'll be okay. We'll be back soon. I promise."

Mom came in as Bryan left. She gave me a hug and whispered, "I love you" in my ear. I held her tight showing that I loved her back. After we let go, Mom stood up and went back toward the kitchen, but said, "be strong," before she disappeared.

The tears began to flow again for some reason. Harder than they had ever flowed before. I missed Amy and Liam so much that it hurt.

I heard footsteps and noticed Dad coming down the hallway.

"Luke is pretty hyper and needs to get some energy out. Do you want to go on a run with him around the property? I'm sure he'd like that," he said. I needed exercise, so I nodded. I'd been sitting around too much.

"You'll stay with Liam?" I asked.

217

"Yep," Dad said and came to sit on the other side of the bed, the side closest to the door. "You go get some energy out. Luke needs to, too."

I smiled and ran out to Luke who sat in the kitchen, twiddling his thumbs.

"Come on," I said. "Let's go run."

"Where? We can't leave, though," Luke said.

"Just around the property. We both need exercise. Come on," I held out my hand for him. He got up and took it, smiling.

~ ~ ~

My heartbeat finally slowed down after running around the barn, through the fields, and after making an obstacle course for the two of us. Luke and I sat at the kitchen table. We had laughed, finally letting go of every bad thing. But as we sat at the table, I realized how hard it was to laugh. I finally felt like I had achieved something for the day, though.

Dad was still in Liam's room, and I wanted to go in there but decided it was best to just wait and calm down first. I hoped that Liam would wake up soon. Maybe the herbs Mom brings back will help. Hopefully, they find some.

I thought about the angel and my armor of God. I longed to see him again. He had shown me how blessed I was and how, even in the bad parts of life, there's good in the midst of all the bad. I had released all my pain and all my stress to the Lord, but it was still hard to think about what Bella put us through.

I remembered something that a pastor told me. He said that forgiving isn't forgetting. You may forgive someone, but that doesn't mean you forget what they did. It's like a debt. If someone owes you something, and you forgive that debt, then the debt doesn't need to be paid anymore; however, you can't forget that debt. It didn't make sense to me when I first heard the pastor speak those words to me, but now it made complete sense. I had forgiven Bella and her father—at least I think I did—but I surely hadn't forgotten what happened, and I never would. It's impossible to forget that your sister died on someone else's account.

"Kyara?" Dad said, coming out to the kitchen.

I turned my head to look at him. "Is everything okay?" I stood up when I noticed his perplexed look.

"Yeah, of course. His heartrate is heightening so I thought I'd come out here for a bit to see how you're doing?"

I sat back down. I wanted to go into Liam's room, but I knew God was protecting him. I didn't need to be with him every second.

"I'm okay," I said.

Dad came to sit next to me, and across from Luke. "How was the run? I heard you laughing out there." He smiled.

"Yeah, we made an obstacle course!" Luke said, a little more enthusiastic than I would have expected. He started explaining the type of obstacle course we did, and I looked toward Liam's room every so often.

"You worried about Liam?" Dad asked, obviously noticing how I kept looking toward his room.

I nodded.

"Well, there's an angel watching over him. I'm sure he'll wake up soon. We've just got to trust God," he said.

"Kyara," said Luke after a short pause.

"Yeah, bud?"

"I want you and Liam to get married," he said.

I smiled. It was the most wonderful thing I've ever heard from my little brother.

I made eye contact with Dad again and he smiled widely. That was all the approval I needed. Liam was the one for me. The only problem was: would we ever see our wedding day?

~ ~ ~

Bryan and Mom came back around one o'clock—based on the position of the sun—with enough food for an army. They had a wagon full of fruit, various meats, vegetables, bread, and cheese.

"How'd you find more food?" Dad asked, surprised.

"There was another abandoned house." Bryan began. "The one on the corner, Dad. We got all the food from there."

"Well, we'll need to wash all the fruits of course," said Mom.

Dad helped Mom and Bryan take the food out of the wagon.

"Did you get anything to help Liam?" I asked and looked over at Liam who was still in his coma. Dad and I had brought his bed out again, so that we wouldn't have to keep going back and forth from the room to the kitchen.

"They don't have any onions, garlic, or ginger. Or not that we could find, at least."

I sighed and looked at Liam. Was he dreaming? Or could he see us, like how those movies were where the person in a coma could see outside of his body. Or was he simply at peace, seeing nothing? I hoped he was at peace, but not to the point where he was about to die. I wondered how he was still alive. Usually, if someone goes into a coma, they usually have oxygen breathing tubes in their nose and an IV in their arm or hand that keeps them stable. But Liam didn't have either of those. He must have a strong will to live. I hoped Bryan was right in thinking it was me. It made me feel special.

I sighed again deeply and then got up and went to look at the food. I picked out a piece of cheese—looked like cheddar—and a piece of bread and plopped it into my mouth. I hadn't had cheese in what felt like ages and, man, did it taste good.

Mom came to join me and picked out some food to eat and sat down at the dining table. I followed. Dad Bryan, and Luke had been talking about the phone and we joined their conversation.

"Where do you think it is?" I asked.

"Luke came up with an idea, actually," Dad began. "You want to tell them?" He turned his head to look at Luke.

"Sure. Well, I think it could be with a family member," Luke said.

"That would make sense. . ." I said. "Bella did say that her father always had it land with a family member.

"But who in our family has black hair?" Dad asked.

Mom was an only child. Dad's brother was dead. I had no grandparents. My parents had cousins, though, that we never saw. Could there be a child of a cousin that had black hair?

"No one," Mom said.

"Then what?" I said. I liked Luke's idea, but we had no family members left.

"Bella. . ." Bryan spoke softly, but I heard it perfectly.

"What, Bryan?" I asked, slightly confused.

"We need to find Bella," he said louder.

"I agree," Dad said.

"How are we supposed to find her? She could be in another time by now," I said, with slight anger.

"I don't think so," Mom said, softly.

"Why don't you?" I asked, bewildered.

"Because I saw her."

Chapter XVIII
Lost Then Found

"What?!" We all said simultaneously.

"Why didn't you tell me?" Bryan said. So, Bryan had obviously not seen her.

"How could you go on without telling us?" I asked. And for the first time in my teenage years, I was actually mad at my mom. She and I had always had a great relationship. But now I wasn't even mad; I was pissed. And I knew Bryan felt the same way.

Mom took a deep breath. Dad looked at Mom slightly angry. Luke seemed confused.

"She told me not to tell you." Mom said, and it looked like she was about to cry.

"Not tell us!" Bryan said, angrier than I knew he wanted to say it.

"Why?" I said, a little less aggressive than Bryan.

"How did you see her? We were together, like, the whole time today," Bryan said.

"Not when I went to the well." And Mom then explained how she went to the well while Bryan was filling the wagon with food at the house at the corner of town. She had started filling the water in a bucket when Bella came up to her. Bella told Mom that she was sorry she had to leave, and to not tell anyone, especially not Bryan, that she was figuring everything out, and soon it would all be okay.

"She promised me." Mom finished.

"How does she know it will all be okay?" I asked, still bewildered, but not at Mom anymore—more with Bella.

"We need to find her. We can't just sit here waiting, twiddling our thumbs until Bella comes to our rescue!" Bryan used heavy emphasis and disdain on her name.

"I agree," Mom said.

"Then why did you let her go?" Bryan asked, still aggressive.

"Because I didn't want to push her. I knew I would tell you guys, I just was waiting for the right moment. Apparently now was not the right moment," Mom said and looked down at the ground.

"It never would be the right moment! You should have told me—ugh," Bryan cut himself off.

"It doesn't matter. Bryan. We need to go find her. Now." I said.

"Agreed," Bryan said.

"No. Bryan, you are not going. Kyara and I will go." Dad said.

"No! I'm going," Bryan started towards the door.

"Bryan! No, get back here," Dad went after him and held his arm to keep him back. "We must do everything together as a family. We must not get mad at Mom for trusting Bella. Remember, Mom has only been here with us for four days. She's probably a little confused about everything. I know that because it was just you and Kyara with the kids, for a few weeks, before I came along, you feel like you need to be in charge." He took a breath. "But now that Mom and I are here, you need to obey us, and do as we say." Dad held Bryan's arm tight.

But Bryan was able to pull away from Dad, as he pushed out the door. Dad went after him and I followed close behind.

"Bryan!" I screamed after him, catching up to him and passing Dad. He was heading towards town. "Dad is right!" I caught him and pulled him back. He tripped backwards but didn't fall. He stopped though, anger raging through the veins in his face.

"Please, Bryan." Dad caught up to us, panting slightly.

"Dad's right. It's not smart for you to go after her right now. She's trying to help us. You would make it worse," I said. Bryan leered at me but let me continue. "Yes, Bryan. You would make her not want to help us. I'm telling you the truth because you need to hear it.

"Bella left us because we, *you and I*, were so hateful to her. We made her feel worthless. We made her feel like a coward and our enemy. But she's not our antagonist. Her father is. We must understand that, Bryan. You need to calm down before you see her. Dad

225

and I will go, and we will get her to help us. Please. Let us do that." I finished and looked at him with pleading eyes.

"Fine," he let out a deep breath.

I nodded, and Dad and I helped him back to the house.

Mom and Luke were standing in the doorway, watching us.

As we got closer to them, I told them that Dad and I would go and that everything would be okay.

"Mom. Please help Bryan understand Bella's intentions," I said.

"I will. Thank you, sweetie."

I nodded and once I checked on Liam once more, Dad and I decided to leave.

Before we went off, Mom told me that I was brave.

I wanted to ask why, but I knew why. I figured it had to do with the fact that I was leaving my loved one behind, not knowing what would happen while I was away.

The sun was at its high point and as we walked toward town, Dad side-hugged me. After a few seconds of awkward walking, he let go, and I felt, for some reason, happy. My dad was with me, and I would be safe. I hadn't spent time with him, just him for a while. Not since before the night of the storm. It felt good to be with him.

"How are you holding up?" He asked me. I looked up at him and smiled slightly.

"Better than I would have thought."

"Me too. I think it's because you're doing so well, with everything that's going on. I see a lot of hope in your eyes, and I wouldn't have predicted you'd be like this."

"Yeah. I didn't think I'd be doing so well either," I was unsure what to say next.

"You just have to hold on to the good things. In all the darkness, there is light and it's up to us to bring light to the darkness. God will always give us light, even if we don't see it right away."

I smiled slightly but felt a single tear in my eye, ready to let go. I wouldn't let it fall, though. The same could be said of my life for the past few weeks. I was ready to let go of this painful and tragic life that was becoming so difficult to keep going. But the thing was, I wasn't going to let difficult times defeat me. I wasn't going to fall and become a failure, even though I sometimes felt like I was.

But I realized that my feeling of failure didn't come from God, and that it came from the devil—the great deceiver. The one who makes me feel regret, guilt, and makes me feel defeated. But I would not let him win.

"What have you been thinking about?" Dad asked. It must have been silent for a while.

I took a deep breath. "Just about what you said, I guess. I want to be able to move on and live happy, but it's hard when. . . when. . ." I couldn't bring myself to say the worst. Amy was gone, and she would never come back. Never.

For some reason, the tears did not flow. For some reason, I didn't feel like crying. It was the kind of sadness in which I just couldn't cry. I wanted to scream and shred things to bits rather than shed my tears.

Dad stopped walking, right before we entered town, and I did, too. He faced me, but I couldn't bring myself to look up at him. Amy had his eyes—the only one out of all of us who had his colored eyes. Bryan, Luke, and I had mom's blue eyes. Amy had Dad's brown eyes. The exact same, dark, almost black, shade.

But Dad brought my chin up so that I'd look at him. I looked at his eyes for one split second, and felt overwhelmed with grief, but I still didn't cry. Not one tear.

"You have to stay strong. That's the only way we'll make it through. Liam is going to be fine. He's with Mom—"

"I'm not worried about Liam," I said, not meaning to interrupt.

"Then what is it?" He asked.

I couldn't bring myself to speak. It was too difficult. I didn't know how I was able to speak a few seconds ago. The words just came out without real thought.

What I wanted to say, however, was that I hated that Amy was gone and that no one else seemed as sad as I was. And then I wanted to explain how I felt bad about Bella. It was mostly Bryan's fault, and mine, that made her want to leave. The words, "You'll be better off without me," hadn't left my thoughts. She had already felt bad enough. Why did we have to make her feel worse?

I understood now that she was telling the truth. She didn't know where her father was, and she had wanted to tell us on the Titanic but was afraid her father would find out. I would be afraid, too, if my father was like that—abusive and heartless. I was truly blessed to have my father; one who cared and loved his kids no matter what.

"Kyara?" Dad said, but I shook my head. "Okay." He nodded, understanding that I wouldn't and couldn't talk.

We began to walk again, and I breathed deeply on each step. For some reason, I felt like I was carrying the weight of the world. And I couldn't do anything to shake it off.

As we walked, Dad began to talk again.

"You know, Kyara, it's our choice on how we decide to act. If we just mope around all day and don't hold on to the good things or talk about the good things, then we'll forget what is good. We cannot forget what is good. If we do, then we'll just all be broken. We are already cracked icons; we can't afford to become shattered icons." Dad stopped for a second to let me think about what he said.

Dad had only once explained the "cracked icon" theory before. An icon is a piece of art that shows the image of God. And we are like an icon, created to function as the image of God. We were cracked because we had fallen short of God and his blessing. But we weren't shattered because we still had hope; we still had the mercy God gave us and anointed us with. The reason we weren't all destined for hell was because

God's grace and mercy were there, and because God sent his son to die on the cross for us.

"I don't feel any less than shattered, though." The words came out of my mouth as if they were pulled out.

"I know. But we have to know that the devil is the one putting those shattering thoughts into our mind. We can't let him do that," Dad said.

I nodded but felt sick as I did. Not the puking kind of sick, but the revolting and emotional kind of sickness. I felt gross, and not because I hadn't had a real shower or bath in a few days, but because I was letting the devil get a hold of me. Again.

Would it ever end?

I knew the answer right as I thought it, though. No. It would not end. Not until God won the war between good and evil. I just wish that that could happen sooner than later. Like, right now.

I didn't want to live this life anymore—not because I wanted to necessarily die, but because I wanted to get rid of the pain and suffering and live a life where I didn't have to worry. I wanted Amy back. I wanted to hold her in my arms like I did on the Titanic. And the only way that was possible was for me to die, or for Jesus to come back. I knew that wouldn't happen though. Well at least the latter part of it. I could die. We were in a dying time. And if the worst happened to Liam or any other member of my family, would any of us be able to make it and move on?

As we entered the town I noticed, once again, how barren it was. I hadn't really spent much time in the town, nor had I seen much of the town, other than the well and a few houses.

An eerie sense filled the air and, not only that, but there was the feeling of loss and loneliness. The people who hadn't fled were moseying about, trying to stay alive—though it seemed hopeless.

I looked at Dad and he, at me. I bit the inside of my cheek and breathed heavily. I had no idea it would be like this.

"Where is everyone?" I asked. "Black Death really did kill the life in the town."

I remembered learning about England and the era before Black Death and how it was much livelier than this. Now, there was no one. The few people that I saw had definite fear in their eyes. They were scared that they would be next—next to get the plague.

"Yeah. Come on," Dad said, and I followed him to a more energetic area of the town. Don't get me wrong, it was still eerie, but there were more people around.

Several people were entering the church.

"What's going on?" I asked.

"I don't know," Dad said.

"Let's go see." I said, and Dad nodded.

We sneaked in through the doors and took some seats near the back.

When we sat down, I was able to notice the complexity and beauty of the church. Stone walls and windows of stained glass surrounded the church. Crosses displayed throughout the church, tied it all together.

Two men stood in front and were talking to each other as everyone filed in and sat down in the pews. The noise quieted down and that was when the man on the left turned toward the people.

I looked at Dad. He looked just as confused as I was. Mostly men were sitting on the pews. There were only a few women. No children though.

"Two years it's been," one of the men at the front began. "Since the Great Pestilence came to wipe us out. And the King is at fault! It is time we fight back!"

Fight back? I thought. Fight who? Fight what?

"Hugo is correct. We must put this pestilence to death!" Though I was in the back most row, I could see the spit escape his mouth as he spoke with such vigor. "And we think the best way is to overtake the king!"

Overtake the king? What in the hell was going on here? I looked at Dad. His face showed just as much confusion as mine surely portrayed.

"Who's with us?" Hugo asked.

A resounding "I" pervaded the church. But one man in the front row stood up and cleared his throat.

"Sir. I-I don't understand. The king was sent by G-God," he was stuttering as if he was afraid to speak on. "Why would we want to overtake him, exactly?"

Hugo stood up straighter. "You all believe that this pestilence is a cause of your sinful nature, correct."

Several men said "I" again.

"The reason it has swept across this land, is because the king is in deep sin—deeper than all of your sins. He is the reason this pestilence has wiped out so many of your friends and families."

The man who had stood up said, "So the Great Pestilence is upon us because the king is a sinful man? We are all sinners, too! What does that say about us."

Several men groaned and nodded their heads, agreeing with the man in the front row.

"Well, he started a war with France, that is still going on, ten years later." Hugo began. "He has a mean temper, which I'm sure he's taken out on many of you. He arrested royal officers seven years ago, such as Bishop Chichester and Henry de Stratford, throwing them in prison—a great sin and quite against the law. And last year, your king defeated Scotland and captured their 'Sovereign' king, King David. These are all great sins. How would any of your sins compare to his?"

The man in the front sat down.

"So, I will say again. Who's with us?"

Everyone, this time, said "I".

Hugo stared at the other man, standing beside him, at the front of the church and they spoke quietly to each other. I wasn't able to hear, but I was sure some people closer to the front would be able to.

I turned to Dad. "Was there really a battle between the townspeople and the king? I don't remember anything like that, especially in Edmund's journal. . ." I trailed off not knowing what else to say.

"No. I don't think there was one. Not that I know—" But he stopped, and his eyes grew wide.

I turned around and saw none other than
Bella.

.

Chapter XIX
That Twin Connection

My mouth dropped. I didn't know what to do. I didn't
know whether to hug her or punch her. So, I just sat
there and stared.

"I'm sorry," Bella mouthed.

I was dumbstruck. Couldn't talk. But Mom
was right. She really seemed sincere about her apology.

But Dad somehow was able to speak to her.
"Are you okay?"

She nodded and put a finger over her mouth as
Hugo began to speak again.

"So, here's the plan." Hugo paused and looked
past us to Bella. "Ah, Bella! You're back! Come up here
and tell of what you saw."

Bella nodded and walked quickly to Hugo.
They hugged, and I felt a certain pang of disgust. She
had not already replaced Bryan.

"Yes, well. . ." Bella began to speak about
where the guards were stationed within and around
the castle. But I didn't listen much. I only thought

about the pain she had already caused us and, if Bryan was here, how much pain he would feel now. How was she supposed to help us if she had replaced Bryan!

She was truly a monster. The hug to Hugo was all I needed to be reminded of her cruelty. Surely, she was Blake's daughter.

Bella met my eyes as she kept talking, and though I saw sorrow in them, I did not feel for her. I didn't care what she had to say. I didn't want to know. All I wanted was to leave this place—wherever Bella was, I did not want to be.

I nudged Dad and whispered, "Let's go."

Dad looked at me and squinted his eyes. My mouth was pursed, and I felt the anger rage in my veins. I couldn't be here anymore, so I got up and ran out of the church.

The night air was misty and chilly, but it felt good. The heat caused by my anger needed a chill.

"Kyara. . ." Dad said as he came after me outside.

And not a second later, Bella came out through the double doors and I could see there were tears in her eyes.

"What do you want?" I didn't care how malicious my tone was. I hated Bella, and there was nothing she could do to change it.

"Kyara," Dad said, sternly, but I didn't care. "Bella's okay. This should be good news."

"Did you not see how she betrayed us? Left us with nothing? The "you'll be better off without me" didn't affect you? And how she," I couldn't bear to look

236

at her, "hugged Hugo, the one I'm sure she's already replaced Bryan with!" I turned to her. "You're such a bitch!"

"Please, let me explain," Bella said, but I shot her down.

"You are just like your father—"

But Dad cut me off. "Kyara, calm down. You need to let her speak. I'm sure there's a reasonable explanation for all of this."

My mouth dropped open. I couldn't believe Dad was siding with her. I folded my arms and stared, vindictively at Bella.

"Hugo. . . is my brother. . ."

I didn't think it was possible for my mouth to drop even further.

Hugo came out and stood next to Bella. "Is this Kyara and her father?" He asked.

And that was when I noticed how similar their eyes were. I didn't think it was possible for there to be another being with as perfect eyes as Bella—the bright and oceanic blue. But it was. And Hugo had those perfect eyes. As well as black hair. And then it hit me!

Hugo was the one with the phone!

I wanted to know more. I wanted to scream at Hugo, even though I didn't know him and ask him where the phone was, but instead I kept it simple, "Yes. I am Kyara. But how do you know this?" My words toppled on top of the next and I wasn't sure they understood me.

"I will have to retell the story again, I guess. First to Bella, now to her friends," Hugo said.

"Wait. Why and what did you have to explain to Bella?" I asked.

"Oh, Bella didn't know about me. I'm her twin, yet our mother took me and not her when she left our father."

"What? You have a twin!" My eyes were still wide with astonishment. There had been way too many crazy happenings over the past few days. First, Bella is from the future. Then, she has a twin? That she didn't even know about? What was this nonsense? Would it never end?

"Yes. And I had no idea about him until yesterday. . ." And that's how the story began. Bella thought it would be best if she explained it, for Hugo was too smart—180 IQ—and she could only understand him yesterday because they had that twin connection. Bryan had probably a 130 IQ and the only way I was able to understand him, with my 100 something IQ was because we shared that twin connection.

"Come. We'll go to my house." Hugo said and started walking north. "We can eat and talk, and you can explain the entire story to them."

I followed, and we entered a rather large house. We sat around the dining table and ate lamb stew that Hugo had made before the meeting.

And then Bella began, again, with a story that I knew would cause a ton of questions:

"I didn't want to leave. But I had to. I truly thought you would be better without me. I didn't want to cause you any more pain. I knew I had not had anything to do with the death of Amy, but that didn't matter to you and your brother."

I bit my lip and looked down at my stew and hesitantly took another bite as Bella continued.

"It was bright enough to where I was able to see where I was walking, for I had left right as the sun had risen, but too dark to be sure of where I was going. I felt like I was being guided, though. As I entered the town, I saw Hugo. He was helping a woman, who I came to find out later had just been cured from Black Death, back to her house."

"Black Death is curable?" I asked.

"Please save all questions until the end. We will never make it if there are interruptions. And I want you to get back to Liam—who I'm sure is eager for your return." Bella said.

"He doesn't know. He's in a coma," I said.

"What?" Hugo and Bella said simultaneously. They really were twins.

"Yeah—"

"I need to see him right now, then. Take me to him." Hugo stood up and started toward the door, but Bella held his arm back.

"They should at least hear the story, first. Kyara's mom is with him. I'm sure he's fine. Right, Kyara?"

"Well, it is getting pretty late. As much as I want to hear the story, we should get back to them," I said.

"Yeah, Kyara's right," Dad said.

"You all can stay here, then," Hugo began. "There's four bedrooms in this house and I made one of

239

them a healing room. I'm sure you'll need as much help as you can get, and I can surely help Liam—nurse him back to health, and all." Hugo smiled.

"Thank you, Hugo," Dad said.

And with that, the four of us hurried out of town, and within three minutes, were back at the farm.

Before we went through the door, I suggested that Dad and I should enter first, so that it wouldn't be a complete shock for everyone to see Bella and Hugo. So, we did.

"You're back!" Luke was the first to speak. He ran up to me and gave me a gigantic hug. Bryan hugged Dad, and Mom came to hug both of us.

"Is everything okay? How'd it go?" Bryan was eager to find out everything.

"Well, we have some good news," Dad said, and I nodded slightly. I was pretty unsure about Bella's return, but I knew I would hear the story soon.

"We don't know the full story. What we do know, however, is that Bella is okay, and that her brother, Hugo, can help Liam." Dad said, and Hugo and Bella entered through the door.

I had no idea how Bryan would react to this, but when he saw Bella, he ran up to her and gave her a massive hug.

"I'm so glad you're okay." Bryan's voice was muffled, but I could hear every word. Apparently, Bryan had done some calming down since Dad and I had left.

Hugo stood there, uncertain of what to do. He looked at Liam on the bed, then at Bryan and Bella, and back at Liam.

240

"You can go over there," I said, giving him the okay.

Hugo smiled at me and then went to Liam. A few seconds passed. Bryan hugged Bella more and Dad and Mom hugged, and Luke and I hugged again.

"He's going to be okay." Hugo said and looked up at us, one hand on Liam's forehead, and the other on his neck. "I just need to bring him back to the house immediately. He's as cold as ice. He'll need oxygen tubes and an IV."

"There are oxygen tubes and IV's here?" I asked.

"Not exactly. I'll explain everything when we get Liam to the house."

"We can put him in the wagon," Luke said.

And so, we did. It took three people to move him, Bryan, Hugo, who was actually quite strong for being so skinny, and Dad. And once he was in the wagon, we hurried back to Hugo's house.

The town was absolutely silent. No one was around. They must all lock themselves in their houses when the night comes.

We entered Hugo's house and maneuvered Liam into the "healing" room and onto the bed. There, Hugo put oxygen tubes, that were surely from the future or somewhere near our time, and an IV in him. Then he went to get a hot towel to put on Liam's head and he told Bella that he could handle everything, and for her to tell us the story. Bella nodded, and we all gathered in the dining room. I began to eat out of the stew bowl again, realizing how hungry I was.

241

"Okay. I'll retell my story from the beginning, but please, save all questions until the end," Bella said.

Once we all nodded, Bella continued.

"I didn't want to leave." She was mostly speaking to Bryan. "But I was afraid you would want me to sooner or later, so I decided to make it easier on all of you."

I knew Bryan wanted to say something, for he opened his mouth. But he refrained and shut it.

"I just thought I was doing the right thing. Anyway, I came across the town and saw Hugo, who I had no idea was my brother at the time, helping a woman to her house. He seemed nice, so I began to walk toward him. When he saw me, though, his mouth dropped open and the surprise in his eyes was so immense that I knew something was up. When he said my name, I knew, by the sound of his voice that he was probably a younger version of Blake, my father.

"When he told me he was my brother and even more so, my twin, I believed him. We may look nothing alike, other than our eyes, but I just knew. So, he began telling me his story.

"Our mother took him, and only him, when we were four because she thought I was too much like Blake, I look like him and everything, while Hugo looks mostly like our mom, Josie. So, she left me behind mainly because she wanted to give Blake a reason to "grow up" and "be mature".

"Hugo found out about me when we were eight. Josie kept a journal hidden in her room, and one day, when Hugo got home from school and Josie was at work, she works in a retirement home, he found the

242

journal. Not only was his birth certificate there, but a copy of a second child, born a few minutes before him. Hugo then went onto the computer and found me—he hacked into a few databases to find me. Remember, he has a 180 IQ."

"One eighty-one!" Hugo called from the other room. I laughed, and Bella rolled her eyes.

"I already told them not to interrupt. Yet you decide to interrupt?" Bella yelled to Hugo. Hugo came out of the room and smiled, then went back in. I knew Liam was in good hands.

"Anyway. . . He found me and basically kept tabs on me for several years. He was unable to find out what I was doing when I was in Blake's house, because Blake has such high security, but when I was with friends or at school, Hugo was able to hack into cameras and see how I was doing. He lived in Florida, so he wasn't able to see me in person, until he went to UC Davis School of Medicine in 2008, which is only three miles away from where I lived and three miles from where I went to school, McClatchy High School. He would drive every day at 3:00 to come and see me, but he never summoned up the courage to say hello. He was too scared that Blake or Josie would find out.

"He got his medical degree in the summer the disappearances happened, and he said he was working on a lab when he came to this time. He still had his lab coat, with his name and year of graduation, 2012, on, and was able to tell the townspeople, or what was left of them, that, once he found out the year he was in, Black Death was nearing its end and he could cure those who had it.

"Oddly enough he was working on a medical thesis that could cure highly contagious diseases such as Black Death, Spanish Flu, and some other random diseases that I don't remember. And if they came back, he knew how to cure them. He said now he's working on a cure for cancer, but he hasn't gotten anywhere yet. He's been able to cure twenty-seven people so far, in the last month here, of Black Death. And I think that's about it. . . Any questions?"

Bryan's hand, Luke's hand, and my hand all shot up.

Bella laughed and called on me.

"Liam's vision. That was obviously Hugo!"

"Oh my gosh! I forgot the most important part!" Bella said.

Hugo walked out and said that he could explain. Bella nodded and thanked him.

"You do only have a 142 IQ, so I knew you'd probably forget the most important part—your brother's story," Hugo said. Though he was smart, he surely was funny.

We all laughed, and I asked, "Where'd you get everything you have in the healing room?"

"Just as Bella said, please save all the questions until the end."

We all nodded, and Hugo continued. "When I got here, I knew I would need supplies. But I had no idea how to get them. Yes, I am smart, but the problem with the mid-fourteenth century is that they barely have any supplies at all. Then I remembered I had Blake's first time machine. It had happened to be in my pocket of my lab coat."

Several of us raised hands, and Hugo shot our questions down.

"Bella, of course, told you that a friend had borrowed his first time machine, yes? Well I was that "friend". Blake hadn't known me since I was four, and I wanted to get to know him, as well as keep tabs on Bella, so I made a morph suit and became a "friend" to Blake."

My mouth and several other mouths were dropped, I noticed. We all wanted to say something, I especially had several questions, which I hoped would be answered soon. Bella simply smiled as Hugo continued.

"Well, I stole the first time machine, and completely lost contact with Blake so that he never asked where I was, changing my phone number in the process. You see I had never given Blake any exact information on who I was, so it was quite easy to deceive him. Anyways, I had always kept the time machine with me for safekeeping. So, I, of course, had the phone with me when I came here."

I wanted to ask where the phone was now, but I knew I should keep quiet. Everyone else was surely thinking the same thing.

"Well, I knew I needed to get back to 2012 to get supplies, but I knew that if I went back, when Blake was still there, he would see me. He has a censor thing that tells how many people are on earth, which I actually helped him make when we were "friends". So, I decided to go to the era of World War Two to the General Hospital in England, where I knew there would be enough supplies, as well as keeping a safe distance from when I was born, since you cannot return to a time in which you were alive, for it would create a black hole.

"I was able to get enough supplies, especially because I had picked a perfect time to go to the General Hospital, but I won't bore you with details—"

Dad actually interrupted this time saying, "It's not boring—I'm a World War Two history teacher. Did you go towards the end of the war in England?"

"No," Hugo said slightly aghast that Dad would interrupt, but seemed to go on just as he would have if he had not been interrupted. "It was when they were setting up the headquarters for the US Army Military Mission in London."

Dad nodded. Hugo continued, "September 9th, 1941, I was able to get inside the military mission, before it opened for patients to be admitted, and get enough supplies to take them back to this time. The only problem was, I had no idea what Blake was planning, so I had to stay here until something happened that would give me an idea of what was happening back home.

"About two weeks passed, I had healed a good amount of people here from Black Death—that's why you see so many people in the town. There would only be a few tens of people in the town right now, but instead there are ninety-seven, including us. Anyways, after two weeks, I decided to go back to 2012, to Blake's house. No one was there, though. No one was even on earth. Everyone had vanished. That's when I realized Blake had planned this all along.

"Everything made sense. You see, what had happened was Blake had always been planning on getting back at the Edwards'. He had planned the exact moment up to a tenth of a second, on when he would make everyone disappear, and then make it so that only the four kids were the only ones on earth."
Bella had not heard this part before, I assumed, because she yelled out, "he lied to me!"

"Of course, he did; he lies to everyone," Hugo paused and looked at Bella. He had been looking at the ground the whole time he spoke, until now. He made eye contact with each of us and then looked toward the Healing Room. "One moment," he said and went to check on Liam.

He rushed back out before any of us had time to form a sentence or phrase and begin talking again. "He's fine—just wanted to make sure. The IV is still flowing, but I'll need to change it in two and a quarter minutes."

"Wait, so how did he plan this?" I asked, not caring about anything except the fact that Hugo still had not explained the most important part.

"Blake's whole plan was mapped out on papers in his office. Everything you've experienced, except for this era. He had planned on taking you all home after the Titanic, but instead, you landed here.

"And I have a theory on why you did."

247

Chapter XX
Theories of Time

After Hugo changed Liam's IV, he came back out and started explaining his theory.

"He hadn't planned on me being alive," Hugo began. "He had thought I died in a car crash when I was nine, which I had faked, so that he would never go looking for me. But he found me when I was in his office. He had come back to collect a few things he needed when you all were in Rome, and he saw me. I tried to hide, but he is almost as smart as I am. He noticed straight away that I was his son because I didn't have my morph suit on. He asked me to join him and help with his plans in getting back at all of you. However, after I explained that I had gone through a lot of trouble to let him think that I didn't even exist. I— Well, that's when he began fighting me." He lifted up his shirt and I saw an almost healed scab, about three inches long along the side of his stomach.

"He had stabbed me, and left me to die, but I was able to come back to this time to stitch myself up before I lost too much blood." All our mouths had dropped once again, and I stared at Hugo in sorrowfulness.

Hugo kept on with his story. "I tried to figure out a way to help you all, but for the first time in my life, I was stumped. I decided to sleep on it, knowing that somehow God would show me a sign of what to do, but when I woke up, the phone was gone. I had kept it secure and with me as I slept, and after I looked everywhere, I realized only one thing could take that time machine away from me: Blake. That's when I found a note, from Blake, that said, 'You did this to yourself. I'll be watching you, and, if you change your mind, I'll know.' Meaning that Blake knows that if I joined him, I would not have gotten hurt. And he wants me to change my mind and decide to help him. And he'll know if I do."

Hugo paused again. But this time I knew he had nothing more to say.

"What are we supposed to do now?" Several of us asked in unison.

"We wait," Hugo said. It seemed like he was tired of talking, but we all stared at him, waiting for more—for some sort of answer.

"This has to be a joke," Bryan said, unbelieving.

"Yeah, Blake wouldn't actually do all this to us," I said.

"Well, it isn't a joke, Bryan; and Kyara, he would do this. I've studied my father for far too long." Hugo said.

"What the hell are we supposed to do, then!" Bryan said.

"We're stuck here," Luke cried.

"Not necessarily," Hugo finally said. "There is a way out."

"Where?" Bryan said.

"How?" I said.

"There is a phone here. But it's guarded by several of the king's forces. That's why I planned an uprising with the townspeople."

"How do you know the phone is here?" I asked.

"Blake always leaves a way out. He never wanted to kill any of you, I know that as a fact, but he wants you to suffer."

"But if he knows Amy's dead, why wouldn't he bring us back?" Bryan asked.

"That's why we have to find the phone. We need to figure out the truth."

"But how do you know the phone is guarded and in the castle?" I asked.

"Blake explained it in the riddle he left for me," Hugo said.

And then it all clicked. The poem mom recited to us a few days ago wasn't a poem. It was a riddle. Now that that made sense though, what about Hugo's riddle?

"I can tell you the riddle, if you'd like," Hugo said.

We all murmured our obvious yes's.

He pulled out a piece of paper and began reciting the riddle. We all listened intently.

"Stone walls. A glass case.

Only a plan will lead a race.

Or a battle that will start,

In my eyes, you'll do your part.

One must die to find the calling,

But only one, or you'll be falling,

Down a hole you cannot return from.

You must only use one thumb.

If you believe in that hoax,

Travel once more through The Oaks.

And if you can find me, you'll win,

Only then will I count your sin."

He finished, and I couldn't believe what had been read. Still several questions flowed through my mind.

"So basically, Amy had to die. We get one more chance on travelling through time. What else?" I said.

"Let me see it," Bryan said, outstretching his hand toward Hugo. Hugo gave it to him, and he read it over in his head.

"I don't get it. Explain, Hugo." Bryan said and gave it back to Hugo.

"Kyara's right. You have to get to 2012 this time. One of you, only one, had to die, which is why I'm so intent on saving Liam's life."

"That's the only reason you're saving him!" I asked, disconcerted.

"No, of course not. I am trying to figure everything out, just like you all are," Hugo sighed.

"Then what?" Bella spoke up for the first time in a long time.

"I know how to get back. We just have to do as the riddle says." Hugo said.

"There has to be another way!" Bryan pleaded.

"I know this is hard for you to understand. But there is no other way. My father is cruel and a very malicious man. Unless God softens his heart, he will only retaliate."

"Isn't he watching us right now, though?" Bryan said.

"We could talk to him," I said, slightly hopeful.

"I've tried. Plus. There's no way he can see or hear us right now. There's no cameras here. The only way he knows what's going on is if he travels here. But the last night he came was the night I got this riddle."

"How do you know?" I asked.

"There's been no sign of him. He had left a note for me four nights in a row. The first night telling me he had taken the phone, the one I recited for you. The second night he asked for me to join him again. The third night he left a note telling me it was in the castle. The fourth night he left the riddle. He hasn't been back since."

"Just because he hasn't left you a note doesn't mean he couldn't still come," I said, trying to figure out everything. For some reason I was calm, and I knew it was God helping me stay this way. I had faith, and I knew we could figure out how to get home some other way.

"He can't come back." Hugo said. "That's the thing. He used up all the time machine's uses. Each phone only has a certain number of times you could use it. He's probably busy creating a new one. That's also why I think that the phone that's here, in the castle, has only one more use. Because he says we have one more chance to get back home."

I sighed and looked at Mom. She had a worried facial expression, one with complete and utter misery. "I don't understand how he could be so evil," she said.

"He's worse than anyone I've ever heard of in my entire life!" Bryan said. "He's basically part of Satan's army."

Hugo looked at Bryan uneasily. "I know he's been awful to us, but at least he used Jesus' army to fight against. We will win. We have the most sovereign on our side. We can beat this."

"But why is God doing this to us? Why can't *He* just take us home?" I asked.

"We all wonder that, too, Kyara." Dad said. "Sometimes we just have to sit tight and wait. God gifts those who wait."

Tears formed the corners of my eyes. Hugo went back to check on Liam and I heard him put another liquid tube on the post for Liam's IV. It was silent as we listened to Hugo working and thought through our feelings.

I was scared. No, not scared. Petrified. Blake was behind all this. And I knew that from two days ago, but I did not know the extent of it. Blake was evil. God could never forgive him for this, and I knew I certainly couldn't. He would pay for this, and I hoped that the last layer of hell would be his worst nightmare. Before I could think more on the subject, Hugo came back out with a what looked like a smile on his face—I could barely see because my eyes were so watery.

"Liam's awake."

Chapter XXI
Awake

"Liam!" I squealed and ran to the room to see him smiling, and eyes staring at me as I entered. He was awake!

"No sudden movements, please," Hugo said to Liam.

Liam's eyes squinted as he looked at Hugo.

"Who?" Liam began, but couldn't get much more out.

I would have to explain about Hugo. The past two days he's been out, too much has happened. He looked around the room and I could see his eyes show more confusion.

"I'll explain everything," I said and looked at Hugo asking, with my eyes, if that was okay.

Hugo nodded.

Bryan and Luke came in and said they were glad to see he was okay and awake, then went back out to join the rest of the family because they understood that he would need his rest.

"I'm going to get him some water and food. You've got to be hungry." Hugo said and strolled out to get the food after Liam nodded slightly.

He came back a few seconds later with water in a cup and some stew. He then helped Liam sit up a little more and helped him sip the water. Hugo then began feeding him the stew and he said, "Go ahead and explain everything, now."

I nodded. "You've been out two days," I began. "Less time than we thought you would be, which is good." I smiled. "This is Hugo. He is Bella's brother—" Liam's eyes grew wide. "She didn't know about him, though." And I began to explain Hugo's story. Liam shut his eyes halfway into the story, when he finished eating, but didn't stop me from talking, so I figured he was listening.

Once I finished, Liam opened his eyes and nodded slightly. I could tell he was trying to not get angry, like I knew the rest of my family surely was, with Blake.

"What are we going to do now?" Liam asked slowly, which had been the main question of the night.

"We get the phone in the castle," I said. Liam nodded.

Hugo said we needed to let him rest and that he would check on Liam every ten minutes. As we walked out of the room, though, I heard Liam say to me as we met eyes, "stay."

I smiled and walked over next to his bed and held his hand in mine.

"Let me know if his heartbeat slows or quickens, okay?" Hugo said and then when I nodded, he left the room.

A tear rolled down my cheek, but it wasn't a tear of distress, but rather joy. Liam was going to be okay. And all because of Bella's brother he would survive. This was probably the best thing that could have happened.

"Don't. . . cry. . ." He said in between deep breaths.

More tears fell down my cheek. I wiped them away and clasped his hand. And though it was gentle and barely noticeable, he squeezed mine back. I smiled and lay down next to him. My arm draped over his chest and it held his left hand. My head was nuzzled against his neck and I could hear his heartbeat.

"I love you," I said.

"I love. . . you, too. . . No matter. . . what."

"Save your breath." I said through my tears. "Please," I added.

I could feel him nod against my head.

The silence enveloped us, and his heartbeat sounded perfect. It was finally at the normal beats per minute. He was back, and he would be here with me forever. I would not lose him again. It was true. His will to live was strong, and I knew it was due to my love for him.

~ ~ ~

I woke up to Bryan gently poking my cheek. I had fallen asleep next to Liam and stayed there all night, apparently. Now the sun's rays peeked through the window.

"Time to eat. Come on." Bryan said and hurried out when he noticed I was looking at him annoyed. He seemed happy, or as happy you could be knowing that someone was behind all the pain we've faced the past several days. He had Bella back and nothing could take her away from him. I wouldn't even do anything to harm their relationship. Though I hated Bella yesterday, I felt reconciled with her today.

As I walked out of the room, I took another glance at Liam. He was sound asleep, but knowing he wasn't still in a coma made me happy. I knew my family was waiting for me to eat, so I walked out of the room and into the kitchen. Bacon and eggs were on the table with what looked like spinach. It smelled absolutely amazing. Everyone sat around the table and smiled as I came in.

"Real food, and a feast at that!" Bryan said.

I grinned and sat down, asking how Hugo had gotten all the food.

"I got some from the World War Two era. I used the time machine eight times to go back and forth between this time and that time to bring everything I needed."

"Wait," I started, "how did you use it eight times? We've used our time machine six times already, and you have used it way more than we have, even before the World War Two era. Why is the use of our time machine done, if you used it more than we did? How many uses does each phone have?"

258

"Mine had unlimited uses because it was the first one Blake made. Blake invented the next few to where, I believe, you can only use it seven times."

"Seven was Blake's favorite number, so that makes sense," Dad said.

I nodded, and Hugo then asked me how Liam was, and I told him that he was still asleep. Hugo then took some bacon and eggs and went to check on Liam saying he'd be right back.

"So, what happened last night after I passed out?" I asked.

"We all decided it was best to sleep on it, so we all went to bed as well." Dad said and added, "But before that we realized Hugo was right and that our only chance was to get the phone in the castle. Then we would take it with us back home and find Blake."

"And make him pay," I said, taking a bite of bacon. Then realized that no one else had started eating, I put the bacon back down and waited.

"No. That will only cause more problems." Dad said.

"What?" I asked, confused and slightly angry.

"We need to get everyone back home as well. Remember, the whole world disappeared the night you four were home." Dad stopped. It was hard knowing that there were only three of us now.

"How?" I said. "How are we going to get everyone back?"

"Well, if Hugo is right and we use the phone to get back home, and Blake isn't actually lying in the riddle, then we'll be able to help him get everyone back.

259

We kill him with kindness. That's what Jesus would want."

I nodded. Hugo came back out and smiled as he took his seat and stared at the food.

"I'm sure everyone is hungry and anxious to eat. Kyara, will you bless the food?" Dad asked.

"Sure." I said, while bowing my head and closing my eyes. "Dear Lord. Thank you for this meal and thank you that we are all together. Please bless this food and be with Liam. Thank you for giving a great person like Hugo to us, right when we needed him. Be with us all and help us to find that phone. Amen." I said and looked up.

It took two seconds before everyone started digging in and taking handfuls of bacon and spoonsful of eggs. We all ate silently because we were all so hungry. The food was amazing, and I was so happy that we were all together.

After breakfast Hugo said that he needed to go to the church, for there was another meeting taking place at ten o'clock about breaking into the castle. Bella, Dad, and Bryan decided to go with him, while the rest of us stayed behind with Liam. Hugo said they would be back within the hour and I understood.

Once they left, I went to Liam's room. He had gone back to sleep, so I went back out to Luke, sitting on the chair. Mom had started making lunch.

"How are you doing, buddy?" I asked Luke and noticed he was moping slightly.

"I don't know," Luke said.

"What do you mean you don't know?"

"I guess I just don't understand something."

"And what might that be?" I asked.

"Should we really trust Hugo? I mean, we just met him. And we were all so confused and mad at Bella yesterday. . ." He trailed off unsure what to say next.

"Hm," I hummed in thought. "All we can do is trust them right now. Yes, Bella was deceiving us before, but she was trying to protect us from Blake. And Hugo seems trustworthy especially because of all he's done to save Liam, and I have a good feeling about him."

Luke nodded, not in complete understanding, but in slight comprehension. "Okay," he said finally.

"How are you otherwise? Anything else bothering you?"

"It's just so hard without Amy being here."

"I know," I said.

"But everyone seems okay about it. Like no one seems to miss her."

I nodded. "We all do show we miss her, but how we choose to show it is different for each of us."

"You're right, I guess."

I held him close to me. The way he was able to cope with this—his bravery—made me brave and able to cope with Amy's death.

A tear formed in the side of my eye and I wasn't sure why. Maybe it was because of the feeling of my little brother against me and holding him close made me miss Amy even more. I didn't want to miss Amy so much, but how could I not? She was my little sister and she was gone. Forever.

Luke turned around and looked at me. When he saw that I was tearing up, he hugged me.

"It's going to be okay. Just like you promised me in Rome, I'm going to promise you now," Luke said.

As he said it, several tears escaped my eyes. I held Luke close. He had grown up so much in these past few weeks and I wasn't too surprised to hear him say the words he did. He had always been brave. Even when he was a baby, he barely cried.

The tears that streamed from my eyes weren't tears of sadness, but rather tears of hope. Luke pulled away and wiped away my tears with his hand. I smiled and gave him a kiss on the forehead.

"You're a great kid, you know that?" I said.

He shrugged and said, "Thanks."

~ ~ ~

Bella, Hugo, Dad, and Bryan came back around noon based on the position of the sun—a little later than they thought. They explained what happened at the meeting to the three of us.

"It went a little long because I let people ask questions and I asked one of the townspeople to go investigate around the castle more at the beginning of the meeting and he didn't get back until an hour later," Hugo said.

"But he did come back with good news. A door to the castle was completely abandoned—no guards were there. But when he went to the door, he found it locked. That was a whole new problem because these doors are locked in a different way than doors in 2012 are locked. These doors, especially castle doors, are barred shut. Keys are the only way to open the doors,

262

unless of course you knock down the door. Too many guards would see us, then and come after us, so that's not an option. And with the amounts of tools we have and the people, we wouldn't be able to make or use a battering ram, so the next best thing is to take over the guards and use a key."

"So," Bella continued for Hugo, "we had the townsman, Wymer, count the guards at the main gate. He said that he had counted them on his first mission and said he was able to see eleven. He guessed no more than twenty were within the premise of the gate. So, we needed at least twenty men with swords and pitchforks to raid the castle."

"Forty-two signed up for battle," Bryan said.

"Did you sign up?" I asked Bryan.

"Yes. They need me," he said.

"I signed up to, of course," Hugo said. "Everyone in the town looks up to me."

I knew there would be no getting Bryan out of this.

"Wait," Dad said. "I just thought of this. I should have thought of it earlier, but . . . Anyway. Where is King Edward? What if he is here? We can't have him fighting in the battle, especially because if he dies, we all don't exist."

"Isn't Edmund already born, though?" I asked.

"Still. We don't want to kill the king. That would completely change history."

"King Edward is out of the country currently. Wymer heard a guard talking to another guard about the king being in France."

"Okay, good." Dad said. "Then this will be easier if the king doesn't know about it."

Hugo nodded.

"Then I can help in the battle. They may need me. The more the better," Dad said.

"No." A tear escaped Mom's eye. "I'm not losing you again."

"He'll be safe with us," Hugo said. "We have enough swords for fifty men. Plus, the battle is mostly just a diversion to go and get the phone."

"Please," was all Mom said.

"Our mission is to find the phone. So, I think at least one of you should come with me. We need all the help we can get. And anyway, we'll need to get into the dungeon to get the phone." Hugo said.

"You don't even know where the dungeon is located. How are you supposed to get to it? Surely there are more guards within the castle," Mom said.

"That's why all of us should go, and Hugo, you should come with us to search for the phone," Dad said.

"Okay, so it's settled. All three of us will go," Hugo said.

I bit my lip. "When is it?"

"Tomorrow. We will have another meeting after lunch, in two hours, to plan it out."

I nodded.

"I'm going to go check on Liam," said Hugo.

"I'll go with you," I said and followed him to Liam's room.

His eyes were still closed, and he seemed quite peaceful, sleeping. Hugo went to check his pulse as I stood at the doorway and watched.

"His pulse is almost normal, and he feels warm." Hugo began to get another IV ready and hook it up.

I smiled slightly, but felt, for some reason, that something was wrong or going to be wrong.

"He's been sleeping a lot," I said.

"He just got out of a coma, he needs the rest." I nodded, and Liam slowly opened his eyes.

I ran to the other side of the bed and held his hand in mine.

"How are you?" I asked.

"Hanging in there," Liam said, and smiled.

Hugo finished hooking up the IV and told me he'd be in the kitchen. "If anything happens, come and get me," he said and left the room.

"Okay," I said a little too late, for Hugo had already exited.

"So, what's the plan with the phone?" Liam asked.

"Hugo says it's in the dungeon of the castle," I said, and I explained what happened while he was asleep.

"I wish I could help," Liam said, referring to the planned battle.

"I know but—"

"My leg is messed up and I'll just be sitting here while you all get the phone." He sounded angry, and I couldn't blame him.

The problem that I was facing was the fact that, if we lost the battle, what would be the purpose? If Bryan, Hugo, or Dad somehow died in battle, then home wouldn't work if the riddle was true, and Blake wasn't lying in the riddle. There had to be another way to get the phone.

This had to work. The battle must be won.

Chapter XXII
A New Beginning

An hour or so later, Hugo came in and said that he had
to get back to the church to run the next meeting.

"Your mom and Luke are staying behind with
you. But everyone else is coming to the meeting," he
said.

I nodded and sat up.

"He should be fine. If anything seems
abnormal, however, have your mom come and get me
at the church."

I nodded again.

"Is he asleep?"

"Yeah," I said.

"He's lucky he has you, you know. Bryan was
telling me that he thinks that's why he's still alive.
Because of you."

I smiled. He walked a few steps into the room.

"I just wish. . . I mean, Bella has someone; you
have someone. I just thought that when I finally
summed up the courage to talk to her, she and I would

take off and go live somewhere, like Hawaii, without our parents, and we'd make a living there—"

"Wait. You have a one eighty-one IQ. Didn't you think that there would be problems with that, like implications?"

"Yeah, of course I did. But I just wanted a family. You know my mom, Josie, wasn't home much either. That's why I related to Bella. Though Blake was home often, that didn't mean he cared about Bella. It's almost like our parents didn't care one bit. We were also orphans, in another sense, at least."

I frowned. "I'm sorry." I didn't know what else to say.

"Don't worry about it." He waved his hand down.

"Well. I should probably go. I'll see you later." And with that he disappeared into the hallway.

I lay back down and could hear Liam's heartbeat again. It made me feel safe—hearing his heart and feeling the pulse in his wrist. I don't know why it made me feel safe, but it did.

I heard the door close and the sound of voices decrease. Mom and Luke were in the kitchen and I could hear them talking—I couldn't quite make out the words, though.

Liam took a deep breath and I looked up at him, with my head still on his chest. His eyes were open, and he smiled when we met eyes.

"Can I get you anything?" I asked him.

"Water?" He said, with a little more energy than he had before.

"Of course." I got up and ran to the kitchen.

"Everything okay?" Mom asked.

"Yeah. He's just thirsty," I said and then ran back to the room with the water glass in my hands.

I helped him drink the whole glass. When he finished, he smiled.

"I feel much better," he said.

"Good."

He looked down at his leg under the covers. "I don't feel a thing. It's like all the pain has stopped."

"That's good."

"Yeah, but, I can't even feel my leg. I can't move it. I can't move either of my legs," he said and bit his lower lip.

"Oh no. Mom!" I yelled, and she ran in with Luke on her tail. "Liam can't feel his legs."

"Well he has been out for two days. . ." Mom began. "I think it's normal to feel numb after being in a coma. We will have to ask Hugo when he comes back. Also, we'll keep an eye on it and if, after another day or two you still feel numb, we'll have to do something about it."

I nodded.

"Do you need anything else, Liam?" Mom asked.

"No ma'am, thank you," he said.

"Of course, Liam. I'm here if you need me." And with that, she and Luke walked out.

I sat down on the bed and we held hands. "At least you can feel your upper body."

"Yeah. My arms feel a little numb and tingly, but I can squeeze your hand, which is good." He squeezed my hand and smiled again.

269

"I'm so glad you're okay," I said.

"Me too. I hope we can get that phone and get back to the future soon."

"Yeah. Same. Hopefully we can get it tomorrow, when they raid the castle."

"I hope that goes well and that there's no problems," Liam said, with no anger this time.

"I hope so, too. . ." I didn't know what else to say, so I lie back down and put my head on his chest and listened to his steady heartbeat.

"Everything is going to be okay," he said. "I'm here now. And I'm not going anywhere. No matter what."

A tear fell down my cheek. I was so glad he was okay. These past two days had been brutal. Not knowing whether he was going to wake up, and just stop breathing altogether. But now, I have hope—hope that he's going to make it.

I fell asleep knowing that when I woke up, Liam would still be alive and awake.

~ ~ ~

"Kyara, wake up." I heard Liam say.

I opened my eyes and wiped away the sleep from my eyes. Then I pulled my head off his chest and looked up at him.

"They're back," he said. And that's when I heard Hugo and Bella talking in the kitchen. I heard my name and then saw Bella and Hugo appear in the doorway. Bryan and the others followed.

"We figure that Liam should hear what's going on as well, so we all decided to come in here," Dad said. I sat up, still holding Liam's hand.

"Everything okay?" I asked.

"Yes," Hugo said and sat on the chair in the room while everyone else either stood in the room or sat up against one of the four walls. "Everything is set. We raid the castle tomorrow when the sun is at its highest point."

"Why then?" Liam asked.

"It's the best time to do it. That way we have daylight when we are searching the castle for the phone. It may take a few hours to find it because we don't know where it is exactly," Hugo said.

"So, what's everyone's job?" I asked.

"Hugo, Dad, and I are in the fight," Bryan began. "You and Bella will be in the church, while the fight is happening—"

"Wait. I thought I was staying here with Mom, Luke, and Liam?" I said.

"No, we need you for when the fight is over. You'll be with us in the castle, looking for the phone. We need as many people as we can get in the castle," Bryan said.

"Why?"

"Hugo and Bella will be looking in the east wing, as you, Dad, and I will be looking in the west wing." Bryan said. "Mom and Luke will stay behind with Liam. He'll be safe that way. Also, while you and Bella are in the church, you'll be with all the women and children of the town. There's only about fifty of

271

them. The doors will be locked, and you'll all be safe, just in case the worst happens."

"And if the worst happens, what happens to Mom, Luke, and Liam?" I asked.

"The worst won't happen. We have forty-two strong men against twenty. We'll be fine. But, Mom and Luke will have swords and you and Bella will too." Bryan said.

"But we'll be fine. The odds are against the king," Hugo said.

I nodded. "Okay." If Hugo thought the odds were with us, then we would be okay.

"So, once the fight is over, and we win," Bryan began, "Hugo is going to run back and get you and Bella, we decided that he was the fastest of us all; then the rest of the plan will be in place. Every thirty minutes, if it takes longer than half an hour to find the phone, we will meet at the entrance to see if the other group found the phone."

"Sounds like a plan," I said.

"I think it's a great plan. I will, of course, be useless, sitting here doing nothing," Liam said.

"Liam. Stop. You were in a coma for the past two days. We don't expect you to do anything," I said.

"Yeah. Kyara is right. Don't be so hard on yourself," Bryan said.

"Fine. I'm sorry," Liam said.

I gripped his hand in mine. "You have no reason to be sorry."

"Anyway, this gives Mom and Luke a reason to stay behind and not get into trouble," Bryan joked.

Liam shrugged slightly, "I just wish I could be of help."

"Don't worry about it. We need you to get better. That's the most important thing," Bryan smiled at Liam.

Liam nodded once.

"Alright. We should let Liam rest," Hugo said. "Everyone out."

"I'll start making dinner," Mom said as everyone piled out of the room.

"I need to talk to you about something. . ." Liam said to me when everyone was out of earshot.

"Yeah?" I asked, a bit nervous about what he would say.

"You may not believe me, but I think I may have seen the future, when I was in the coma. And I don't think I'm supposed to tell anyone about it, but how can I not?" He took a deep breath and looked at me.

"Maybe we can change the future, if you tell me what you saw. . ." I said, unsure if I actually believed him.

"Well, some of what I saw is good, and some bad, so I don't know if it would be worth trying to fix it. But. . ." he trailed off. I could see fear in his eyes.

"But?" I asked, and he took a deep breath. "What?"

"The bad is pretty bad. The good is pretty good, but I know it doesn't outweigh the bad."

"Okay. . . Just tell me." I was getting a little frustrated at the situation. Why couldn't he just spit it out? Was the bad really that bad?

273

"Sorry. . ." He took another deep breath. "We go to another time after this, but we have to go to this time in order to get back to our time."

"Why?"

"Because we meet someone." He looked away from me. "I don't know if I should even be telling this, let alone, if I should even know this or if it's even true, but I already started and you're going to ask too many questions. So, I guess I have to keep going . . ." He trailed off.

"Okay, who do we meet?"

"Your ex-boyfriend."

Chapter XXIII
All Apologies

"Trevor's in the next time we go to?" My eyes grew wide.

Liam's eyes met mine and nodded. I could see pain behind his gaze. I felt bad for him. He obviously didn't like Trevor because he was kind of the reason we had a falling out before, on the Titanic.

"Liam, you do know that he doesn't matter to me, right? I'm yours, and nothing will change that. No matter what, remember?" I said and kissed him on the cheek.

Liam said nothing and stared at the door.

"Please say something."

He shook his head slightly.

"Did I get back together with him? Is that what happened? Do I leave you? Because you know that's not going to happen. I love you and only you. You have to understand that. Also, how do we know that what you saw was true. I mean, you were in a coma?"

"I know, Kyara," he said a little harshly.

Harsher than I would have expected from someone who

just came out of a coma. "But that's what I saw and plus, I saw Hugo with the phone in that other vision I saw. So, this has to be true."

"But it won't happen. I'm not going back to Trevor. I just won't."

"How do you know? That's how I saw it in the future."

"We'll change the future then. I'm not going back to Trevor. I promise."

It was silent for a few minutes.

"I need some rest," he said.

"Okay." I lay down next to him and nuzzled my head into his neck.

I could feel his chest take a deep breath. "Alone," he whispered.

I pulled my head up to look at him. A single tear fell down his pale cheeks.

"What?" I felt tears enter my own eyes.

"I'm sorry. But I need time alone."

I nodded and then walked out of the room, slowly, waiting for him to change his mind, but he didn't. As I entered the kitchen, everyone looked up, except Mom, who was cutting up carrots with her back turned. Everyone else sat at the table and the talking ceased when I stopped walking.

"Everything okay?" Bryan asked.

That's when Mom turned around and looked at me.

Tears filled my eyes as Hugo stood up quickly and started toward Liam's room. I held his arm and pulled him back before he got far enough.

"Is he okay?" Hugo asked, quicker than he normally speaks and with fright in his tone.

"Yes. He just wants to be alone."

"Honestly, I don't think that's smart—"

"I think he's fine." I let go of Hugo's arm and he stared at me, asking for certainty with his eyes.

I nodded. "You can check on him in a little bit if you want. He just needs to be alone for now."

Bryan stood up and walked over to me. "What's wrong?"

I shook my head and walked over to the table and sat at an empty chair between Luke and Dad. Dad patted my back and asked if I wanted to talk about it. Again, I shook my head. I leaned back in the chair and let a few tears flow from my eyes. I wanted to be alone, but I knew that I wouldn't be able to go to my room without answering a few questions first. So, I just sat there, listening to Mom continue chopping carrots.

Hugo and Bryan sat back down, and Bella started talking to Hugo about their mom and what she was like. I figured they had already started that conversation earlier and were continuing it now. Bryan listened in, while Dad got up and started helping Mom prepare the vegetables. Luke just sat there, staring at me. He looked back and forth from me to Mom and Dad. He must not know what to do. I felt for him. I didn't know what to do either. I probably could steal away now and go to my room, but I didn't have the energy. I was just too lazy.

What I really wanted was to be with Liam, and to assure him that I loved him and my feelings for Trevor were long gone, at least I thought they were. But now the idea of seeing Trevor again made me a little warm inside; I had to admit. Maybe it was just the thought of bringing closure to the situation. If Liam really did see the future, and we do see Trevor, then what am I going to do when I see him? I had to plan this out now because if I didn't, then what would the point of Liam having the vision and telling me be?

I had to make sure I wouldn't fall into Trevor's schemes. I knew he would try and win me back, especially if there was another guy in the picture. He would do whatever he could to get me to love him rather than Liam. That's just what he did. It was his personality.

But what if he had moved on? Like me. . . What if he had found the girl of his dreams? Just like I had found the boy of my dreams? Liam was mine, forever. Wasn't he? Or would seeing Trevor bring back memories? I mean, I had known Trevor for a while before we started dating. Then he asked me out and we dated for several months before we broke up. Liam and I knew each other for barely a day until we started dating, and we've only been dating for a little over a week. I had only known Liam for ten days. And we were already madly in love? Is that even possible? Was it possible that I was still in love with Trevor?

No. It can't be. I loved Liam and that was that.

~ ~ ~

Later that day, after dinner, and after Hugo had fed Liam, I decided to go into Liam's room and see how he was doing.

"I'm sorry," he said right as I entered.

"Me too."

"You have no reason to be. I messed up, again, and I'm sorry that I thought that you were going to go off with Trevor. It was probably just a dream. I don't even think it's possible to see the future—" But before he said more, I kissed him.

When I pulled away I said, "I love you. No matter what."

"And I love you, too," he smiled.

"How are you feeling?" I asked.

"Pretty good for just being in a coma."

"Good. I've been praying for your healing."

"Thanks, love."

I smiled and lay down next to him. It was silent for a little while and I was okay with it. Silence was sometimes the best thing for lovers.

"So, what did you do when I kicked you out?" He laughed slightly.

I looked up at him and rolled my eyes. He laughed a little more.

"I went to the kitchen and just hung out while Mom and Dad were making dinner. Everyone else talked as I just sat and listened and thought."

"What were you thinking about?"

"Us." I kissed him. I didn't want him to know the exact topic because I was also thinking about Trevor, so I let the kiss linger until he pulled away.

"I love you so much," he said.

"Me too," I winked.

"Hey, could you do me a favor?"

"Anything."

"Could you get me some more water?" He motioned toward the empty water glass on the bedside table.

"Of course." I picked up the glass and went outside the room to the kitchen. No one was in sight, so I stayed out for a little longer, enjoying the emptiness.

I drank some of the water and then filled it up again and went back into Liam's room.

He smiled as I entered, and I gave him the water. He was slowly regaining strength and his arms were able to move without someone holding them, so I let him drink on his own. He drank almost the whole glass and then set it on the bedside table when he was done.

"Thanks."

"Sure," I said.

"Was everyone in the kitchen?" He asked.

"I didn't see them. I don't know where they all are. Maybe all went to bed. It is pretty late."

"Hmmm . . ." he hummed. "I'm not tired."

"That's good."

"I have slept a lot of the day, though."

I nodded and yawned.

"You're tired." It wasn't a question.

"A little, yeah."

"It's been a long day," he said.

"Yeah, with you waking up, the meeting, our little brawl—"

"I wouldn't necessarily call it a brawl."

I laughed. "But yes, it has been a long day."

"Can you stay here with me?" He took my hand in his and pulled me slightly toward him. I lie down next to him and put my head on his chest.

"Definitely." And with that, and his slight stroking of my back, I fell asleep.

~ ~ ~

I woke up with a start, but not because I had dreamt of something bad, but because the sun's rays were peeking through the window and were shining in my eyes. I think that was the first night in a long time I hadn't had a dream.

I heard talking in the kitchen. It sounded like Mom and Luke. They must be making breakfast.

I looked up and saw that Liam was still fast asleep. I slowly got up and tiptoed out of the room and into the kitchen.

"Good morning, sweetheart," Mom said in her quiet voice. Mom was never good at whispering or talking quietly, but I figured she and Luke had been up for a while and I hadn't woken up till a few minutes ago.

"Hey, Sis," Luke said, a little quieter than Mom.

"Good morning," I stretched. "What're you guys making?" I walked over to Mom.

"Same as yesterday. We don't really have much else." Mom shrugged.

"True, but yesterday's breakfast was good, so I'm sure it'll be good again," I smiled.

Luke sat at the table and watched as Mom and I prepared the eggs and bacon.

"How's Liam?" Mom asked.

"Still asleep. He's doing well though. I'm so glad he's not in the coma anymore."

"Me too. That was hard for all of us, so I can't imagine how you were feeling."

"Yeah, well. I'm just glad he's okay now," I said.

Dad came into the kitchen then and said, "Good morning" to all of us. Luke got up and gave him a hug. Mom gave him a kiss and hug and I gave him a hug.

"Smells good," he said.

"Same food as yesterday. There's not much else. But there are a ton of eggs." I said.

"Yeah," Dad began, "Hugo had talked to me yesterday about almost bringing back an entire chicken with him to this time, but then realized that the chicken may die by travelling through time, so he decided against it. Instead he just filled up bags full of pork, bacon, eggs, and vegetables."

"There were chickens in the hospital?" I asked, confused.

"No. There was a farm somewhere near the hospital, I think."

We nodded as Bella and Hugo came in next. Bryan must still be asleep.

They sat down and yawned simultaneously. I laughed and then went back to stirring the eggs.

"Thank you so much, Hugo, for letting us stay here," Mom said. "I don't know what we'd do without you. Truly."

"It's not like I would have made you wait at the farm. Not since I found my twin sister and her new family." Hugo smiled.

Mom smiled, and I almost started crying. If it weren't for Hugo, Liam would still be in a coma, or maybe even dead. If it weren't for Hugo, we'd still be lost and wandering with no place to go or stay and have no lead on finding the phone. Now we were okay, and we were all together, united as a family. And today we would find the phone and hopefully get back home.

I hadn't felt this content in a long time. Though we hadn't found the phone, I knew we were going to today and that soon we'd be home. Liam was getting better every hour and, though we had lost someone along the way, I knew she was happy and in a better place.

"All right, they look good," Mom said, and that's when I realized the eggs I was stirring were perfectly scrambled.

I picked up the pan and put it on the table and sat down next to Luke.

Bryan entered the kitchen and smiled at each of us after saying, "Good morning."

We all greeted him back.

"I'm going to go check on Liam." I said, stood up, and walked to Liam's room, which had also been mine last night as well. Just thinking about that made me happy.

I reached the room and entered to see Liam just opening his eyes.

"Good morning, beautiful," he said, and I blushed. I loved when he talked to me that way.

"Hey. How'd you sleep?" I asked.

"Great. I woke up in the middle of the night and the feeling of you by my side, your head on my chest, was probably the best thing in the world."

My face turned even redder and my heart skipped a few beats. I felt my eyes water as I walked over next to him, but I didn't let the tears fall—though they would be tears of happiness.

"I can feel my lower body now. Look." He looked down at his legs, and under the blanket I saw his leg move slightly.

"That's great!" I took Liam's hand in mine.

He squeezed my hand and smiled up at me. "I love you. So much."

"I love you, too." I said. "No matter what."

He pulled me closer and before I knew it, we were kissing.

I heard someone clapping from the door, so I pulled away and turned to see Bryan applauding us. I laughed, and he said, "Breakfast is ready."

I nodded, gave another quick kiss to Liam, told him I would bring food in for him in a second, and then joined Bryan to walk to the kitchen.

I got some food for me and then put some extra food on another plate for Liam.

I turned to go back to Liam's room when Dad asked, "How is he?"

I smiled, turned back around, and said, "Great. He can move his legs again."

"Does that mean he feels the pain of the stitches?" Hugo asked.

"I don't think so," I said.

"Hmmm. That's strange," Hugo said. "Let me go to the room with you."

"Okay," I said and together, Hugo and I went to Liam's room.

When we entered, Liam looked at me confused, probably wondering why I had brought Hugo. I don't know why, but it didn't seem like Liam liked Hugo—which didn't make sense, especially when Hugo basically saved Liam's life.

"What's up?" He asked.

"Kyara told me you can feel your legs, but can't feel the pain of the stitches?"

"I feel pain, but it's not enough for me to whine about," Liam said, a little nastier than I would have expected.

"Liam. Hugo is trying to help. Let him," I said.

"Sorry. . ." he seemed sincere about it.

"It's imperative to know when you are in pain, so that I can help and make sure the stitches are doing their job," Hugo said.

Liam nodded.

"Can I check your stitches?"

Liam nodded a second time.

Hugo walked over to the end of the bed and lifted up the covers. His face turned pale when he saw the stitches, but I knew mine turned white when I saw how bad it looked. His leg was purple and green, and it

285

looked like mold was growing out of his leg. I almost threw up.

"What's wrong?" Liam asked.

I swallowed back the puke. "It doesn't look good. Not at all."

"We need to get that phone, so we can get back to the future. This infection will get worse if we don't get to our time." Hugo said.

"Can't you do something?" I asked.

"Not with the tools I have. We can wash it, but we're going to need clean water and strong soap. That'll help the infection, but as for the swelling—" that's when I realized how big his leg was compared to his normal one— "that's why we need to get to the future. As soon as possible."

I nodded, and Liam lifted his head slightly to try and see what his leg looked like. Thankfully he didn't see it because he couldn't lift his head more than a few inches.

"So, do we need to raid the castle sooner? Or. . . ?" I trailed off, not knowing what else to say.

"We need to wash it first. I'll send your mom and Bella out looking for clean water and soap."

"Okay. What can I do?"

"Stay with him. I'll be back in twenty minutes." He began to walk out of the room, but I stopped him.

"Where are you going?" I said.

"Trust me. I'll be back soon. Just keep him stable." And with that, he was gone.

"But . . ." I groaned. "Why are smart people so stubborn?" I asked to no one in particular.

Liam answered me. "Because they think other people know what they mean when they say something obviously too smart for normal people to understand."

"Sometimes I don't understand you, either," I said and laughed slightly.

Liam didn't laugh—he seemed off in another world.

"Are you okay?"

"Just in pain," he said.

"I'm sorry." I took his hand in mine, but he didn't squeeze it like he normally did. "It's going to be okay. I promise," I told him.

He didn't say anything, just looked at me, and then closed his eyes.

"Can I get you anything?" I asked.

"Hugo said to stay with me, so you should probably do what he said," Liam said, still with his eyes closed.

It took a second for me to realize what he said, and once I did, I became slightly angry. "Okay, number one, one minute away from you to get you breakfast will not change anything. And number two, why do you hate Hugo so much? He saved your life."

Liam finally opened his eyes, noticing my anger. "Sorry."

"It's okay. I just. . . I don't know what to do anymore." I sat down on the bed, flustered.

"I don't either. It feels like the world is coming to an end."

"So, did the people who were living in this time. But we've lasted seven hundred more years.

Maybe it's about time the world ends. . ." I trailed off not knowing what else to say.

"Maybe so."

And then silence took its way.

What if this was just the beginning of the end of the world? What if the end really was coming? What if we couldn't get back to the future because there was no future? Maybe everything ended in the time of the Titanic, and that's why we can't get back home. It made sense in a satirical sort of way. Like someone was playing with us. And I knew exactly who it was: Blake.

But if he was in the future, like Hugo thought he was, then there wouldn't be a black hole and it wouldn't be impossible to get home. Or would it be? Blake could make it impossible. He could keep us here for an indefinite amount of time. Especially when Liam said that we had to go to another time before going home.

"What's wrong?" Liam said, breaking my train of thought.

"What?" I asked, trying to remember what I was thinking about.

"You're face. It was all scrunched up. Kind of angrily."

"Oh. Sorry. I, uh, was thinking about Blake."

"Don't. It'll just create more problems. We have to think about us and getting back to the future."

"But Blake is the only way we'll get back to the future," I said.

"I know but we have to worry about us, too. If we worry about Blake, and what he's doing back home, then we won't be able to make it there."

"Why?" But before I could ask more someone interrupted me.

"Has your mother come back yet?" I heard from the door.

I turned around to see Hugo holding a bouquet of several different colored flowers.

"I don't think flowers are going to help my infection. Unless you're going to make a "Get Well" sign too." Liam sniggered.

Hugo opened his mouth to speak, but nothing came out.

"You went to get flowers? Really? I thought you were going to get something to help Liam's infection," I said.

I was starting to understand why Liam had his doubts about Hugo. I mean, it was a nice gesture, but did he really need to spend time away from a dying Liam, to get flowers?

"What's going on?" Mom came up to the door, with Bella on her tail, who held a bucket full of water.

"We got soap—oh. Hugo. Flowers. How nice," Bella said, but had definite perplexity in her tone.

"They're not flowers," Hugo almost shouted.

"Oh," Bella repeated. "What are they then?"

"They're plants to help Liam's infection."

My mouth dropped. Hugo really did want to help Liam. He went out of his way to find plants that would help Liam's infection.

"We should clean it first, right?" Mom said.

"Yeah. Go ahead," Hugo said.

Mom and Bella squeezed around Hugo who stood frozen at the door.

"I'll be right back," Hugo said, and then unfroze, and turned around to go to the kitchen.

Liam stretched his hand out to hold mine while Mom and Bella cleaned Liam's cut. He winced when the soap touched his skin, but didn't budge until they finished, in which he exhaled deeply.

Hugo came back in holding a bowl full of chopped up plants and some type of liquid making it look like a paste.

"This may sting, but it'll cure your infection," Hugo said as he reached Liam's leg. Mom and Bella moved out of the way and let Hugo be the doctor. "Good job on cleaning his leg."

Mom and Bella said, "Thanks," simultaneously and watched as Hugo began to apply the flower paste to his leg. Right as the paste touched his cut, Liam clenched my hand tightly and gasped heavily, almost kicking Hugo in the face. Blood spurted from his leg, through the stitches.

"That's not supposed to happen, is it?" I asked to no one in particular as Liam clenched my hand tighter and tears streamed down his face.

"He's having a reaction! It's getting worse!" Hugo said.

I looked at his leg and noticed it swelling like a balloon being blown up. Puss seeped from the stitches, and an unknown, green liquid started gushing onto the bed.

"What's in that!" Liam asked, clenching my hand tighter with every word said.

"Goldenseal, thyme, calendula, lavender, rosemary—"

"I'm allergic to rosemary!" He said and let a few cuss words fly from his mouth.

"What do we do?!" I asked. This was not happening. It absolutely couldn't. I would not let this happen.

"We need to clean it—now!" Hugo said and started to apply the soap and water again.

Tears streamed down my face—I could barely see Liam through the moisture that engulfed my eyes.

But I was able to see Liam go limp as his hand dropped from mine.

Chapter XXIV

Death Revisited

"Nooooo! Liam! Please, no!" I could barely breathe. His loss of breath caused me to lose mine.

Mom began doing CPR, but it wasn't working. Hugo shouted, saying something that I couldn't understand because my ears were not working. If he were dead, I would be, too.

~ ~ ~

I felt something cold on my forehead, and then heard a voice, which I couldn't quite make out, but knew who it belonged to. Something didn't make sense. Liam was dead. Why was he saying something that I couldn't understand? Was I dead, too, then? No, I wouldn't have that cold feeling on my head and the pain in my chest.

"Kyara," I heard, clearly this time.

Why couldn't I open my eyes? Why did nothing make sense?

The cold substance on my head moved and that's when I noticed it was a hand, for it started stroking my hair.

"Why isn't she waking up?" I heard from the voice that could only belong to Luke.

"She hit her head pretty hard," Dad said.

Hit my head? How? I don't remember anything, other than Liam's breath stopping and me. . . falling!

My eyes opened at once.

"Kyara!" Liam said, with a little more enthusiasm than I would have expected from someone who wasn't breathing just a few seconds ago.

"What—what happened?" I asked.

"When Liam lost consciousness, you fainted and hit your head on the bed frame," Dad began.

So, Liam had stopped breathing, then? But why was he okay now?

"How. . . How long have I been out?" I asked, and tried to move, but couldn't feel any part of my body. All I could do was stare at the ceiling and listen.

"Almost seven hours," Dad said and slowly the feeling in my lower body returned. I moved my legs a bit and noticed that I was under the covers. I felt the warmth of my lover by my side.

"Careful," said Liam. "My leg is propped up and I don't want it to get kicked out from under me."

I stopped moving my legs and turned my neck slightly to look at him. His dark brown eyes stared into mine and he smiled at me. I tried to smile back, but my head started pounding.

"Don't move your neck too much. You have a concussion," Mom said.

"What happened? Did you raid the castle?" I asked, urgently, wanting to know what happened.

"Yes, we did," Dad said. "But it didn't work. There were guards that we didn't see when we sent the lookout. Several townspeople died, but only a few guards were injured. We were able to steal a key from a guard, but we don't know which door it opens or even if it would open any. Hugo is trying to figure that out now. Because it's dark, he has more of a chance of figuring it out without being detected."

"Is he alone?" I asked, slightly confused.

"No, Bella is his lookout," Dad said. That's when I realized I hadn't heard Bella's voice.

"Liam was able to regain consciousness a few seconds after you fainted," said Mom. "He's been stable for about five hours. The flowers Hugo got have really helped the infection."

"But isn't he allergic to rosemary?" I asked, still confused.

"Yes, but Hugo was able to get it cleaned out and reapply the other anti-infection herbs to his cut. It looks much better now. We also re-stitched it and put some cloth around it so that it would stay enclosed," Dad said.

"So, if Hugo finds the way in, what's he going to do?" I said.

"He's going to come back and get us to help him search for the phone," Bryan said. Why hadn't he talked until now? "But you, Liam, and Luke are staying here."

"What? No way!" I sat up, a little too quickly because it felt like all the blood rushed from my head, but the pounding stopped finally.

"Kyara—"

"No! I need to help! I feel fine—"

"You have a concussion," Mom said.

"So? I can rest when we get to the future! The phone's the only thing that matters right now! We could get home." They had to let me go. I couldn't just stay here cooped up with Liam. . .

My family all looked from one to the other and didn't say anything for a few minutes. Finally, Mom said, "Maybe she's right. We need everyone we can get. And that way we have three groups of two rather than two groups. We can cover more ground."

"Thank you." I said releasing a long breath.

"But, I need you to tell me exactly what you're feeling right now. Any unusual pain?"

"My head hurts a little," I felt the bump on my forehead that had surely formed in the last few hours. "And the light is a little annoying, but otherwise I feel fine."

"Okay," Mom nodded. "It's a minor concussion. You can go." She smiled.

"Yes!" I hollered and stood up and hugged her. I was able to walk fine, which was good.

I looked back at Liam, who stared down at the blanket I had just escaped from, frowning slightly. He looked up at me and smiled when our eyes met.

"All right. Kyara, I want you to rest until Hugo and Bella get back. We'll all be in the kitchen," Mom said and started out the door.

"I'll get you water," Dad said and followed Mom.

Bryan smiled slightly and walked out after them. Why wasn't he saying much?

Luke gave me a hug and then joined everyone in the kitchen. I went back to the bed and climbed back under the covers.

"Everything okay?" I asked.

"Yeah."

"Somehow I don't believe that you're really feeling okay."

"I don't know. . ." He trailed off. I let him think and snuggled my head up against his chest and listened to his unusually steady heartbeat.

Dad came in and set the water down on the bedside table, grinned, and then walked out without saying a word.

It was silent again and that gave me time to think about everything. We were about to get the phone, at least hopefully. We all thought we knew where it was, so that should count for something. I didn't want to think of the possibility of not finding it. I couldn't. We had found it in all our other times, so we had to find it this time. We just had to.

"Kyara?" Liam said.

"Yeah?"

"What if we don't get to the future? Like, ever?"
He said.

I sighed heavily. I hadn't thought about that.
Well I had, but not for a few days. Not since. . . A tear
fell down my cheek. Did I even want to leave? I mean,
Amy was here. We would be leaving her, to rot, all
alone. She was buried in this era. Why should we
leave, especially if we are just going to be transferred to
another time?

"Sorry. I shouldn't have said that." He began
stroking my hair. That's when I realized I was leaving a
puddle on his shirt. I lifted my head up and wiped
away my tears.

"I. . . I just can't think about that. I don't want
to," I said.

"I know. I'm sorry. Let's talk about something
else. Something good."

"What is good? I don't even know what that
word means anymore. It feels bitter when it falls off my
tongue."

Liam frowned. "This. This is good." He wrapped
his arms around me and held me close.

More tears fell down my face. Why hadn't I
thought about that? I pulled away slightly and kissed
him. His lips felt cold and dry, but I didn't care. I still
loved him. And I was just happy he was alive. And I
was glad I was too.

"I love you. So much." He said when I pulled
away and put my head on his chest again.

"I love you, too."

Silence stole over the room again as I listened
to his heartbeat—probably my favorite sound in the

world. I closed my eyes and thought some more. Before I could get very far, though, Bryan came in.

"Hey," I sat up. "Everything okay?" He looked sullen.

"Can I talk to you? Please," he said.

"Yeah," I crisscrossed my legs and stared at him.

"Alone?" He said, slowly and hopefully.

I knew that tone. He needed to talk. Desperately.

"Yeah." I stood up. "I'll be right back, Liam. Love you."

I followed him out and across the hallway to the room Bryan and Luke slept in.

"Everything okay?" I asked, though I knew the answer.

He shook his head and took a deep breath. "I feel like I'm a curse. I know it's crazy, but we first lose Amy, and then Bella, and then almost Liam and almost you. Mom didn't want to tell you, but when you fell and lost consciousness, you weren't breathing for about a minute. It's like you had lost the will to live. Because you thought Liam was gone. I started doing CPR on you and told Mom to keep trying on Liam. And then at the exact same moment, you both start breathing again. You were still unconscious, but Liam was conscious, slightly. He was loopy for about an hour until we saved his leg. For a bit, Hugo thought we would have to cut it off. Then it started getting less swollen and the infection went away. But you were still unconscious. For six more hours. . . And I had to go fight in the battle where every single guy fighting by my side, died or got terribly injured. I just," he took a breath, "I feel like I'm losing everyone. I kept thinking, why don't I just die in the battle? There's no point anymore, you know?"

"There is a point. You, me, Liam, Mom, Dad, Luke, Bella. We are all still alive! And there's a reason for that!"

He shook his head again. "Not if we don't find the phone tonight."

"But we will!"

"How do you know?"

"I have faith! Don't you?" I said.

"No. And I haven't since Amy died. A god who loves and created the universe wouldn't cause an innocent girl like Amy to die. It's not fair."

"Life isn't fair!"

"How are you okay with this? It's like you don't even care that Amy's gone!"

"I do care! I'm devastated! You have no idea," I was beginning to get angry. "And you're not a curse. You can't blame everything on yourself. It's not any one person's fault."

"If I had just come to the farmhouse right after I woke up that morning Amy was kidnapped, rather than stay and enjoy time with Bella, maybe things would be different. Or what if we had just left Bella in Rome? Why did we have to bring her? Since she's Blake's daughter, she helped bring all the trouble on us."

"You can't think that way. It'll just cause pain and more problems."

"Then why do I feel so impure?"

"Because that's what Satan wants you to feel!
You can't give him the foothold—"

"Too late—"

"No, it's not! It's never too late," I shook my
head and a tear fell down my cheek.

Bryan closed his eyes—I could see the anger in
his rigid stance, boiling up like a grenade about to
explode.

I took a step back. Something wasn't right.
Bryan had never looked this livid before. But it wasn't
long before his legs buckled beneath him and he was
on his knees. I heard a loud and tearful cry come from
Bryan. He was fighting it. He didn't want Satan to win;
I knew it. And right now, there was a huge war going
on between demons and angels.

I sprinted from the room and got Mom and
Dad. They ran back in with me and saw Bryan on the
floor gasping for air.

Mom reached his side and held him close. I
leaned against my father and he put his arms around
me. No one said anything. Somehow, they knew that
there was a huge battle going on right now.

Mom began to sing. I couldn't figure out what
it was at first, but then I realized it was the worship
song, "Forever Reign." Though I couldn't sing well, I
began singing along at the chorus, for I knew the
chorus well. It was one of Bryan's favorite songs.

Bryan was shaking under Mom's grasp.
Something spiritual was definitely going on above in
the Heavenly realms. I knew God would win, but I
couldn't shake off the feeling, "what if He didn't?"

Maybe Bryan was right. Maybe God didn't care? He took Amy. He's kept us from going home. He caused the worst man of all to be my dad's arch-nemesis. I mean, what had this family done to deserve it? I didn't think we were that bad. Yes, we had sinned, but not as much as some people. Or was there something I didn't know about? Did we deserve this? Even if we did, why did Amy have to die? She surely didn't deserve this.

My faith began to slowly fade just as Bryan's did. Come to think of it, it really didn't make sense that a loving god would put us through this. I may have felt his presence several times, but it seemed like he was not here now. I may have met him in Bethlehem, but it felt like he was not real today. And I may have helped turn someone to him, but what if Anna turned to no one?

I didn't know what to do anymore. Everything seemed out of whack. Something in the back of my head was telling me I was wrong, but another voice was telling me I was right. It could be Satan, but it also could be the truth, telling me that I was right about God not existing.

However, if I didn't believe in God, what would I believe in? I've believed in him ever since I could believe in anything. If I believed in something that wasn't real, then why had God sent His angel to tell me about the armor? And why did Liam have a similar dream that same night? It could not just be coincidence. There had to be some greater power that would do that, and some great, but lesser power making me feel so hopeless.

I wanted to ask for a sign, but I knew that wasn't fair—He had already given me several reasons to believe. Reasons that would make anyone believe. I couldn't not have faith in God's existence, not after all I've gone through. God was there. I knew it now as I thought it through. And I asked for forgiveness for doubting Him. That's when Bryan started breathing normally again—he took a deep breath and looked up.

"I'm sorry," he said. His eyes were red, and he rubbed away the tears from his eyes.

"No," Mom, Dad, and I said all at the same time.

"There's no reason for you to be sorry," Mom said, and helped Bryan stand up. "You should be proud."

"God just won the battle. He just won you back," I said and smiled.

"He sure did. And thank you," Bryan said and smiled back. He walked closer to Dad and me. I let go of Dad and hugged him.

"We can't let that happen again," I said when he let go of the hug. "You scared me, and made me start doubting, too."

"Sorry. And it won't happen again."

"We can't know that," Dad said. "There may be days where we do doubt. But if that happens, we just got to hold on to each other. Be on our guard. "

"We have to hold on to the truth," Mom said.

"You're right," said Bryan. "We can't know if that will happen again. Satan tries his hardest to get us to not believe, and he will try again, especially at our weakest moments."

I heard the door to the outside open, running footsteps, a slamming door, and then Hugo yelling, "I found the right door! What's going on in here?" He held the key in his left hand, tightly, as the smile slowly faded from his face. Bella came in after and stared at all of us, with confusion.

"We just had a run in with the devil, but we're good now. You found the right door?"

"Run in with the devil? And Kyara is okay? Wow, we missed a lot in the past two hours." Hugo said.

"Yeah you did. And yes, I'm okay. Liam is too," I said.

"And we're ready to go, if you are." Bryan said, a little giddier than I would've expected, especially after having a crazy panic attack.

"Okay, then let's go," Hugo said.

I started out the door to go say bye to Liam. No one stopped me, and when I got to Liam's room, he turned to look at me, a smile on his face.

"Did you hear all of that?" I asked.

He nodded. "You have to go, don't you?"

"Yeah," I bit my lip and nodded slightly.

"Be careful."

I reached his bed and leaned down to give him a kiss. "I love you."

"And I love you."

"I'll be back soon. With the phone. We'll be okay. I promise," I said.

"You better be," he said and gave me another kiss.

When I pulled away, he said, "You're beautiful."

"Thanks," and with that, I was out the door, promising something to Liam that may become a broken promise.

Chapter XXIV
Reunited

"So, Bryan and Kyara will team up and go west. Hugo and Bella team up and go east, while the two of us," Dad pointed to him and Mom, "Go straight through the castle toward the north."

"Sounds good," I said as we walked up toward the castle. It was a pretty long walk. We had already walked half a mile, but we were almost there.

Bryan looked at me and nodded. "We got this," he held his hand out in a fist for me to pound. I did so.

It was dark out. The full moon was our only source of light. Our eyes had adjusted quite well. Before we had left the house, we made sure that Liam and Luke were okay to stay behind.

Luke and Liam were probably talking right now, worried about us, but trying not to be. Mom was going to stay back with them, but if we had three groups, we'd cover more ground, and be quicker to find the phone.

It felt odd carrying a knife in my hand. I surely didn't plan to use it on someone, unless it was self-defense. Everyone had a small knife in his or her hands, just to play it safe. It made us all feel a little more protected.

We made it to the door, finally, and Hugo unlocked it to pull it open. We entered and looked around. There were two statues of knights on either side of the door, and there were three corridors, one to the right, one straight ahead, and one to the left. Perfect for three groups. There were also several torches that lined the walls.

"Alright. Let's do this," I said as Bryan and I started for the left corridor.

"Wait." Dad stopped us. "We need to meet back here at the chime of the bell, to make sure we are all okay. If we find the phone within that time, good job. If not, then we go for another thirty minutes. And so on. Got it?"

"Sounds good," Bella said.

"Everyone take a torch, too," Dad said. We did as he commanded.

"All right. Be careful." Mom said after we had all grabbed a torch, and we all shared hugs with one another. After everyone gave each other a hug, we were off.

Bryan and I started speed walking through the left corridor. It came to a dead end after about a hundred yards and cut to the left. We followed it. We had, so far, seen no doors, but Bryan said that every door we see, we needed to check out.

Another fifty yards later, we came to another left turn, and right as we turned, we found a door.

"Come on." Bryan said, and we entered it. Thankfully it was unlocked.

The room was about the size of our house back at home—the downstairs part of it. There was a huge table in the center of the room with stacks of books on it, and rows of books outlined the walls.

"This must be the library."

"You think?" I said, a little sarcastically.

"Let's look around. Just to make sure the phone isn't in here."

I nodded and went to my right. I was in awe of the number of books that this place held. I was also in awe of the idea that there were these many books in this era. I picked one up but couldn't read it. It was in a very confusing font and language. I put it back and started looking across the shelves.

"Hey Bryan? How long do you think we've been looking? We need to make sure we're back when the bell chimes."

"We're about ten minutes in, I think."

"Okay." I started walking through the aisles faster.

After a few more minutes, I met up with Bryan at the other end of the library. He had found nothing, same as me. We exited the library and started going through the hallway again. It had been a little more than ten minutes and we hadn't found a single thing.

"You think we should run?" I asked.

"Yes, but just remember. The distance we run, we're going to have to run that distance back to the first door."

"That's fine."

"You sure you can do that? Is your head okay?"

"Yeah. I feel fine."

"All right. Let's run then," and Bryan started to run. I followed his lead.

"Just don't fall. We have knives and torches, remember?" He said.

"Yeah, of course." I held my knife up slightly and torch steady and watched where I stepped to make sure not to fall.

For the amount of room this castle had, there were not many rooms, or doors leading to rooms. After about twenty seconds of running, we found another door.

It was locked, and it was probably a good thing because I had a bad vibe about it.

"We should keep going," I said.

"Yeah. You feel that, too, don't you?" He was referring to the bad vibe I had.

"Yep." We started running again. The door that was locked, opened and the second I looked back, a man shot an arrow, which flew by my face, missing me by not even an inch.

"Faster!" Bryan said, and we turned a corner. The man we fled from hadn't even said a word, and he had a bow and arrow, ready for use.

"That was weird." I said. "He didn't even yell at us."

"Yeah, he just almost killed you, without asking who you were. Something doesn't feel right."

"What if he knows? What if all the guards know that we were coming back? And they're waiting for us?" I asked.

"I don't think so. They would have found us sooner."

"Bryan. . . We have to go back that way—to get back to the first door. What should we do? We can't kill him."

"He almost killed you!" Bryan said a little louder than he should have. But the guard didn't come after us, so I figured we were okay.

"How long has it been?"

"About twenty minutes."

"How long will it take to get back?"

"About five minutes if we run."

"All right. Let's figure out if the guard went back into his room. If he didn't, we'll find another way back."

"There is no other way back, we have to go the way we came."

"Fine then let's pray for safety," I said, and started going back toward the corner that we came around to flee from our captor.

"Let me look around the corner first," Bryan said.

I rolled my eyes and said, "fine," giving him the way ahead.

He peeked his head around the corner and made a thumbs-up with his hand. "We're good. He's out of sight."

308

"Should we run past his door?" I whispered.

"No, we need to be as quiet as possible."

I nodded, and we started walking down the corridor, past his room, making as little noise as possible. Our footsteps echoed slightly, but not enough to wake someone up or give someone behind a door a reason to come out. We passed his door, on the far side of the hallway and started speed walking to the corner where we would turn right. We made it, after what felt like the longest walk in the history of walks.

I took a deep breath when we rounded the corner; I hadn't realized I had been holding it.

"We should run back," Bryan said. It's now about twenty-five minutes.

"Okay," I said, and we began to run.

We passed the library and then turned right once, then twice, ran a hundred more yards, and we were back at the beginning door.

We were the only ones back.

"How long has it been?"

"We're basically at the thirty-minute mark. So, they're not late or anything." And the chimes sounded, making me realize how much of a time savant he really was.

I nodded and sat against the wall.

"I hope one of the two groups found it. I don't know what we'd do if we didn't. At least we know our corridor goes nowhere. I have a good feeling that someone found it. Don't you?"

"Yeah, but something feels wrong, too. I don't know."

I bit my lip. For some reason, I felt as if someone had been captured. I'd soon find out I was right.

~ ~ ~

Bella and Hugo came running back. Hugo's knife was dripping with blood, and Bella didn't have her knife with her, but she held her torch. I jumped up from my sitting position.

"What happened?" Bryan and I asked, our eyes wide with concern.

"You're parents. They've been taken," Bella said.

"What? How! We have to go after them." I began toward their corridor.

"They found the phone."

"What? Where?" Bryan asked.

"It's being defended by the king and two guards," Bella said.

"Wait. I thought the king was in France?" I said.

"Apparently not. Anyway, they found us. We were fighting off other guards. They must've known we were coming."

"It was us two against four guards, until your parents came. Hugo stuck one of the guards in the arm with his knife, and I threw a knife into the other guard's gut, but the two other guards took your parents with them, back toward where the phone was—at least that's what the guard said. We told the two guards we were fighting to tell us what was going on, or else we would kill them. The guy I hit with my knife couldn't breathe, so the other one told us about the phone—he didn't know exactly what it was, but we found out that he was talking about the phone. He asked to take the other guard to the infirmary, and we said yes, and that's when we came back."

"So, what do we do? We have to get that phone," I said.

"The only problem is that it might be defended by more than just the king and those two guards that went back to where the phone was. And now that your parents are with them probably, we have to get them and the phone," Hugo said.

"We have to go now then!" Bryan said.

"Do you know where they are?" I asked.

"The guard pointed us in the right direction, so yeah," Bella said, and with that, we were off through the corridor that Hugo and Bella had just appeared from.

We ran for what felt like a mile, but I knew in my head it had only been a couple hundred yards. We stopped and stood outside the largest door I had ever seen—a wooden and gold painted door.

"This is it," Hugo said.

"We need to think of a plan. There could be hundreds of guards in there," Bryan said.

"We have to get Mom and Dad, and the phone, too." I said. "We can't do anything but charge in and demand for them to be released. We don't need a plan." I started to push the door open, but it was too heavy, I could barely move it.

Bella began to help me, and then Hugo, then Bryan, understanding that we did not need a plan. Once we opened it, we saw the king and two guards guarding something in the center of the room, but no Mom and Dad.

I held my knife up, as Bryan and Hugo held up theirs. Bella stood behind us.

The guards and King Edward took out their long swords, and as they did, Hugo and Bryan at the exact same time, threw their knives and hit the guards straight in the chest. They fell backward, knocked over the case that held the phone, the glass broke on the stone floor, and the guards fell on the broken glass, starting to heave for breath.

"Give us the phone," said Hugo.

"Where are our parents?" Bryan said at the same time as Hugo.

I handed my knife to Bryan, because he had better aim than me, but told him not to kill him, and that I had an idea.

"We know about Edmund," I began. "Your son that you had with Marguerite, one of your maids. And we will kill you if you don't tell us where our parents are. You also better give us that device."

"How could you know about Edmund?" King Edward said. But then his eyes grew wide. He then pushed the guard away, picked the phone up, and tossed it to us, and held his hands up in surrender. Bryan caught the phone and started smiling. We could go home now.

"Where are our parents?!" I screamed at the king. I didn't care that he was my very great grandfather and that I should respect him. I only cared about my parents.

"I'm sorry," was all he said.

"What do you mean?" Bryan said.

The king said nothing.

"Tell us!" I took the knife out of Bryan's hand and held it up high, ready to throw at the king. It didn't matter now, if I killed him. Edmund was already born. Edmund was our true ancestor.

"They've been executed."

My heart stopped, my knees buckled, and I fell to the ground. If only we had been faster and hadn't taken the time to listen to Bella and Hugo tell the story.

"You're lying!" Bryan said, but as he did, his voice cracked.

"I'm sorry. But your friends at home will be executed, too, if you don't get them quickly."

"Liam! Luke!" I found my voice, shot up, and started running out of the castle. I heard Bella, Hugo, and Bryan, following me, but didn't look back.

This could not be happening. Luke and Liam had to be okay. Mom and Dad were most likely dead. Amy was dead. We had lost everyone. And whose fault was it? Blake's. Not Bella's—she had nothing to do with this. Not Hugo's. Blake's fault. I would kill him if I ever saw him.

"Kyara!" Bryan said, I could hear him fighting off tears. "When we get Luke and Liam, we have to leave. I'm sorry, but we can't go back for Mom and Dad. Once we get home, and we will this time," he caught up to me, and I could feel him staring at me, but I wouldn't look at him because I know I'd start crying, "we have to get Blake to get our parents out of this time."

"Bryan!" I looked over at him for a split second and felt the tears come to my eyes. "They're dead. Along with Amy. We just have to accept that." I wiped away my tears as we entered the town. The town was completely empty, and once I reached the house where Luke and Liam were, I crashed through the door and screamed for them.

"Kyara!" Liam was okay.

Luke came running out, "Is everything okay?" He said.

Bryan stood next to me, holding onto the phone, tears streaming down his face. Hugo and Bella ran in after us and started to catch their breath.

I ran into Liam's room and once I saw him, the tears fled from my face, quicker than I thought was possible.

"Kyara, what's wrong?"

I sniffed and managed, "My parents are gone. We got the phone though. We have to get back to the future now. Or else Mom and Dad will be long gone. The guards are coming after us."

Bryan came in carrying Luke in one arm, and the phone in the other. He handed the phone to me. Hugo and Bella ran in and told us they were ready. Everyone held onto me and I looked at the phone. I turned it on and prayed for us to get home. I could barely see the letters—my eyes were too watery.

I then typed in the words, "The future, please," hit send, and the six of us began to spin—faster and

314

longer this time. I began to get quite dizzy and it felt like we were never going to stop. Then, at last, we stopped.

I fell to the carpeted floor, as everyone else let go and fell as well. I looked around after I regained my vision.

We were in a large room but only one thing was in this specific room. There were doors that led to other rooms, probably, but this room had only a large steel box, about the height of me and the width of three of me. I decided I would check that out later, and right now I needed to make sure everyone was okay.

Liam was right next to me; Bryan, who was on the other side of me, still held Luke, but Luke got up and crawled over to me. I hugged him. Bella and Hugo were about five feet away, still laying on the floor and staring at the ceiling. I looked up and saw a glass roof. Beyond was the night sky. Stars everywhere, with a bright full moon. I thought I saw something zoom past above, but I figured it was just my imagination.

I let go of Luke and stood up, the lights instantly turned on. Not that it was that dark before, because the stars and moon were light enough.

"Motion censored, probably," Bryan said. "Maybe we're back in the future."

My eyes widened, and I wanted to smile, but for some reason, something seemed off.

The phone was, of course, nowhere in sight, so either we lost it again, or we were back in the future. I hoped it was the latter of the two.

I looked at the steel box again. It had a knob on one side of the box, the side facing me. I walked over to it and the view outside the window stunned me. We were about two hundred feet above ground. My mouth dropped, and I stepped backwards—away from the window.

We were in the future, but the year we were in was unknown. What was known, however, was the fact that we were not in our time. We were after our time.

Chapter XXV
The Future

"Kyara?" Bryan said and joined me at the window.

"Whoa." He said and looked around outside.

I noticed something speed by the window, and I fell backwards. Bryan caught me before I hit the floor.

"What was that?" I asked after I regained my balance. It was the same type of thing I had seen before when I looked outside through the roof. It almost looked like the outline of a person.

"I don't think we're in our time. I think we're several years after," he said.

Hugo and Bella joined us. Luke stayed with Liam. He seemed slightly scared.

"Kyara," Liam said. I looked over at him, and saw that he was staring at his wound, which began to bleed again and stain the carpet below.

I ran over to him and asked Bryan to find something to stop Liam's blood flow.

Bryan, Bella, and Hugo all chose doors and opened them at the same time. There were four doors in all, so I went to the last door on the right side of the room. My door led to what looked like a closet, but inside was what freaked me out. Clothes were there, yes, but they were not hanging on hangers, which hung on clotheslines. Instead the clothes were hanging in the air, as if something was holding them. But I could see nothing holding them.

I took the first thing I saw, a black shirt, and as I touched it, it fell onto my hand, as if gravity had kicked in. I ran to Liam and put the shirt over his wound to stop the blood flow.

"I think that's a bathroom," Bryan said as he came out of his door. "I found some type of healing ointment." He shrugged and came over to Liam and me.

I took the tube that looked like a toothpaste bottle out of his hand and unscrewed the top.

"There's no rosemary in there right?" Liam said.

"It just says 'HEAL' on the tube. Nothing else," Bryan said.

I turned the tube over, assuming that it was paste in the tube and that when I turned it over, nothing would come out. But, instead, a clear mist came out and, as it hit my arm, it disappeared. I felt a cool sensation and then a ton of energy surge through my veins as every sore bone and muscle in my body felt completely cured.

"You okay?" Bryan asked.

"I feel great!" I said and jumped up. The headache I had when we left England had entirely gone away.

Bella and Hugo came out of their rooms at the exact same time and looked at me with similarly confused expressions on their faces.

"Well," Bella began and pointed back toward the room she was in, "there's tons of weird tools in there that make no sense to me but look kind of awesome. I want to try them out."

"My room has to be the bedroom. But the bed looks nothing like a bed," Hugo said, walked over to me, and held out his hand.

I handed the tube to him and he looked at it. He smelled it and squinted his eyes to look inside the tube. He poured a bit of the mist on his hand, and his eyes immediately opened wide and his expression turned excited.

"It smells like water and feels cold when it touches your skin, but it does great justice to you." Hugo handed it back to me.

I kneeled back down next to Liam and took the shirt off of his leg and unwrapped the soaking cloths. The wound began gushing blood and I quickly poured the mist on his leg. When it touched his leg, Liam screeched in pain for a split second and then stopped. The bleeding ceased, the wound vanished and, though there was still blood all around his leg, it looked like there never was a deep sever on it.

"No way," Liam said.

"Impossible," I said.

"How?" Bryan said.

"That's not normal," Hugo said.

Bella and Luke had their mouths dropped and they were both speechless.

"See if you can walk," I said and helped Liam up. He was hesitant to put any weight on his leg, at first, but after a few seconds he did. His eyes grew wide and I knew he wasn't in pain anymore.

I helped him walk around the room until he said he could walk on his own.

"Impossible," I repeated as he walked around, smiling.

"I love the future!" Liam said and jumped up and down a few times.

"Me too," I grinned. I felt more energy than I had ever felt before.

"Kyara. We have to think logically here. We aren't in our time. We've lost the phone again, I'm guessing. And Mom and Dad aren't with us. We have to figure out what to do," Bryan said, bringing me back to reality. I had to fight the Healing Mist to realize the truth. We were, once again, lost, and we needed help. But who would help us? We knew nothing about this time. How would we be able to get through this time without knowing anything about it? We had been lucky in the times before because we knew about them, but this was different.

"You're right. We should figure out what to do." I started toward the door, but a big whooshing sound caught me off guard—almost the exact same sound that we had heard the day of the storm when everyone allegedly disappeared.

"What was that?" I turned around and everyone stared at the steel box.

The knob began to turn, and my heart started to pound. I wanted to say something, like, "run," or "who's there," but I couldn't sum up the courage to say anything.

The door on the box began to open and a man, about ten years older than me stepped out. He had blue hair, but wore all white—a white coat, white pants, and white shoes. He wore circular goggles, but they were not—I came to realize—attached to him. Instead, when he moved to look at us, the goggles moved with him, as if gravity was not a real thing anymore.

His eyes grew wide as he checked out each of us. None of us moved. We had no idea what to do, nor could we do anything. We were in his house, and we were trespassing—if trespassing was even a real thing in this era.

"I can't believe it!" He said. "My father told me that I would be the one to witness it, but I still can't believe the day is actually here."

I had not a clue what he was talking about, but I don't think anyone else did either.

"I'm sorry," Liam said and walked over to me— how was he able to walk and talk? I sure couldn't. "Who are you?"

"Oh, right. You, obviously, don't know who I am." He smacked his head with his hand and the goggles disappeared for one split second, and then reappeared when he dropped his hand back to his side. "I'm Philo, your great, great, grandson," he pointed to Bryan.

The Journey

The Terminal Sacrifice

The incredible end to *The Journey Trilogy*

Chapter I
Philo

December 30th, 2120 (9:37am)

Bryan's mouth dropped from shock at what Philo had just said and he looked at Bella. I could hear him thinking, hoping that Bella would be the one who was going to bear his children.

"What year is it?" I asked, barely able to hear my own words.

"Almost year 2121, for tomorrow is New Year's Eve," Philo said, as if he could hear my question as if I was screaming it.

"So, um, you still celebrate New Year's and Christmas and all?" Liam said, a little more audible than me.

"Christmas isn't a holiday anymore," Philo said.

"What! No Christmas! What has happened to the United States?" I said.

"Look, I wish we could stay here and talk, but we need to get back to The Oaks where no one will find us," Philo said and looked around and then at his watch, which looked nothing like a watch—more like a bracelet with words flowing from the top screen. When Philo looked at it, the words appeared in mid-air, long enough for him to read, and then disappeared back into the screen on the watch.

"How do we know we can trust you?" Liam said.

"Good question. And I don't have a good answer, but you have to trust me, or else they will find you."

"Who's the 'they'?" I asked.

"The Watchers. Now come into the Teleporter. We must go. I can explain everything back at my home."

"This isn't your home?" I asked.

"It is, but—" There was a loud bang coming from outside the main door. "We must go! Everyone in the Teleporter. Now."

We all followed him to the box by the window. I wanted to ask how we would all fit, but when he opened the door to the Teleporter, there was a lot more room than I would have expected. Almost as if size didn't matter anymore, we all fit into it with enough room for at least two more people. Philo closed the door and I was able to take everything in.

It looked like an elevator inside. But instead of buttons with numbers on it, there were buttons with letters on it, some of which formed words. I wanted to read them all, but before I could think more on the fact, Philo pressed the button that said TO and an enter button. Everything vanished, and it felt like I was falling several feet into oblivion.

~ ~ ~

"Most humans pass out their first time, but I'm surprised you didn't," I heard someone say, sounded like Philo, but I hadn't heard his voice enough to decide.

"I'm different, I guess," Liam said. I opened my eyes and felt an agonizing pain as I did. It wore off after a few seconds and I looked around, not sitting up yet. I was in a room about the size of the room we were in before, but the ceiling wasn't glass as it was last time. It was gold.

I sat up finally and saw Liam and Philo a few yards away from me. Everyone else was scattered on the blue carpet, still passed out.

"Kyara." Liam walked over toward me and hugged me when he reached me. I hugged him back. Philo had followed him and held out a cup for me with blue liquid inside it.

"Drink this. It helps," Philo said, and I took the cup, which was more the size of a shot glass.

I drank the blue liquid and though the liquid was cold, I felt a warm sensation flood through by body on its way down my throat. It tasted like blueberries, but like the sweetest blueberries I had ever tasted, and with a hint of mint.

I felt instantly better and more awake. Liam helped me stand and I hugged him again.

"How long was I out?" I asked, wondering how long it would be until the others woke up.

"Five minutes. We had just brought everyone out of the teleporter when you woke up," Liam said. I nodded.

"And what about the others?" I asked.

"It depends on the age and athleticism to determine the amount of time they stay passed out," Philo said.

I nodded again and looked around. We were in what looked like quite a large kitchen. Cabinets lined the walls, which were all pure white and completely clean. They didn't look like normal cabinets either; there were no handles on them. There was also a triangular table in the center with three chairs around it. On the table were four more shot glasses filled with the blue liquid.

Everything in the kitchen was white or blue, like the door. The door seemed to have a center break in it, and I assumed it opened only by the blue button that was on the right of the door.

Bryan, then, sat up quickly and then fell back, banging his head on the carpeted floor. He grunted and the three of us ran to his aid.

Liam helped him sit up and I asked Philo to get more of the blue liquid. Philo jogged over to the table and picked up another shot glass and brought it over. Philo handed it to me, and I helped Bryan drink it.

"What happened?" Bryan asked after he finished the liquid and blinked a few times.

"Most everyone passes out on his or her first time through teleportation. You will get used to it eventually," Philo said, matter-of-factly.

"That was weird, though. I don't think I want to teleport again," Bryan said as Liam and I helped him stand up.

Bryan looked around and saw Luke, Bella, and Hugo still knocked out on the floor.

"They'll come to. Don't worry," said Philo, smiling slightly.

"So, what's going on? Who are you and where are we?" Bryan asked.

Bella woke up, then, before Philo was able to explain anything, and said, "help."

Philo went to get another blue liquid from the table and brought it to Bella. There were only two liquid shot glasses left. It seemed as if Philo was waiting for us.

Bella sat up slowly and drank the liquid. She then stood up and went over to Hugo.

"Don't wake him," Philo said. "It'll only make it worse."

Bella retreated from Hugo and that's when Luke opened his eyes.

Philo went through his normal routine and helped Luke stand after he had drunk the liquid. Luke looked around and then at each of us.

"What's going on? Why is Hugo asleep?" Luke asked.

"He'll be fine soon. The smartest stay out the longest, and from what I remember, Hugo has a 180 IQ?" Philo said.

"One eighty-one," I heard from Hugo; he sat up and Philo gave him the last blue shot glass.

"So, can we get back to my question?" Bryan said looking at Philo.

"Yes, but first, let's go into the living room. You'll want to sit down to hear all of this." Philo said and went over to the door, pushed the button on the side of the door three times and the door opened, the lower side of the door disappearing into the ground and the upper side disappearing toward the gold ceiling.

We all followed him through the door and entered the "living room," yet it looked nothing like I would have expected. It was a bare room, with four blue, leather couches squared in the middle of the room. Yet the couches were suspended in midair and when I went to sit on the one closest to me, and Liam sat next to me, we didn't move down, rather it lifted us up a few inches so that our feet didn't touch the ground. I pulled my legs up and sat with my legs against my chest. I felt more secure sitting this way.

"Woah," Bryan said when he sat on the couch to the right of us, with Bella next to him. Hugo and Luke sat on the one across Liam and me, and then Philo sat on the couch to the left of us. Only Philo's couch did not move upwards when he sat on it. Instead a robotic voice succumbed the room.

"Philo," it said.

"This is Robataus," Philo said to us. And then to "Robataus" he said, "show me the computer. Our friends are from the past. I need to catch them up to speed."

The center of the floor opened up and a large clear table was pulled out of the ground.

"The computer is on," Robataus said.

"Thank you," Philo said, and his couch moved forward to the table.

Blue letters appeared on the table to create the word, "Welcome."

"Now I will show you exactly what we need to do, in order for you six to get back home, save your parents, and stop Blake."

The Journey The Malevolent Curse Playlist

"Hopeless Wanderer" by Mumford and Sons: Their first night in the medieval times when Kyara and Liam go look around.

"Raging Fire" by Phillip Phillips: When they find the creek in the beginning of the third chapter.

"Dead Hearts" by Stars (karaoke): As they are walking through the town and move up toward the farm in chapter three.

"Mad World" by Gary Jules. When Kyara sees the body in the farm house.

"Everything" by Lifehouse: When they realize Amy is gone and start searching for her.

"Heal" by Tom Odell: When Bryan and Kyara bring Liam back to the barn and they try to keep him stable.

"Unsteady" by X Ambassadors: When Dad and Bryan bring Amy back and they realize she's dead.

"The Funeral" by Band of Horses (karaoke): As they are burying Amy while Dad and Bryan are telling the story of how they got Amy.

"Goodbye" by Secondhand Serenade: When they give their speeches for Amy.

"Who I Am Hates Who I've Been" by Relient K: In the middle of chapter nine when Bella is explaining to Bryan that she does love him and wants to explain everything.

"Drown" by Bring Me the Horizon: In chapter eleven when Kyara starts punching the walls and screaming, wanting to kill Blake.

"Not About Angels" by Birdy: When Liam is having his panic attack after his seizure.

"Dancing in the Moonlight" by Toploader: When Kyara is having her dream about Liam and her dancing and racing on horses.

"Let You Go" by The Chainsmokers: The next morning when Bryan sees Bella left.

"Breathe Me" by Sia: When Liam falls into a coma.

"Every Breaking Wave" by U2: When Dad and Kyara are walking into town to go find Bella.

"Heart of Stone" by Iko: When Kyara sees Bella hugging Hugo and runs out of the church.

"When I Look at You" by Miley Cyrus: When Liam wakes up, when Liam and Kyara are talking, and throughout chapter twenty.

"What Hurts the Most" by Rascal Flatts: In chapter twenty-one when Kyara is in the kitchen after Liam kicks her out and she's thinking about Trevor.

"Leave Out All the Rest" by Linkin Park: When Kyara faints after Liam is being treated with rosemary, which he is allergic to.

"Ashes of Eden" by Breaking Benjamin: When Bryan is having the breakdown with Kyara after the fight with the king's army.

"Verge" by Owl City (karaoke): When Bryan and Kyara are running through the castle trying to find the phone.

"Strong Enough" by Matthew West: Credits.

Made in the USA
Columbia, SC
26 October 2024

44755246R00200